Romancing the Dark in the City of Light

Romancing the Dark in the City of Light

ANN JACOBUS

THOMAS DUNNE BOOKS
ST. MARTIN'S GRIFFIN NEW YORK

This is a work of fiction. All of the characters, organizations, and events portrayed in this novel are either products of the author's imagination or are used fictitiously.

THOMAS DUNNE BOOKS.
An imprint of St. Martin's Press.

www.thomasdunnebooks.com
www.stmartins.com

Designed by Steven Seighman

The Library of Congress Cataloging-in-Publication Data is available upon request.

ISBN 978-1-250-06443-1 (hardcover)
ISBN 978-1-4668-7050-5 (e-book)

First Edition: October 2015

10 9 8 7 6 5 4 3 2 1

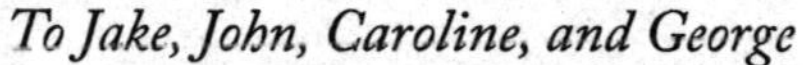

To Jake, John, Caroline, and George

ACKNOWLEDGMENTS

This novel was started in 2006, but some elements and characters are recycled from a shelved manuscript that dates back to the late nineties. So many people helped bring this story to life, and others helped resuscitate it when there was no discernable pulse. Each deserves not only acknowledgment but also all-you-can-eat Nutella crêpes.

On the journey with it longest and closest is Erzsi Deàk, who was my Paris BFF and critique group partner long before she was my agent. And she doesn't even like dark stories.

Gros bisous and a lifetime supply of assorted French pastries to Kat Brzozowski, my editor, for falling in love.

Champagne for everyone at Thomas Dunne Books/ St. Martin's Griffin! Special thanks to Mitali Dave, Stephanie Davis, Eva Diaz, Justine Gardner, Jessica Katz, Michelle Cashman, and Karen Masnica.

Tim Wynne-Jones read a nascent draft while he was my advisor at Vermont College of Fine Arts and encouraged me publicly. Paris writing group members Claudia Classon, Sandra Guy, Pedro de Alcantara, and Melissa Buron gave me excellent input on early drafts, as did Tracey Adams and Emma Dryden, psychologist Dr. Alex Cook, and Lacy Jacobus.

VCFA readers Stephanie Greene, Miriam Glassman, Nancy Bo Flood, Stephanie Parsley Ledyard, Dianne White, Candy

Dahl, Jen White, Caitlin Berry Baer, Angela Morrison, Jonathan Rich, and Kelly Barson all provided invaluable direction and encouragement. Deb Gonzales did, too, plus created the ace discussion guide.

I'm especially grateful to Jane Resh Thomas who gently counseled me on delving into the dark heart of my protagonist, and to Richard Peck who shared his story-telling genius repeatedly.

My San Francisco writing group, Beyond the Margins, lavished me with guidance and support. Cases of Bordeaux and *mercis* to Annemarie O'Brien, Christine Dowd, Frances Lee Hall, Linden McNeilly, Helen Pyne, and Sharry Wright.

Joy Neaves of namelos helped deepen this story significantly, and Deborah Halverson's expertise polished the manuscript to a shine.

I had astute young adult readers along the way including Caroline Kordahl and Jessie Papaglia for early drafts, and later, Nell Dayton-Johnson and Jacqueline Wibowo—thanks to Nancy Sondel's PCCWW.

Un grand merci to Chef de Service of the Police Municipale de France, Jean-Louis Le Touze who advised me on all things criminal in Paris, and Dr. Christian Jacobus, MD, who was cheerfully on call 24/7 for his expertise in medicine and emergencies. *Shukran* to Zayna Hindi, Shoka Marefat, Layla Al-Ghawas, and Wael Elbhassi, who helped assure me that Moony was all I believed him to be.

In memory of Mom and Dad, and their unending faith in me; and with devoted love to Catherine, the Kordahls, my wild and crazy sibs, my dear kids; and of course, to Jim, who has been stalwart, patient, and beside me every step, in this as in all things. Chihuahua Louis XIV kept me company (slept) through countless hours at my desk.

And finally, to the grand, eternal, and dazzling City of Paris, with undying admiration and respect—I trust it can handle the optic of a depressed adolescent that results in something a little less flattering and laudatory than usual. Summer's views are not mine.

ONE

Paris Métro
Charles de Gaulle–Étoile

The train rounds the turn in the tunnel and the interior lights flicker off. Summer Barnes, pressed by the crowd against the doors in the second car, regards the brightness of the station ahead. This must be how it looks when you have an NDE, she thinks. A near-death experience. You're rushing through a dark tunnel toward *The Light* ahead. Where Dad and Grandma wait with smiles and open arms.

A whiff of the garlicky breath of the old lady leaning into her brings Summer back to the moment.

Nearby, a young Goth girl lays her head against her boyfriend, closing her kohl-rimmed eyes. His pierced and studded face softens as they entwine like tangled wire.

That's the answer, Summer thinks. Three feet away.

Love.

If you're passionate about someone, and they feel the same, everything else must fall into place.

And have purpose.

She's in the most beautiful city in the world and all she can think about is getting on the next flight out. Or finding a pair of ruby slippers and tapping her heels. It's not that she doesn't appreciate it. Paris! *La Ville Lumière.* City of Light, endlessly cool. Where Mom lives, although seems to spend very little time.

Maybe being *stuck in the tunnel* has to do with coming to Paris unexpectedly. One minute she was sprawled on her dorm room bed, the next she was staring out an airplane window at the icy black north Atlantic far below.

Or maybe it has to do with the fact that lately, she's always solo. Whatever, the November cold and the short, sunless days weigh her down like a ton of snow.

She just needs to find someone in Paris to hold hands with.

A train thunders by in the opposite direction. Her ears pop.

Brakes screech. Her train jerks to a halt and Summer slams into the garlic lady. They've stopped before reaching the end of the crowded platform.

A woman screams. The rawness vibrates through the station and tunnels.

A trill of panic zaps her. The train doors open and no one moves for two beats. Then she and the others rush out. What if it's a bomb?

No, there's been some accident. Two Métro employees jog down the stairs and force their way through the jittery crowd. One opens the white electrical closet against the wall and the other scurries down the stairs at the end of the platform to the tracks.

Everyone waits. No one leaves. A little saucer-eyed girl grips a man's hand. Summer smiles reassuringly at her. That stupid dad needs to get his kid out of here instead of gawking at the show like a big-mouthed bass.

The Goth girl points at the tracks, her face frozen with shock.

The edgy mob surges forward and people crouch to peer between the cars at something under the train.

Probably a person. Summer struggles to think of . . . Little Red Riding Hood, equilateral triangles, unfurled lilies.

It doesn't work. The tracks are practically yelling, *Look over here!* Plus people are hyperventilating up all the oxygen. She gropes for the silver flask of mandarin orange vodka in her pocket, unscrews it, and takes a deep swig.

Time to *partir.* She turns and collides with a tall guy in a dark wool coat and hat. "*Pardon,*" she mutters, looking up at him.

He's her age and breathtakingly gorgeous. The kind of guy who would normally look right through her.

"Do you speak English?" she blurts out.

"I do." His dark, sympathetic eyes seem to say, *Isn't this strange, isn't life awful?*

"What happened?"

"That's a woman on the tracks," he says somberly. "Were you on the train?"

"Yeah." Summer rubs her eyes with her gloved hand. It's weird, but she's close to tears. "Did she . . . fall? God, I hope she wasn't pushed."

"Here," he says. He nudges people out of the way by the edge of the platform between two cars. She leans in to look. Two Métro guys are straightening the cloth that is already covering the body.

A black, patent-leather, low-heeled pump lies on its side in the gravel between the rails. "Oh," she breathes. That solitary shoe makes her knees go rubbery. "How horrible."

The guy tilts his head. "Not necessarily. If she jumped, it may have been a release." He pauses. "A deliverance."

Summer blinks at him, then pivots and pushes her way to the exit stairs, heat creeping up her neck. That's exactly what she was thinking—that the lady is so lucky to be out of here. She knows the guy can't read her mind and doesn't mean anything by those words, but there it is: the real, and growing reason why she's got to find someone to love.

TWO

The next day at lunchtime, Summer stands in the skylight-lit atrium of the Paris American International High School (aka PAIS). She's pretending to study a large bulletin board. Her search for someone to be with ought to start here even though she's likely the oldest student in the building. She's scoped out the guys in her classes, but needs to look again.

She puts in her earbuds. Her favorite urban blues singer-songwriter, Kentucky Morris, croons to the cello riffs and gospel back up on "Love Me Back 2 Life." She hums under her breath.

Her thoughts drag to the incident in the Métro the evening before. It's like a piece of chewing gum stuck to her shoe.

That round-eyed little girl couldn't see the body, she's sure. Still—people shouldn't off themselves where little kids are, for chrissakes. But what's the best, surest way to do it?

"Ever been in a musical?" says a deep American voice over her shoulder.

She spins around with a frown and steps back. "No." She pulls out her earbuds. "Are you joking?"

"Nope. You were reading the announcement." A guy with a big smile, olive skin, and dark hair that covers his ears stands a little too close. One brown eye looks off about ten degrees in another direction.

"Actually, I wasn't." She had noticed it though: *The Unsinkable Molly Brown*.

"Going to be a great show. Tryouts Tuesday." He lists slightly to one side. His right arm hangs limp, the fist curled in a tight knot. And his words have the faint imprint of an old speech impediment.

"I'll, uh, make a note of that." She touches her nose ring. He's the guy who limps in the halls. He's in one of her big classes, too.

He grins good-naturedly, warm and real. "You're Summer, right? Got Concert Choir with you." A hanging fern behind his head gives him a bright green aura. "Just arrived?"

She can't help but smile back. "Day eleven, but who's counting?" He's a nice guy for a drama geek, and is obviously making an effort.

"From where?"

"Boarding school." She wants to bolt, the better to avoid any questions about flaming out of St. Jude's School for the Hopelessly Messed Up. But a pack of guys leaving the gym look toward them and one yells, "Yo, Moony!"

"Moony?" she asks. Must be a drama nickname.

The guy jogs over. Three more follow, but hang back. The jock—blond, meaty, and undoubtedly A-list—leers at Summer. Her whole body tenses. She knows what comes next.

"Aren't you going to introduce us?" he asks Moony.

With reluctance in his voice, Moony says, "Uh, Summer Barnes, meet Josh MacDougall."

Josh says, "Hey, hey, hey, Summer breeze, where have you been all my life?"

Heat floods her face. "Seriously?" That's his setup for the punch line?

He blinks. Leans back. "Wait," he says, frowning. He puts his finger to his chin. "Aren't you related to the chicken Barnes? Weren't they, like, giving the birds bad drugs, and exploiting illegal aliens?"

Somebody must have googled her. Few people have the nerve to bring up the family chicken business notoriety to her face—poultry mistreatment and undocumented worker scandals from long ago. It was her grandfather's business.

"Josh?" she says, through gritted teeth.

"That's me." His lips stretch back from his teeth and, unbelievably, he makes a soft hen-clucking noise. "Bawk bawk."

"Clearly, your *mother* was given bad drugs. Or you'd know not to freaking accost someone you just met with such rude questions. Oh, and dumbass sound effects."

The other guys laugh. So does Moony. "Burned you, Josh," he says.

"Wha?—I—no."

"My god. Look at that top hat," Summer exclaims, pointing. When they all turn, she disappears.

So much for holding hands with any high school boys.

THREE

Summer's phone dings in the rest room where she's hiding. A text from Missing Mom, who, as far as Summer knows, is on another continent. But on top of certain details as usual.

Don't forget Mme. LF. Ask about colleges for January.

Crap. She did forget. She's late for her appointment with the college counselor.

She peeks out the door then leans her head heavily against the cool jamb. What's his name—Josh—wasn't trying to insult her. At least at first. She was supposed to say something witty or flirty back.

Not burn him.

Twenty–sixty hindsight.

But she will have to hunt beyond the International School if she wants to meet someone. Where and how is going to take planning.

The coast is clear and she dashes.

Madame Laforge is an American, married to a Frenchman. She sits behind a blond wood desk in a small office that smells like pickles, frowning at Summer's tardiness.

"Sorry about that," Summer says, plopping into the chair. She's still revved from her unsocial encounter. Deep breath.

Madame rifles through Summer's file, purple-framed glasses perched on her nose. "I spoke with your mother, who was *quite* insistent that I help you as soon as possible. And she's out of the country, I understand."

"Yep." Exhale.

"I have received your transcripts." She adds, "You were a straight-A student in eighth and ninth grades."

Summer knows the shocked tone well. Her average has declined a tad since then. Her last school was for disabled, unable, and unwilling rich kids. Ironically, her one relationship experience, if you could call it that, was there.

Madame goes on, "I understand you'll actually finish at the end of this semester." She glances at the IB art students' calendar on the wall. "In five weeks."

"Yes, ma'am." Thanks to her mother's high-level negotiations and maybe a large donation, the school will let her graduate—even with her abysmal record.

If she passes everything.

Madame's expression says, *Good luck with that*. "Your academic record is one thing, but I'm not sure how we can downplay this disciplinary history." She purses her lips. "Being asked to leave four schools will be problematic any way we cut it."

Summer gazes out the window at the gloomy day. At Verde Valley School in Arizona, at least the sun always shone. She was there for eleventh and most of her *first* senior year. It's the only one she misses. St. Jude's was a train wreck.

"While we're on the subject, you do understand that PAIS will absolutely not tolerate the use of drugs or alcohol?"

Summer knows to look directly at her interrogator. "Yes, I do."

Before shuttling her to the airport, the disciplinary committee at St. Jude's played her the grainy clip that some brainless freshman videoed—and the dean confiscated—of her staggering hammered across the dorm lobby and then face-planting outside in the hedge.

If only someone were casting for a last-one-standing party reality show, she thinks wistfully. She'd be a shoo-in.

Madame regards Summer over her glasses. "Is your father here in France?"

Why is she asking? "No." Now *he* had some drinking issues, but Summer doesn't say that. "He died. Six years ago, next month."

"I see. I'm sorry. Normal procedure is a first meeting with a student's parents, but we'll have to forego that." Madame focuses back on her laptop screen. "We'll be targeting only US colleges, as UK or EU universities are out of the question. If you can bring your grades up for this semester—and there isn't much time, it'll all be over December twentieth—we might be able to swing it." She sighs.

"Right. I've turned in more homework in the last two weeks than I did in the previous year." Totally true.

"Well." Madame licks her thumb and flips through several more pages. "You desperately need some extracurricular activities."

"That could be a problem," says Summer drily.

Madame beams her a look of disbelief.

She shifts in her seat. "Okay, not a problem. I was actually just thinking about helping with the school musical."

"You understand you will need *high* grades to prove that you have a new attitude."

Remembering Mom's instructions, Summer asks, "Are there any schools that start late January that I could apply to fast?"

"*This* January? May I ask why?"

"Because my grandpa wants me to." She doesn't clarify that he's dead and left her money that she'll receive only if she graduates from a four-year university by age twenty-two.

"First-semester grades won't be out in time. And based on your records, no." Madame observes Summer over her glasses. "You do understand that we cannot give you another chance if you fail to pass all your classes in the next weeks."

"Yes. I *do* understand. Everything." She notes that familiar cold, falling feeling. But it's not leaden. It's wispy. Like snowflakes.

When she was eight and on a family skiing trip, she and Dad glided off trail and stopped beneath a ledge. He wanted a nip from his flask. They sat side-by-side in a soft, protected hollow, her body leaning into the safe warmth and weight of him. They watched through the evergreens as snow fell silent and graceful against darkening skies.

Madame says, "Your mother mentioned Arkansas State in Jonesboro, but that would be a 'reach' school for you. North Central Mountain College of the Ozarks in Whipperwillville is a potential safe school."

I'm on to you, Summer thinks. You made that place up. "The Ozarks are awesome," she says cheerfully. "Let's aim for that."

"I'll be checking with your teachers. Please fill out the personal statement form for me online and I'll see you in two weeks."

Probably a whole 'nother year lost now. The thought occurs to Summer, as she shuffles out of the office. She might make a good tabloid headline, though. FORMER HONOR ROLL GRANDDAUGHTER AND ONLY HEIR PROVES WORTHLESS, FLAMES OUT, AND FORFEITS FORTUNE.

At least she didn't get the "choices" lecture today. It is so time to be finished with high school and she has screwed up long enough. The good thing about this bad news is it makes her want to prove everyone wrong. She'll bust ass for the next month, and graduate if it kills her. Then worry about where to apply.

And she still wants to find someone to hold hands with. Or else she might as well chug a can of motor oil now.

FOUR

In the kitchen the next morning, Mom's little dog, Camus, barks at Summer when she sits down. She ignores him despite the pain it blasts through her headache. Mom's elderly Moroccan housekeeper mutters and puts him on the other side of the pantry door, then places a plate of scrambled eggs before Summer.

"*Merci,*" Summer says. Mom's still out of town. The *International Herald Tribune* and *Le Monde* lie before her. By the gray light from the courtyard window she searches the city section of the French paper looking for any mention of the lady who died at Étoile station. Fire, robberies—nothing looks close.

"Ouaiba, I'm looking, uh—*je cherche . . . un accident.*"

Ouaiba dries her hands on a violet linen dishtowel and approaches.

Summer holds up the paper. "*Une femme . . . etait mort . . . dans le Métro.*"

"*Sacrebleu!*"

"Can you help me? Find the story? *L'histoire?*"

Ouaiba takes the paper and scans the two pages of short local police reports. "*Hier?* Yes-ter-day?" she asks.

"Thursday. *Jeudi soir.*"

Ouaiba shakes her head. She doesn't see anything either.

No mention, as if it never even happened. It was a suicide then,

Summer thinks. If it had been an accident, or a murder, it would be a *story.*

Summer dresses and heads out. Public transportation is one of the best things about Paris. She's had free run of the city since her first visit at age thirteen. A ton of homework awaits her but she has tomorrow, too. She gets that she has to graduate. She needs to find someone to be with.

As she descends the Métro stairs, her pulse quickens. She stops. Something huge and dark and cold and deadly waits patiently below for her.

Great. Trainophobia. Just what she didn't order.

She grips the grimy handrail, as people push around her. It's as if the lady on the tracks is still there, emitting a repelling force field. She inches forward. Shallow breathing makes her light-headed. She grabs a seat on the train, then concentrates on slow, deep breaths and listens to Kentucky's *Safety Glass.*

A couple of sips from her silver flask help. It was given to her dad by his fraternity brothers at the University of Arkansas. He kept it filled with scotch. She's a vodka girl, herself.

She emerges in the eleventh arrondissement, gulping in fresh air and proud of her fortitude in overcoming this new little anxiety.

A twenty-foot wall rings the outside of Père Lachaise Cemetery, but she enters by a side stairway. Her mini guide has a fold-out map showing the locations of all the noteworthy residents: Oscar Wilde, Frédéric Chopin, Edith Piaf, and . . . Jim Morrison.

"'Hot American lead singer of The Doors and big partier who overdosed in Paris in the seventies,'" she reads. That's the guy to visit.

Hands deep in her ski jacket pockets, she walks along a gray cobblestone main drag. Soot-darkened, elaborate tombstones, ten-foot angels and obelisk monuments, and shed-sized mausoleums crowd together like bad teeth. Dried leaves cartwheel alongside her, and a solitary man in a dark coat crosses her path in the distance.

So beautiful this place, she thinks. Like something out of a poem. Or a dream.

When she finally finds it, Morrison's grave is deserted, simple and anticlimactic. Wilted flowers in cellophane, a bourbon bottle, two beer cans, and folded notes litter it. On his tombstone, a mysterious line underneath his dates reads, *KATA TON DAIMONA EAUTOY.*

A patch of dry grass and a park bench catch her eye, and even though she must climb uphill to sit, she's ready for a refreshment break. She sips vodka from her flask to clear her head, then pulls out her phone from her backpack. She opens her to-do app and taps:

Scope out classes. Again. Then she deletes it.

Join a school club? Doubtful on that one, too.

Bars. Clubs. Not ideal.

Ballroom dancing lessons?

French dating sites. Expat dating sites.

Prisons?

Volunteer somewhere. That would be good for her French, too. But finding something could be a major undertaking and she's not up for it.

Through the bare trees, crowded, slate rooftops stretch out to the horizon beneath ashy skies. This would be an excellent location for eternal rest, she thinks. Assuming the inhabitants are actually *resting.*

The anniversary of Dad's death is December 17, less than a month away. She closes her eyes and her twelve-year-old self is sitting in the hard front pew of his quiet memorial service.

"'I shut my eyes and all the world drops dead.'" A guy is standing at the other end of her bench.

"Ex-cuse me?" She clenches her fists. Some English-speaking crackhead has zeroed in on her. She has a green belt in tae kwon do, only it's been over six years since she's thrown a good kick.

"The poet you're reading," he says. "Plath." His cologne wafts up her nose. Heavy, spicy, undertones of cider vinegar? He looks about nineteen, maybe twenty—although hard to tell with his unnecessary sunglasses—and he's wearing jeans and hiking boots, wrapped in a black wool coat. Maybe the guy she glimpsed over on the main drag earlier.

"Oh." She stares at the front cover of her book, as if she forgot.

He says, "Let me guess. I bet you like Dickinson, too, maybe even Virginia Woolf?"

Without making any sudden moves, she slips the book into her backpack and her phone in her pocket. "I'm going to speak to you as if you're not insane, because I've heard that's the best way to handle a lunatic."

He looks taken aback, then laughs. "Sorry. Didn't mean to startle you. I don't often run into women reading Plath in Père Lachaise."

She has to give him credit. She would appreciate it if everyone took her sharper remarks this well.

His gaze makes her feel like a smear under a microscope. She pulls off her ski hat and runs her hand through her uncombed hair. He's tall and broad shouldered, with full lips and silky skin. His hair is eighteenth-century-English-poet-like in its thickness, length, slight curl, and suggestion of unkemptness.

"You hang out here regularly?" she asks, zipping her backpack.

He smiles with perfect, straight white teeth. "I'm new in town. Just had some time in between appointments."

As a rule, guys who hit on her have tossed back a half dozen shots, some X, who knows what else, and are no great shakes themselves. Heathcliff here seems sober, so *why* is he talking to her?

Oh, yeah, she thinks, I've slipped below the *magic weight*. Deflated my chipmunk cheeks. Even though her clothes are all oversized on her lately, she feels no different. People are nicer to her though.

"You're American." She crosses her arms. Maybe this is some kind of prank. Or the guy's a predator.

"Among other things. I'm here for a while on business." There's something familiar about him. Like when you see a stranger on the street and the shape of their eyes or mouth reminds you of a relative. "And you?" he asks. "May I?" He sits on the end of the bench.

He looks like the guy who loitered in the corridor outside of her father's hospital room. Waiting on someone in one of the other rooms. He kept smiling sadly at her.

But there's no way. This guy would have been too young.

She says, "I'm originally from Arkansas. Little Rock."

"No kidding. I've spent time there. Nice city. You don't *sound* like you're from Arkansas."

"Been gone too long, I guess." She's only visited a few times in the last five years, most recently for Grandpa's funeral. "You're here on *business*? What kind of business are you in?" she asks.

"Sales. International." The wind tousles his hair.

"International sales?"

Yeah, right. Unless he means drugs, which might explain the expensive clothes and that flashy Swiss watch. Maybe he recognized her as a potential client. Good radar if he does. She's never bought any drugs in France, though. The laws are harsher here.

And jail would really suck.

"My name is Kurt, by the way." He doesn't extend his hand. Neither does she.

Summer blinks.

He looks familiar because he's the guy from the Métro.

FIVE

"You were at the accident!" Summer cries, springing up from the cemetery park bench. "At Étoile the other night."

Kurt's smile fades. "That was you, then. I wasn't sure. Also wasn't sure whether to bring it up or not."

"Her scream has been bouncing around my head ever since."

"That was a witness," he says quietly.

"Oh." Ding dong. Of course. Someone who saw it and was alive to scream. "I looked but never found anything about it. In the paper." She sits on the bench then stands up again. "So, I guess it was a suicide?"

"Yeah. An accident or a homicide would be a story. Suicide isn't news since it happens every day. Plus no one wants to hear about them. Unless it's a celebrity, of course."

She nods. "I know, right? Why wouldn't people be totally fascinated?" She smiles to show she's kidding. Kurt looks into her eyes, as if searching for something. He is so hot, her cheeks warm. "Um, do you always stare at people like that?"

"Was I staring? Sorry," he says, looking down, almost shyly.

A slight dizziness knocks her. She needs to get out of here. Which way?

Downhill.

"I was just heading out," she says, slinging her pack over her shoulder.

"Mind if I walk with you? I'll grab a taxi outside the main gate." He actually seems sort of lonely.

"Fine." She steers toward a wide lane through the grand, iron-colored mausoleums.

He scrambles to catch up. "I don't want you to think I'm sketchy. I'm just happy to find a fellow American. A literary one." She glances at him now. There's that grin again.

Moving relaxes her a little. He keeps stride with her, his tall form strong, his movements graceful and confident. Brown leaves whirlpool before them.

"Have you been here long?" she asks, pulling her shoulders back and sucking in her stomach. Yay for being thinner.

"Just got here. How about you?"

"A couple of weeks now."

"What are you doing here?"

"I'm a student." She is *not* going to say she's in her *second* senior year of high school.

"How's your French?" he asks.

"It sucks," she says. "Yours?"

"I have to speak it for business."

"Oh, right, sales," she says. She glances at him sideways.

He pulls out a package of fancy British cigarettes and offers her one.

"No thanks, I quit."

"Are you sure?"

"What the hell. Might as well." Just one. She sniffs the fresh, rich tobacco. He lights hers, then his.

"Ah, nicotine," she says, exhaling. "What my life has been missing. Whoo—head rush."

He laughs. She's not sure she's really that funny but she's liking him better by the minute. They smoke and walk the last half block without talking.

"Here we are," Kurt says. They're under the huge stone arch at the main entrance, and a taxi idles at the stand on the street.

He turns to her. His dark, soulful eyes say, *You're gorgeous, I want you.*

Like a hen eyeing a june bug, she thinks. But sincere. And intoxicating.

Here he is. A made-to-order ten. New in town. *Très* sophisticated. A guy Mom would probably not only approve of, depending on his business, but lust after herself. Actually a strike against him.

Someone to hold hands or drink champagne with. Someone who could make life a little more meaningful.

"Thanks for keeping me company," he says. "It's been a pleasure . . ." He waits, a not-so-subtle hint that he doesn't know her name.

"Summer. Summer Barnes."

"Barnes." He frowns in thought. "Of Little Rock. Any relation to the chicken Barnes?"

"Ha. No," she lies, crossing her arms. She doesn't want him to like her, or not like her because of—or even to have to discuss—her stupid family, the chicken Barnes. If she ever sees this guy again she can explain. She also doesn't want him to kidnap her for ransom, if he isn't already planning to. When she was six, her parents hired a firm that specialized in personal security. They trained her how to avoid kidnappers.

Rule number one: Never talk to strangers.

He opens the taxi door and before she can say good-bye, he slides in. Then he leans out to see her and says brightly, "I'm going to Place de la Concorde. Can I drop you anywhere on the way?"

"I'm in the sixteenth. Near Place Victor-Hugo," she says. Considerably farther.

The taxi driver turns to look at her, too. Is she getting in or not?

"You can get the one at Place de la Concorde. Change at Étoile."

"Yeah, I know." No need to inform him that she and the Métro are having issues. She has to get back to Mom's and do her work. This will be faster.

Like their old golden retriever, Polly, she follows him into the waiting car.

SIX

Inside the warm cab, they aren't touching, but the heat of Kurt's body and the slightly funky smell of him permeates Summer's clothes and settles on her skin.

It's already dusk, and car lights and neon signs burn bright in the gray dimness. Kurt chats about the differences between the French and Americans, as she studies his handsome profile and shiny, disheveled hair. She's never been this physically close to someone so gorgeous. The warmth in her cheeks says she's blushing.

Kurt gestures with his large but elegant, smooth, tanned hand, waving perfectly shaped fingers and nails. He displays those white teeth, and she imagines running her tongue over them.

Place de la Concorde is lit up like a rock concert and traffic zooms in giant pinwheels around the Luxor Obelisk. Kurt has no small euro bills, so she pays the taxi fare.

"Thanks. Sorry about that," he says as they get out. "May I offer you a glass of champagne to show my appreciation? This hotel has an awesome bar. Quiet, soft lights . . ." He tilts his head in the direction of the *très cher* one at the end of the block.

"Champagne!" she exclaims. "What a great idea." She's giddy already. Long live the French who let you drink wine and beer at eighteen. And her flask is empty.

They walk past the Métro entrance. A bum wrapped in a dirty gray blanket sits on the sidewalk and she drops a euro coin into his paper cup. He nods at her, and then raises two fingers in a sort of salute at Kurt. "*Beau chapeau,*" the bum says.

Kurt nods in return. Nice hat? she wonders, looking at Kurt's bare head.

"Do you know him?" she asks.

"We're old pals. I'm staying nearby."

He doesn't strike her as kindhearted. He's hot, not warm, she thinks. But who cares? Just as they are about to enter the brass revolving door, she feels his hand on the small of her back. Through her jacket, fleece, and T-shirt, an electric jolt of hard iciness spreads through her middle.

Fear jitters her nerve endings. It's like when she and Katie were fourteen and convinced two townies they were college students. They realized they were in over their heads when the guys drove them to a scary apartment complex, and they bolted at the last minute.

No, it's more than that. Something about his touch is both hot and freezing, terrifying and soothing. Violent and peaceful.

She plucks her France Telecom phone from her pocket and scans the screen as if there's new information there. "Oh, shoot," she says. "I—I've got to go home."

He pouts. "Are you sure? Not even a quick coffee?"

"I can't. Sorry."

He thrusts a card into her hand. "Here. Since we're both new in town, if you ever want to catch a movie or something, call me."

She stuffs it into her coat. A nineteen-year-old with a business card. Kind of impressive. "Okay! See you." Greatly relieved, guilty, and a little disappointed, she skids past the startled doorman and sprints for a taxi.

SEVEN

Monday, Summer sits alone at the end of a long table in the steamy school cafeteria, trying to appear coolly oblivious to the three sophomore guys at the other end whispering and shooting her furtive looks. Their clothes, their slang, their zits are the same as at any other American high school, except that there are more kids from more countries here, and apparently they come and go more frequently. It's not even weird that she arrived in the middle of the semester.

All she has to do is get through this lunch, then this week of classes, then three more. And finals. She massages the bridge of her nose.

The important thing is to stay focused. Persevere.

Honestly, would a boyfriend help her do that? Or hurt? And where *is* she going to meet someone?

She pushes the chicken nuggets around her plate, thinking yet again about Kurt. His intense stare and cold heat. That fluffy hair. Her wish practically dropped in her lap. The hottest guy she's ever seen, let alone talked to, and she totally blew it. Freaked out for nothing, probably.

Withdraw and retreat.

She absently cuts a nugget in half then nibbles the edge of a piece. Yuck. They do *not* know how to fry chicken here.

She's had very little practice with hot guys. With any guys. And that's because she's chunky and doggy. Or was. Even at parties where everyone else is hooking up, she's always the odd woman out. She freezes up or says dumb things. Or offensive things.

He seemed so genuinely interested though. Eyes don't lie.

And out of the corner of hers she sees the drama guy, Moony, limping toward her. She doesn't look up, hoping he'll go by.

"Mind if I sit here?" he asks. She does, and is about to respond with something about head lice but checks herself. His eyes are bright and his lopsided smile wide.

"Okay. Just don't try and recruit me."

He grins and places his tray across from her.

It really is raining men.

She's five eight and usually weighs in around 175 pounds, which sounds better as eighty kilos. But in tenth grade she was briefly down to 133 and was amazed, alarmed, and then distressed at the attention she got. She must be there or near again. Which is weird, because for the first time since she was eleven she hasn't even been trying. But she also hasn't much wanted to eat.

Moony falls into his seat ungracefully, holding his leg out at a funny angle.

"What's up with your leg, anyway?" she asks.

"Bad car accident," he says, forking a French fry into his mouth. "Age ten."

"Whoa. What happened?"

He smiles. "Cousin was driving. Totaled the car. Obliterated my right side. Didn't do my left any good." He sticks out his foot and, with his right hand that she now sees is thin and deformed, clutches his jean pants leg up to midcalf. Masses of thick and thin scars crisscross his skin. A few dark leg hairs sprout in between the silver lines and byways. Some sort of plastic brace supports his ankle, and his right high-top sneaker has a three-inch-thick false bottom. "Could show you more, don't want to ruin your lunch."

"Jeez." She exhales. "Sorry, I didn't mean to be rude."

He shrugs, no problem.

"Did your cousin, um, survive?"

"Yeah. Smashed up, too, but fine now. He's a paramedic." Moony looks pleased.

He works well with his left arm and leg, and from far away moves almost normally, except for the limp. His shoulders are broad but uneven. His face would be classically handsome but the one eye is funny and the right side of his jaw is lumpy like it's made of Lego pieces. That right arm under his long-sleeved T-shirt is thin and misshapen. He makes a huge effort to compensate and it almost works, but he's seriously messed up.

A buff black guy brushes by them. "Yo, Moony," he says.

"Javier," says Moony back.

"Is Moony, like, a nickname?" asks Summer.

"Yeah. For Munir."

"Arabic. Are You Muslim?"

"Yeah. I'm Christian, too. Father's Kuwaiti. Mom's American. Teaches third grade in the lower school."

"Is that allowed?"

"She's fully qualified."

"No." Summer smiles. "Being both religions."

"Depends who you ask." He laughs, and takes a bite of lasagna with the fork in his left hand. He rests his thin, scarred, curled right one on the table near his plate, exhibiting good European table manners.

"You're pretty relaxed about something a lot of people freak out about. At least in Arkansas. Religion, I mean."

"I guess," he says through ricotta and meat sauce.

"Don't people usually ask about . . . your leg?" He showed her his scars with an almost enthusiasm.

"No. I like people to ask. Better than pretending I have no disability."

"May I?" she asks. He nods and she takes a French fry with her fingers, bad European table manners. "So was it here? The accident? In Paris?"

"Kuwait City."

"Oh. What happened?" She leans forward as the cafeteria is now full of gossiping teens and clanking cutlery.

"Don't remember anything. Abdul went too fast, lost control."

"How old was he?"

Moony looks down. "Thirteen."

"Ohmigod!" she squeals.

"Was a maniac," he explains patiently. "Didn't have permission."

"Obviously."

"Changed him a lot." He resumes eating. "I woke up in hospital three days later. Mom holding my hand."

"Good for her."

"Was transferred to Paris. Many months in Necker."

"What's that?"

"Big kids' hospital in the fifteenth." He means arrondissement, and points to the back wall of the cafeteria, like it's on the other side. "Lots of operations, still do therapy. Learned to walk, talk, eat all over again."

"Wow. That's incredible." Talk about perseverance.

"Not really. Just wanted to be a normal kid. Next goal, make the soccer team."

"How's that going?" she asks carefully.

"Not so well." But he smiles slyly. Or maybe all his smiles look sly. "What about you, Summer?"

She pauses and touches her throat. "Last year I went to a boarding school where my nickname was 'Back.'" She owes him something for all that he disclosed about himself. "Short for 'Razorback.'"

One scarred eyebrow lifts higher than the other. "A wild hog?"

"It's the mascot for the University of Arkansas. Where I was born. The state."

He nods and bites his garlic bread. "Mom's from Missouri."

"No kidding. The Show Me State. But there are a couple of reasons." She flips up her hair and stretches the collar of her T-shirt down in back to show him her scar. It's small and insignificant compared to his, a ragged pomegranate-colored patch at the base of her neck.

He leans forward to study it. “Nice.”

She laughs. “I could show you the one on my butt from the skin graft.”

He guffaws. “*Would* liven things up in here. How did you get it?”

“I pulled a pan of boiling spaghetti sauce on top of me.” She can’t believe they showed each other their scars. And that they’re laughing at them.

“On your back?”

“Yeah, I ducked or something. I was five.” She doesn’t mention that her dad was supposed to be giving her dinner but had passed out drunk.

“That sucks.” He pauses. “Said there were other reasons? For the nickname.”

“They also called me Razorback because I was, um, fat.”

He looks surprised. “You’re not now.”

She studies the fork on her plate. “And kind of an asshole.”

He presses his lips to keep from smiling. “Not you,” he says, his eyes crinkling with the effort.

“It’s okay. You can laugh.”

He does. She does, too.

EIGHT

It's almost time for classes. Summer and Moony stroll outside from the cafeteria to the upper school. Even though the wind is icy, the sun breaks through the clouds and floods the grassy suburban sports fields with golden light.

When she noticed Moony before, he was always walking by himself and now she understands why. He's slow and it's unnatural to keep pace beside him. She doesn't mind.

"So your mom teaches third grade here, huh?"

"Yep. Your parents?"

"I'm staying with my mom," she says. "She lives here most of the year."

"Dad?"

"He died when I was twelve." She looks away so he won't ask more.

Moony turns toward her. "Sorry."

"What about your dad?" she asks.

"Divorced post accident."

"That sucks."

"Reembraced Islam, lives in Kuwait with new wife and kid."

She tucks a strand of hair behind her ear. "But he can marry a second wife and still be married to your mom, right?"

"Over Mom's dead body."

"Ha!"

They enter the long upper school building and stop at Moony's white locker. He twirls his padlock with his good left hand. A pale, wiry guy jogging by calls, "Hey, Moony. Three thirty, right?"

"Bro. Yeah."

Two girls strolling in the other direction giggle. "Hi, Moony," they sing.

"Anna. Rose. S'up?"

"What do you have now?" asks Summer, bouncing on her toes, trying to win back his attention. He pays it fully and she already misses it.

He turns back to her. "Theory of Knowledge. You?"

"French Two. I'm flunking it. She goes so flipping fast."

"I tutor French. Satisfaction guaranteed." He winks.

He's flirting with her! "That's good news," she says, pulling out her cell phone. "Number?"

He recites it.

"Last name?"

"Al Shukr."

A petite girl with big brown eyes and highlighted hair squeezes in next to Moony. "*Salut,*" she says as she stands on her tiptoes to kiss him on both cheeks. Her hips are impossibly thin and her haute couture blouse could be hocked for a pair of concert tickets. "Hi, I'm Jackie," she says, looking at Summer defiantly.

"This is Summer," says Moony.

Summer forces a weak smile at the thought that she could sit on this girl and smush her.

The three-minute warning bell rings.

Jackie puts her long glossy fingernails on Moony's deformed arm, and tosses her hair. "I'll call you later," she says.

"Good," he responds.

Summer scowls at Jackie's back as she minces off. So Moony and Mini-Barbie are together? Disappointment sinks through her. She doesn't do well in competitions, but maybe she'd like to be in this one.

Moony's thick, boyish hair falls over his dark brows, emitting waves of limey shampoo scent, as he rifles through his locker. He's hot. If it weren't for getting smashed up he would be godlike. She wants to hold hands with *him*.

No, that's silly. She doesn't even know him, and he is disabled, she reminds herself.

So is she.

She's pinching herself painfully and stops. Maybe she *does* want to be in this competition. Raw, aching fear stabs her at the realization. Fear of the inevitable. Fear of failure.

"Well, see you," she says, hugging her backpack.

Moony asks, "Come to tryouts tomorrow afternoon?"

"Oh. That."

"*Really* need techies and crew."

"When's the show?"

"April."

"I won't be here."

"You won't?" He frowns.

"Um, I mean at PAIS. Not the world in general." She clears her throat. His left eyebrow rises. "I finish at the end of this semester."

"In a month?"

"Technically, I'll have enough credits to graduate."

He shakes his head. "Doesn't matter. Help 'til then."

She lets out a sigh. "I'll think about it."

Moony struggles to pull a huge book from his locker, but it slams to the floor. She lunges to retrieve it, then hands it to him, smiling. His jaw is tight and his eyes flash furiously.

"What?" Her stomach drops. "You're welcome!"

"Don't. Need. Help."

"Do I look like a flipping elf?" she asks loudly. "Jesus, next time I'll punt it down the hall for you. You just asked me for help with the stupid play!"

"Fine, Back."

"Watch it, gimp."

His eyes go wide and he covers his open mouth. Then a laugh explodes from deep within him.

Summer joins in. They laugh so hard, kids rushing to class give them worried looks and a wide berth.

NINE

That evening, Summer unlocks the front door to the apartment and grins. She's thinking of Moony's handsome face and hearing his deep laugh when she said she'd punt his book. Even though he only has one good hand to hold, and he's a tad touchy, she'd like to hang with him more.

Mom stands in the gilt and marble foyer. Shoot. Summer was really hoping they'd avoid each other. She swallows.

"Hi, darling. I'm just heading out." She's wearing an ice-blue dress and low-heeled black pumps.

Like the one on the tracks.

Summer crosses her arms as the dog barks at her. "Hi, Mom. What's up?" After Dad died, Mom moved here and Summer went to boarding school in the US. She hasn't lived with Mom since she was thirteen, and spends most school breaks with Aunt Liz.

But here they are. Mom's dyed blond hair is bigger than normal, swallowing her bony face.

"Oh, hush, Camus," says Mom.

The little dog circles Summer, barking like mad. With one or two exceptions, they've pretty much ignored each other since Summer arrived, but he must be taking a stand as the contested object of their affection is finally between them.

"So antisocial," says Mom. "Chihuahuas are one-person dogs. I guess that one person is me, isn't it, sweetie? Come here, Mu-mu.

You are such a good guard dog." She picks him up and kisses him on the snout.

"Ewww. Mom, please." Camus resembles a long-haired rat, with a *My Little Pony* tail. Summer offers him the back of her hand to sniff. He barks once to prove he's no pushover, then sniffs.

"I'm family. Your sister," she says. "No guarding necessary." They both know he's the precious child and she's a burdensome houseguest. He trots off with his nose in the air. "Um. How was Dublin?" Summer asks, recrossing her arms.

"That was two weeks ago. Last week I went to check on things in Cameroon and the Côte d'Ivoire. And they were fine. I think I have a little tummy bug, though." Mom checks her phone.

"Oh. Sorry to hear that." Summer focuses on her own empty stomach. Busybodies Without Borders. Mom works on a village-girls-staying-in-school project in Africa. Which is cool, of course, and Summer's proud of her.

"What did you do? What's it like—the Ivory Coast?" She wonders how she ended up with so much—why American and French kids *all* have so much—compared to the kids in those villages, who barely have enough to survive and are dying to get an education to better themselves. Someone should tell them that it's all highly overrated.

"Hot." Mom slips her phone into her shiny black bag and focuses on Summer. "How's school going?"

"Um, great." She wiggles her nose ring. Madame Laforge and the iceberg of finishing high school and getting accepted at some university crystallizes into thousands of singular, six-pointed flakes, and blows away.

"Good." Mom stares at Summer's piercing and frowns. Summer woke up after an epic party with no memory of how it got there. She likes it now especially since Mom doesn't. It's dramatic.

Drama. Hmmm. She could go to Moony's auditions tomorrow.

"Sweetheart, Winston's coming to town this weekend."

Summer snaps to. "Winston? Why?"

"For one thing, to make sure you're on track. He'll be here Friday."

He's the family's lawyer, the executor of her grandpa's will, and Mom's ex-boyfriend, just to keep things interesting. Summer hasn't seen him since her grandpa's funeral. And before that, her dad's. This can't be good. "Why can't he just ask you, or even me? Give him my cell phone number."

"I guess he has to see for himself. For legal reasons. There have also been some recent developments. A lawsuit challenging the will."

"By who?"

"Whom. Your father's great-aunt and her son. What's-his-name." Mom pulls her coat from the armoire.

"Dennis." Summer chews on a ragged nail. One of many people who would be pumped if she flames out.

Mom's studying Summer's jeans and T-shirt, as Summer peels off her own coat and tosses it on the marble-slabbed hall table. Mom changes the subject as she always does when Dad comes up. "We should go shopping. Pick out some cute things to show off your new figure. Those jeans are not flattering." Mom thrusts her arms into her fat fur coat.

"Okay." Summer lets the jeans comment float away. Having a chubby daughter drove skinny Mom up the wall. Even though she's glad to be thinner, the long-sought victory is hollow. It hasn't changed how she feels one ounce. Plus if she gets new clothes she'll probably just expand out of them again.

On the other hand, better fitting clothes should be part of her holding-hands strategy. Although Moony doesn't seem to care.

She will. She'll go to Moony's auditions. She doesn't have to sing or dance, just help. She takes a deep breath.

Mom says, "I've got to run. Ouaiba has some stir-fry in the kitchen for you for later."

"Long as it's not chicken," Summer quips, expecting a smile.

But Mom's gaze is steely. "It's prawn. And what is wrong with chicken?"

Summer swallows the anger that erupts in her. But she hits a lob. "I can't help but think of the millions who have already sacrificed their lives so that you can live here in Paris."

Mom doesn't blink and lobs it back. "If you aren't careful, dear, all those feathered lives will have been in vain. Well, taxi's waiting. Kiss, kiss." Mom touches the tips of her fingers to her lips and firmly pulls the ten-foot door closed behind her.

TEN

In the dark, Summer walks up to Place Victor-Hugo and the nearest *tabac* for cigarettes. They'll help with all the studying she has to do over the holiday weekend.

She passes red awnings and plate glass–windowed *très cher* restaurants packed with people oblivious to the fact that the day after tomorrow is Thanksgiving.

She wonders what Moony and his mom will do for the holiday. Today at auditions she did sign up to help with props, against her better judgment, mainly because Moony said they might hunt for some together this weekend.

At the end of their street, a woman in short shorts, a fake fur vest, and shiny black thigh-boots stands with attitude on the corner. Another woman similarly dressed is across the street. Hookers! She's never seen a real live prostitute before. That she knows of, anyway. Mom's building is not far from the Bois de Boulogne and according to Ouaiba, all sorts of sexual activity goes on there. But this is too posh a neighborhood for them to hang in very long before the *police nationale* chase them off.

Why are they so scorned when it's clearly not a first-choice profession for the vast majority of women? They're forced into it, usually at really young ages, by circumstances and abuse. They aren't strong enough, don't have the resources, the education, the contacts, to avoid it or get out of it. And yet they're reviled. Even in the Bible. It has never made sense.

No one has their backs.

As she passes the woman, Summer takes out her earbuds and says, "*Bonjour,*" in a sort of sisterhood hello. Just like Fantine in *Les Misérables,* or Nancy in *Oliver Twist.* She could give her some money, but then vetoes the idea. She feels sorry for the woman and doesn't want her to know that.

The woman replies with French and gestures, the equivalent of, *You want some?* She's older up close, tired looking.

Summer's face heats. She shakes her head. "Just being neighborly," she mumbles.

In her room, she peers out her window at the fur vest woman, who's relocated like a walking stereotype under the streetlight on the corner. The other one is gone. A slick black Peugeot stops and the passenger window glides down. The woman leans in to talk. Straightens up, pauses, then opens the door. An interior light blinks on, illuminating a man. Summer doesn't want to be a voyeur, but she can't pull away. The woman gets in and before she closes the door, the man stares up through the moon roof at Summer's third-floor window. Like he's looking right at her.

It's Kurt. Or his doppelgänger.

She jumps back. Ohmigod. Is he freaking following her?

No, she never said what street she lived on, just the area.

The car drives off. She looks again. Wait. The man is older, gray-haired even. Or is that moonlight bouncing off his head? She's seeing things. She leans against the wall, closes her eyes, and takes two deep breaths.

Was it him? If it were, so what? Picking up a prostitute in her neighborhood . . . maybe it's some sort of game.

She's so clueless. Is she supposed to be outraged, or turned on? Or scared.

ELEVEN

On Wednesday, Summer thumbs through a *Marie Claire* without registering the fashionable contents. She's in a high-ceilinged waiting room in an old apartment building on Parc Monceau in the eighth arrondissement. Dr. Garnier, in a chic gray wool suit with pink piping, smoky stockings, and high heels, opens the door to her office. Summer shuffles in.

This is Mom's idea of punishment for getting kicked out of school.

Again.

She just wants to get through the hour without getting all her blood sucked out.

"Hello, Summer," the doctor says with her accent. "Please. Be seated." She gestures at one of two chrome-and-dark-leather chairs, a glass coffee table between them. Tall windows look out over the bare trees in the park and the chilly dark Paris evening.

"What's up, doc?" Summer says.

"But it is you who must tell me what's going on." It's her second visit. Last week they covered the fact that St. Jude's expelled her for possession of alcohol, pot, and medications that weren't prescribed to her. And the huge fit her mother had.

Today, she tries to run the clock down with babble about each of her classes at school, spinning the fact that she will be involved in the musical. She already knows what her issues are. And what she needs to do: focus, buckle down, work, pass. Eat right, sleep right, exercise. Try not to think about . . . escaping.

She should be home doing all that and not wasting time here. She wonders if Moony ever went to a shrink, like while he was recovering from his accident.

"And how do you feel about it?"

"About what?" The room is paneled with wood and packed with books, including leather-bound sets of the works of Voltaire, Dumas, and Sartre. Not that Summer's read anything by them, but she knows who they are and that she's supposed to be impressed.

"Being in Paris. Attending a new school, doing theater. Living with your mom. Any of it."

She has to give her something. Not too little info, and not too grim or bright a picture. She's not sure about Dr. Garnier but most shrinks love to set off unnecessary alarms. Balanced and "realistic" is the key. This is a tiresome game that costs hundreds of euros an hour.

Come on, say something honest. "Well, a little . . . overwhelmed," Summer admits. "It's an adjustment."

"*Mais, oui.*"

"I don't want to be here."

"Where would you like to be?"

She contemplates this unexpected question for a moment. Père Lachaise Cemetery? She can't joke about that here. "Maybe in California. Not far from the beach. My aunt Liz lives in San Francisco."

"But is this not your first response to difficulty? To withdraw and retreat? Or escape? We discussed this last week."

"Is it not?" Summer echoes, trying to keep sarcasm out of her voice. "I guess." She thought her problem was anger. And she only retreats to cut losses. She doesn't back down when it matters.

"What is Aunt Liz like?"

"She's real," Summer says, picturing her aunt in one of her lumpy, uneven, hand-knit sweaters. "She's Mom's younger sister but she's very different. She accepts herself and others for what they are. Plus, she thinks I'm awesome."

"What would you do there?"

"I could read. Walk on the beach. Maybe give swimming lessons?" It's a dumb answer, but at her third boarding school, she did just that with kids for the Red Cross. After two weeks, she had the whole lot of them swimming like guppies. "Um, I could sleep."

Dr. Garnier shifts in her seat. "Are you having trouble with sleep? Too much, too little?"

She is, but Summer says, "No. I just like to."

"Your mother mentioned you have slimmed down. Is this on purpose?"

"I'm always dieting." She is proud of her new figure, only it doesn't feel like self-control. It really *isn't* on purpose, but who cares?

Dr. G makes a note. "It sounds as if there would be less pressure in San Francisco."

"Yeah. For sure. No having to finish school. This term anyway. I could maybe do it later."

"Tell me something that you enjoy."

"I like to read."

"What do you like?"

"Almost anything. Romances. Gothic or otherwise. Fantasy. Poetry. Biographies. Nonfiction. Just not so much lately." She's always read a lot, even when she was flunking. Until the last few months.

"You don't read now?"

"Not really." A fascinating book on near-death experiences, and some clinical stuff on death and dying, but for sure if she mentions that, the doctor will get her panties in a knot. People are so weird about death. It's actually a rich and interesting subject, across cultures and history. Egyptian, Viking, and Parsi customs have interested her most recently.

The cool thing is that pretty much everyone agrees: something happens afterward.

The doctor makes another note on her writing pad. "Tell me other things you love?"

"Things I love?" Summer asks. Despite Herculean efforts, her eyes roll. "Kentucky Morris."

From her expression, the doctor isn't sure where that is.

"A singer-songwriter. You know—*When you've gone 'round the bend, and the world comes to an end*?" The woman looks at her blankly. "'Absolute Zero.' It's a popular song."

"*Ah, bon.*" Dr. Garnier nods. "I'm an old Beatles fan myself. 'All You Need is Love.' And?"

Summer forces a smile, "*Lord of the Rings.*" It was really more her dad's favorite, but she'll claim it. "*Les Misérables.* Snarky YA. Um, schnitzel and strudel? Walking in the rain?" Sour cherry nitro-martinis pop into her head. She and Grace snorting lines of cocaine last year on senior skip day before their big falling out.

Dr. Garnier folds her hands. Waits.

"Like I said, I like romance. In books and movies."

"What do you like about romance?"

"I don't know. I guess because *I* would like to meet someone." Nothing wrong with confessing this.

Dr. Garnier brightens. "You had a boyfriend before?"

This old French woman just assumes she likes guys. She happens to be right, but still. And Summer has no intention of discussing he-who-shall-not-be-named. "No," she says, chomping a fingernail. "Boy *friends,* yes. A boyfriend, no."

"What would this change?"

"I wouldn't be lonely?" Duh.

Back in tenth grade, her best friend Katie met Justin and suddenly the two were planning their joint futures. It straightened Katie out and gave her life focus and meaning. Or maybe it just got her away from Summer's worsening influence. Whatever the reason, they're still together.

The doctor asks, "Do you feel lonely?"

Tread carefully, she tells herself. Rational, cooperative, mature.

She definitely doesn't want to get into her propensity to lose friends, her current complete lack thereof, or her abysmal record in love. "I'm new in town. I've been to, um, a lot of schools in the last few years. Plus I want to have sex." Good sex. She had sex and knows by all the hype that it could be much better. Plus, this has got to be a suitable conversational thing to say in France to change the subject.

Dr. Garnier smiles. First one all day.

"Have you met any boys?"

"Maybe. There's a great guy at school, only he's . . . I do really like him."

"What do you like about him?"

"He's smart and funny and handsome. Has clear boundaries, that's for sure. He's not easily put off, and I like that. Because"—she clears her throat—"sometimes I put people off. Also, he's got this energy, totally positive." She thinks a moment. "He's got *purpose*."

Dr. Garnier tilts her head. "How do you mean?"

She shrugs. "He just knows why he's here and what he needs to do."

"*Ah, oui*. He sounds like an impressive boy."

"Yeah. And I did run into a guy this past weekend, very hot, kind of, um, alarmingly so." Probably best not to say she saw him outside her window in a car with a hooker. "But out of my league. I guess." Time to exit this subject. "Another thing I love is quiet. And peace. Away from the roar of the world."

The doctor frowns. Maybe that was a little too abrupt.

"I mean, sometimes I think I'd like to live in a simpler time. Be apprenticed to a shoemaker or something. Or live in an Alpine convent."

Dr. Garnier says drily, "No boyfriends allowed in a convent."

Summer smiles. She should just give the doctor what she really wants. "Lately, I miss my dad." It's true. The words came out surprisingly easy, but sit there all heavy. She pauses. "We're very much alike. But I think I was a disappointment to him, too. Then he was . . ." She trails off. Does the doctor know anything about Dad or his drinking? Or his strangely quiet and muffled death?

Such a can of worms to open, but maybe she should. He's been on her mind a lot.

"Ah," Dr. Garnier says, looking at her watch, "we shall discuss your father next time."

"Oh."

Dr. Garnier scribbles more notes. "Are you taking your antidepressants?"

"Uh, yeah," Summer lies. She's tried several kinds and they all suck. She didn't even bother getting the French prescription filled last week. She's not big on pills other than occasionally for recreation. Liquids are another matter.

"I think you are an excellent candidate for them now, during this time of transition. I'll give you another prescription after the holidays. Do you take walks?"

"Not if I can avoid it."

"Consider it. Paris is a lovely city for walking," she says proudly. "It is also my prescription. Dress warmly. Wear trainers and walk for twenty minutes." She means tennis shoes.

"Okay. Why?"

"It stimulates the system, makes you exercise, releases good chemicals in the brain. Helps you sleep. About our appointment next week?"

Summer rises to go. She needs a nap after all this work. "Thanks," she says. "Oh, shoot, I can't make it next week because of the play. And it goes on for a while. I can call to make another appointment when I better know my schedule?" Shrinks she's known in the US aren't so bossy or overdressed. Plus, she has no intention of coming back.

Dr. Garnier pauses, but says, "*Très bien.*"

TWELVE

PAIS is closed for Thanksgiving. Mom is having a dinner party this evening and Summer plans to avoid it. She's just returned from the large Monoprix nearby, wheeling the blue plaid plastic shopping caddy heavy with bottles to sustain her through the coming weeks. She's going to pass all her classes come hell or high water but she'll need a little help from her good friend Vodka.

The checkout lady didn't even look twice. *Vive la France.*

Her cell phone dings with a text from Moony:

Hunting props at Les Puces. Métro Porte de Clignancourt 13:30. Come with?

She texts back fast as white lightning:

Okie-dokie. See you then!

The day brightens like a meteor shower.

Summer descends with determination into the Métro, but her breathing speeds to panting, and the crowds swell and threaten to suffocate her. Bad trainophobia. She about-faces and climbs back up to ground level, leaning against a news kiosk until she's steady.

She finds an ATM, withdraws some euros, and hails a taxi. Then waits for Moony outside the Métro entrance near a bedraggled café and a phone card store. She's so happy he invited her, but her palms are sweaty, and she can't stop fidgeting. It's gray, cold, and drizzling. North African immigrants stroll by in distinctive long clothes and head ware. Summer uncorks her flask and takes a deep pull. Liquid courage. Then she pops a piece of cinnamon gum.

Three young men, Arab gangbangers by their tracksuits, bling, and attitude, are eyeing her. The French call them *racaille.* She tries to ignore them but clenches her teeth. These North African guys think a woman by herself is against the law. That it means you're a prostitute.

One of them walks closer to her and says something; she has no idea what. "Go away," she says, looking him in the eye.

He makes rude kissing noises at her.

She gives him the finger knowing full well that the gesture is much more shocking in France. His friends hoot.

The guy's furious. "Fook you."

He picked the wrong girl to diss. "Fookez *VOUS* and your friends. You seriously want a piece of me?" Her mouth has gone dry so she spits her gum on the ground near his shoe. His track pants are tucked into his socks.

He hesitates. Confusion and fear play in his eyes, Summer notes coolly. Definitely not what he expected.

Poor guy. He has no idea that she has nothing to lose.

He takes two quick steps toward her as if to compensate for his delay. More skinny homies, looking amused, slink up and surround them. Now he's feeling braver and rattles off a bunch of chipped and broken-sounding French, an ugly sneer on his face. The others laugh.

Adrenaline courses through her veins, as she fleetingly wishes she were her old weight. *Never corner something that's meaner than you are,* her dad used to say.

A half dozen guys inch closer. She probably can't vanquish them all but she could do some damage. She's threatened people numerous times, but has only come to blows twice. The possibility of sexual violence distracts her. Six on one. But surely not here on the sidewalk in front of the Métro entrance in broad daylight. Although pedestrians are now keeping clear of them.

She steps toward him, watching herself move in slow motion. Every detail of the scene assaults her senses—garlic and grilled onions from a nearby restaurant, diffuse gray light reflecting off the chrome of a parked Honda, the guy's hi-def patchy facial hair, his flickering eye movements.

"In that case, don't forget to fook your *maman*." She pronounces *maman* with her best accent so he is sure to understand. He does, and snarling, fumbles to grab at something in his jacket. Fortunately, it's extremely unlikely to be a gun here. And she has a Swiss Army knife in her pocket. She can slash them with the corkscrew. Plus her flask is in an inner coat pocket over her heart, so at least if they stab her there, they'll bounce back.

Summer assumes her tae kwon do fighting stance.

THIRTEEN

"Summer!"

"Moony!" Summer cries. He's at the top of the Métro stairs. "These turkeys are annoyed that I'm not covered up with one of those . . . long *black dresses*!" She fails to smooth the shake in her voice. "Oh yeah, I did *clash* them and their moms." *Clasher* is a slang French verb she picked up.

The gang collectively observes Moony's limp and posture like the pack dogs they are. If they try anything with him, she vows to pop their eyes out.

Moony rattles off something in Arabic. They frown and look back at her. Summer holds her stance and lifts her chin. Moony pats his coat pocket and keeps talking, now in French that flies over her head. They look alarmed, exchange glances, and slink away.

Summer lets her breath out. "What did you say?" she demands when he reaches her side.

He scowls at her. "You mean 'Thanks for saving my butt.'"

"I was doing fine."

"Think so?" His right arm hangs, but he's shaking his left hand in her face. "Outta your mind? What you said—way more offensive than in Arkansas."

"I know it's not nice. They started it. They wouldn't leave me alone."

"You really can't back down," he states.

"Look, it's my training. *Sell* chicken, don't *be* one."

"What?"

"My family is—was—in the chicken business."

He shakes his head. "Oh. Right. Explains stupidity."

"I don't need someone to protect me!"

Moony looks at her like that's the dumbest thing he's ever heard. "Everyone needs someone to watch their back."

She blinks. "Whatever. So what did you tell them?" She is kind of drained.

"You're my violently insane cousin. Have your medication here." He pats his pocket and the left corner of his upper lip pulls suspiciously toward a smile.

Her mouth drops open. Then she laughs, and pulls out her flask. She offers it to Moony. "Just a splash? To calm our nerves."

"No, thanks."

"Don't mind if I do." She takes two sips then puts it away. "And, um, thank you." She does totally appreciate that he had her back. Plus it's just nice to be near him.

Moony says, " 'Black dresses' Muslim women wear, for modesty, are *abayas*. Men cover their heads and wear long *thobes,* too. In the Gulf."

"I know *why* they wear them. I just didn't know what they're called."

He herds her in the direction of the freeway overpass. The flea markets start on the other side of the freeway, la Périphérique. His eyes have dark circles, and his face is pale and pinched. At the risk of another fight, she asks, "Are you okay?"

He sighs, but doesn't get mad. "Yeah. Rough night."

"I know what you mean. Post-party penance."

"No. Not that."

"Oh."

They walk at a snail's pace past dozens of narrow collapsible stalls and blankets spread on the sidewalk. It's a mini-souk full of used clothes, shoes, cell phone covers, posters, and cheap red, blue, yellow, and white plastic bowls, tubs, and pails. Whiffs of grilled meat and ripe garbage float in the drizzly air.

Something is different about Moony today. His movements are stiffer. He looks sort of beat up. Maybe he's in pain. Maybe that's why he couldn't sleep last night. Jeez.

"You know, we could do this another day," she says carefully. "What with the sucky weather and all." The altercation left her feeling a little wrung out. Moony may feel the same. They could just sit in a café and talk.

"I'm fine." He frowns, clearly annoyed, then mutters, "Thanks to modern pharmacology."

"Okay, okay, just checking. What's on the shopping list?"

He pulls his phone from his jeans pocket and thumbs through a couple of screens. Small white French delivery vans and compact Renault hatchbacks zoom by as they wait to cross the road. The south end of the huge flea market area starts on the other side.

"Clothing, accessories," he reads. "Rifles."

"Rifles?" she asks. Maybe they are easy to get at Les Puces.

"Old ornamental ones. Probably too expensive."

"Oh. But we can check."

"Antique plate or bowl. One piece to wave around so audience thinks it's all old. Period clothing. 1910. Ladies' hats maybe."

"Isn't the costume designer in charge of that?" she asks. Graffiti that looks just like American graffiti covers the buildings, the walls, and the overpass above them.

"Yeah, but said I'd look." The light changes. They step into the street. A guy on a big French scooter rounds the corner and narrowly misses Summer. Moony grabs her arm.

"Truth or dare," Summer says, taking a chance.

"Truth. I avoid dares." He smiles.

"Ever been in love?"

"Madly."

She waits. "Aren't you going to give me a little more?"

"Frame questions better."

"Okay, with *whom* were you madly in love and when and what happened?"

"Nurse Sophie. In hospital. Met her my eleventh birthday." He grins. "Saw me naked."

"Ha!" Nurse Sophie probably helped givc him a reason to recover. Good for her. Summer's also relieved that he's not madly in love with petite Jackie-who-fondled-him-at-his-locker.

"You have a distinctive way of talking, you know."

Moony nods. "Used to be harder. To talk. Habit. Your turn."

"No, it's cool. Efficient," she says. They enter a covered walkway that goes past dozens of bright antique stores full of crystal chandeliers and massive wood and gilt furniture. "Um. Truth."

"Same question."

She hesitates, but knows she can trust him with the story. Wants to trust him with it. "It was more of an infatuation, hardly love, and I was unceremoniously dumped . . . and humiliated."

Moony regards her with surprise.

"Remember? I was bigger." She fills her cheeks with air to show him. "Last June—boarding school number four, for misfits—I had a crush on the debate team cocaptain. Not much to look at, but a very witty guy. Probably sociopathic."

"Here we go," says Moony.

This area is open air but covered from the light rain. A stall straight ahead displays stacks of soft piles of mostly white old French quilts, sheets, table linens, and dish towels. A rosy-cheeked woman is folding.

"And?" prompts Moony.

She's glad he's still listening. "One evening we, um, hooked up"—she glances at Moony—"then I was scared and avoided him for a couple of days. He dumped me kind of . . . publicly." She's never told anyone the full story and won't get into all the details now. It's more complicated. The dickhead posted a horribly unflattering fat photo of her, eyes half-closed, clutching a vodka bottle, with the caption at the top, DRINKING TO FORGET . . . At the bottom it read, I'M A SLUT. He shared it with his 743 friends. At least he got in trouble. But so did she. And at the time, it smashed her to an unprecedented low.

"Turn here," he says. "Stupid guy."

"Thanks." She froze it away months ago. It took a while, though.

A glint catches her eye across the courtyard to her left. At a stall crowded with gleaming silver candlesticks, bowls, and frames, a man in dark glasses and a fedora holds up and examines an ornate flask. It's exquisite and she's now dying for a slug from her own. He looks at her, expressionless, then smiles.

It's Kurt.

Summer stumbles on a crack in the sidewalk and almost pulls Moony down.

"Sorry!" she says. Whoa, what is he doing here?

"What?" says Moony. He turns toward the stall.

Kurt raises a gloved hand. He's looking at her like at a lavish layer cake.

Moony's eyes widen.

She nods at Kurt, but turns away. She's with another friend now. Could he have followed her? He's as hot as she remembers, but she will not think about him.

"Do you know that guy?" Moony's eyebrows are low and a scar between them is squeezed into a new shape.

"That's—I think I met him once. Let's just move on." And she drags him in the other direction.

FOURTEEN

Late the Saturday morning of the Thanksgiving weekend, Summer sits at her desk organizing her notes and assignments. She has a major French exam on the following Tuesday. Perfect. She texts Moony. She's been wondering how to see him again.

Can we schedule French tutoring?
Sure. Next week?
ASAP. Test Tues. Today?
I've got a football game this p.m.

He means soccer. She knows he's not playing. Maybe he can miss it. She calls him.

"Hey. You're going to a game this afternoon?" She'll talk him out of it.

"Have to. I'm manager."

"Oh." He's so *involved*. "Could we study tomorrow then?"

"Sure."

"How about four o'clock?"

There's a pause. Moony says, "Want to come watch the game today?"

"Is the hog's ass pork?" she says.

"What?"

"It's a rhetorical question. It means, 'yes,'" she says. "In Arkansas."

He laughs. What a great sound. A hum starts in her, warm gold notes in triplicate from violin strings, a cello, and a sax. Like the opening notes of Kentucky's "Looking for Grace."

Summer waits for Moony on the same corner where she saw the hooker, flanking one of the ubiquitous six-story limestone buildings with black wrought-iron balconies. She repeatedly zips and unzips the navy wool jacket she took from Mom's closet as she scans the street for her ride. She also pulled her hair back and swiped on some pink lip-gloss for the first time in months. Her stomach aches even though she's psyched. Probably because she's psyched.

For some reason, she thinks of an illustration of Pandora from her seventh grade unit on Greek mythology. A wispy girl with pouting lips in a white silky dress, trying to close the lid of the box she's just opened. At the time, she thought Pandora should have been prosecuted on criminal charges, like a huge oil company, for letting all that shit out into the world. Her twelve-year-old self couldn't get past the idea of how nice life might have been if Pandora had just minded her own flipping business.

A big American minivan with diplomatic plates stops and the side door opens automatically. Summer smiles when she sees Moony and slides in next to him. In the front is team captain Josh, the jock she met the day she met Moony, and Josh's mom. In France, no one can get a license until they're eighteen.

Josh turns around to look at her. "Truce?" he asks.

"Peace," she says.

But it's forty-five minutes of excruciating small talk with Josh and his mom out to the burbs and their game with a French team. They park at a gated club in Garches, with sweeping lawns and fields. The day is overcast.

Outside the van, Summer gulps in fresh, cold air, then sees

Moony limping toward her from the other side. "What's up with the cane?" she asks.

"Security blanket. No big deal."

She's not sure what he means, but she helps Josh carry a duffel bag of soccer balls and a case of blue sports drinks to their field. Gold leaves from towering trees flutter to the ground as she stands on the sidelines while the team warms up. The game is thinly attended.

Moony talks to the coach, clipboard in hand. The guys gather and at one point Josh glances over at Summer and says something. Everyone turns around. There's laughter and Moony looks down sheepishly. Perturbed, she looks away.

The whistle blows and the game starts. Moony spreads a bright yellow rain poncho on the damp ground and he and Summer sit. It's like they're perched on a giant egg yolk.

As he adjusts his bad leg, his hair swings off his right ear. A clear plastic hearing aid nestles inside.

"What did Josh say that was so funny?" she asks, trying not to stare at his ear.

"Called you my girlfriend."

"Poll results are in. He's a jerk."

"He thinks you're hot." He looks at her out from under his dark eyebrows in a way that she knows he thinks so, too. His brown irises have chlorophyll-like flecks of green.

"Dysfunctional way of showing it," she says, surprised. She wishes she could just enjoy the new attention, but it's hard to forget old defenses.

"He's got good taste. Speaking of"—Moony pulls a package from his jacket pocket—"Gummy bear?"

"Thanks." Summer takes a red and a white one. She should have brought her flask. Being with Moony is awesome, but these other people are annoying, ADD jocks on steroids.

Moony asks, "Know the game?"

"Yeah, I played until I was eleven." And her friend Katie was a nationally ranked midfielder in tenth grade. Supposedly, Katie *and* her boyfriend, Justin, showed up as freshmen at Dartmouth in September.

"What position?" He pops gummy bears into his mouth.

"Defense mostly."

"Why'd you stop?"

"Um, just got sick of it. Might have had something to do with when I finally got my dad to a game. Playoffs. He made a scene," she says, matter-of-factly.

"What happened?"

She picks at her jacket zipper again. "He was drinking from his 'water bottle,' um, actually full of white rum."

Moony's cheek twitches.

"I'd gotten the wind knocked out of me and was lying on the field. He wasn't watching. The coach helped me off and sent in a replacement. Only now, my dad stands up in the bleachers and yells, 'Get back out there, Summer!'" She doesn't mention that he added, *you pussy!* because it makes him sound so awful, and he wasn't. He was just loaded. She continues, determined to finish the story. "Then he yelled, 'Never everr, everrrr back down' and then he fell *backward* into a row of parents." She chuckles. "You see the irony, right?"

Moony looks horrified. "Uh."

"Probably no one in your family drinks, since your dad is Muslim. Am I right?"

He shakes his head. "Sweeping generalization. Dad drinks occasionally. Mom, too. Her dad had some issues."

"Happy to hear it. So you have a clue."

"Yes." He looks at her for a moment. "*I* had issues. With painkillers. Last year."

"Really? What kind of issues?"

He pulls at his collar. "Was taking too many." His look says, *obviously.*

"Sounds like fun." She grins.

Moony smiles in spite of himself. "No, it wasn't." He prompts, "Said he died, when you were twelve . . ."

"Yeah."

"Alcohol?"

She knows it played a part—the ball bullets past them. Three players suddenly surround them. Six muscular legs, in shorts, high blue or white socks and shin guards are jumping and straining in front of her. One of the French team players has to throw the ball back in from where they're sitting, in the way.

Summer stands up. Moony struggles and she gives him her hand. He hesitates, then takes it. She pulls. The moment she registers how nice it is to be holding his hand, she lets go too fast and he almost keels over. "Sorry!" she says. Her cheeks heat as he stands on his own.

"So yeah, my dad," she says, "he died of a stroke. By the time I got to the hospital, he was already brain dead. They unhooked his life support late that night." She remembers how cold it was. And the nice guy in the corridor. Light snow flurries swirling beneath the tall hospital parking lot lights.

Tomorrow is December already. Seventeen days until the anniversary.

Moony's looking at her. "I'm really sorry."

"Thanks."

Moony says nothing, but she can tell he's listening.

"He would have lived if someone found him sooner," she adds, thinking of Mom, never where she's supposed to be. "He was unconscious in the bathroom for hours before anyone even realized." Summer massages a dark tightness between her eyebrows, then turns it into a dozen bright snowflakes and sends them off.

"What about you?" she asks. "When did your folks split up?"

"After I got out of hospital. Was eleven." Like a Brit, he doesn't use an article before 'hospital.'

"Really? What crap timing."

He looks down at his deformed hand. "Accident was a huge strain."

"That sucks."

He nods but focuses on the game now. The other team is close to making a goal. "New goalie," he says. "Got to get it out of there—whoa! See that?"

A PAIS player just kicked the ball and it's soaring through the air deep into enemy territory. Moony bellows, "Go, Tobias!" as a guy heads it to Josh, easy as pie, who shoots it straight into the French team's goal.

Everyone explodes into cheers. The guys body-slam each other and hoot. Moony waves his cane. Even Summer claps and high-fives Moony.

Now it's one to zero.

She dares to ask, "Were you . . . ever afraid . . . that you *wouldn't* get better? Be able to walk again, and all?"

Moony says, "No. I knew I'd get better. Could stand any pain, was a matter of *when* I'd be back to normal." He pauses. "Not quite there yet." The corners of his mouth turn up. "Once I could walk without help, like eighteen months after the accident, *then* I had mental problems."

"You still do."

He laughs for real. "I know."

"I'm kidding. But why then?"

"Not unusual. At all. You've recovered, but reality sets in. Realize you're always going to be a gimp. Have pain, memory, bowel problems."

"Thanks for sharing."

"Certain things forever out of reach." He says all this so evenly, she realizes he's working not to sound down. How *does* he keep so positive and energetic about school and activities, she wonders. About life.

It's raining by the time the ref blows his whistle. Game over. PAIS won, 1–0.

On the ride back, the boys discuss and rehash each play. Tired and sinking, Summer sits quietly and wishes the middle seat didn't separate her from Moony.

Josh's mom lets them off at the avenue Foch entrance into the Étoile, across from the Arc de Triomphe. Summer observes the madness that is right-of-way in the six-lane, twelve-spoke roundabout and blurts out to Moony, "Want to . . . go have a coffee or something?" She doesn't want the time with him to end.

"Got a doctor's appointment," he says.

She believes him, but her disappointment spasms like he just said she's a fat, vicious liar and drunk and he never wants to see her again. Then tossed in a foul Sicilian curse on all her future offspring.

What is she thinking? It's hopeless. She already knows she can't do this. Be with someone. And find flipping purpose. It's absurd. She can't even keep a friend.

She will never get better.

Moony's watching her closely. "I'll limp you to your train," he says. "And see you tomorrow. 16:00."

She puts on a smile. "Oh, I'll just walk home from here. I'm close." She's still not capable of the Métro. She can't help herself—she scans the crowds, half expecting to run into Kurt.

As if reading her mind, Moony asks, "What about that guy? At Les Puces?"

"Which guy?" But she knows.

"That . . . Arab guy."

"At the silver stall?" He's not Arab. Maybe it was hard to tell with Kurt's shades on.

"I don't know him. Just ran into him once."

"Where?"

"Out doing touristy stuff." She doesn't feel like sharing this info with Moony. She's divulged too much for one day. Anyway, it's her business.

"Think he's following you?" Moony asks. "Don't engage him," he says sternly. "In any way."

"Please. He's not following me. It was just a coincidence." She looks down at the sidewalk, then back up at Moony. "Don't worry, I know my way around the block."

FIFTEEN

Sunday afternoon, December first, Summer watches a Tibetan sky burial on YouTube while she unravels the crocheted afghan on her bed. She should be studying French and preparing for Moony's impending visit but can't focus on irregular verbs and political vocabulary.

The Tibetan family is bringing the bundled body to rest it on a few rocks so it's not on the stone floor of the tower. Seated monks ring the area. Everyone sits out of the way so that the birds—vultures, actually—can do their work. Although they don't show that part. It's not morbid at all. *Jhator* is the practice of offering your body to animals as a final act of kindness. You don't need it anymore. They get nourishment. Everybody's happy.

The building buzzer sounds.

She startles, clicks off her computer and jogs out to the apartment door. The front entrance to the building is open during business hours, but locked at night and on weekends with a code pad. She already texted Moony the outdoor code. Once in the building, a second main door has a buzzer for each apartment and video camera for viewing visitors.

The video screen in their apartment is lit up and a black-and-white image of Moony's face flickers there. She hesitates, then presses the intercom. "Come on up. Second floor. Only door."

He smiles as she jabs the button that remotely opens the inside door to the elevator and stairs. She wishes she'd studied more French. He's going to think she's dense.

Oh, and sloppy.

She runs back to her bathroom, pulls a brush through her hair and dabs on some lip-gloss. Then she shoves a pile of folded, laundered underwear into her armoire. The front doorbell chimes. She trots out in time to see Ouaiba open the door.

"*Monsieur Moony est là,*" Ouaiba announces with a big smile.

Moony stands inside the foyer craning his neck at the fifteen-foot ceiling, the chandelier, the gilt mirrors, and the antique French furniture.

"Hey," she says, grinning. Her anxiousness evaporates on seeing his face. They kiss cheeks. He's the only person she's liked doing that with. It's not a great custom as far as she's concerned.

"Bling crib," he says.

She gestures vaguely at the room. "Thanks to all the brave chickens. Um, come on back this way. Mom's got a soirée going on in the living room, best avoided. Tiptoe." Last thing she wants to do is to expose him to Mom.

Moony has no cane today, but points to his right leg and thick shoe bottom and reminds her, "Tiptoeing's not an option."

"Right. My bad."

As they walk past the open double doors to the living room, Mom calls, "Summer? Come in, darling, and say hello." There are about seven or eight people in the huge salon, all gripping champagne flutes. A two-foot-tall cone paved with rows of beige caramel and pale pink strawberry *macarons* topped with icing roses sits on the coffee table.

Summer rolls her eyes and leads Moony in and introduces him to Mom. Mom holds out her hand and looks surprised when Moony offers his left to shake. Summer observes her mother sizing him up, a disabled Arab kid in a hoodie, and silently dares Mom to make any condescending comment or gesture. But Mom doesn't.

A familiar but unidentifiable beefy, balding man bounds up, sloshing a crystal tumbler overfull with scotch. "Hello, gorgeous. I don't know what that thing is in your nose there, but you sure shed some pounds, you skinny thing." He grabs and hugs her, spilling more of his drink. Summer steps back, scowling. Too bad she can't say the same for him. She didn't recognize Wild Winston because he's gained thirty pounds and lost most of his hair since the last time she saw him.

He adds, "And nice of you to get dressed up for this. Har-har."

She looks down at her old, too large Alcatraz T-shirt. A comeback involving his inability to remove his belly or put on another head of hair pops in her mind, but she just says, "Har-har yourself. This is my friend, Munir Al Shukr. Moony, this is Winston Thomason, Houston resident and chicken lawyer."

Moony says, "Nice to meet you." He shakes hands again with his left.

A catering woman offers them hors d'oeuvres. Summer takes the nearest, a gray slab with flecks of parsley spread on a thin slice of baguette.

Winston turns to her and says in a serious voice, "So how's everything going?"

Summer says, "Fine. I'm working hard. Moony's here, in fact, to help me with French. Yuck! Liver." She spits the masticated hors d'oeuvre into a napkin then sticks it on the tray of a passing server.

Winston grimaces. Then says, "Are you on track to start up somewhere in January?"

"I don't know."

Winston's eyebrows shoot up and his chin sinks back into his second one. Just answer him, she thinks. "Probably Jonesboro. We're working on it. The college counselor is helping me."

Moony's staring down at the carpet. Mom pulls him over to meet one of the French guests.

"Awright," drawls Winston. "Then we'll see about transferring you. Assuming you keep your grades up."

"Right," says Summer, turning away. The other guests resume chatting all at once. They must have been enjoying the show.

She pulls Moony out of the room, grabbing two full champagne glasses from a tray on their way out.

"Sorry about the grand inquisition in there. I hate these things. They bring out the thirteen-year-old in me."

"No kidding," Moony says drily. "Jonesboro?"

"That's where Arkansas State is."

"You start in January?"

"Um, probably not. More likely next fall, at Whipperwill U. Or some place like that. At least, that's the plan, for now." She sighs. "First, I have to graduate. For that, I have to pass my French test."

"*Insha'Allah*."

"What's that mean again?"

Moony smiles. "God willing."

"It's going to take more than God." She pauses at her door, and turns to Moony. "My grandpa left me money when he died. But I have to graduate from a private high school and a four-year university by the time I'm twenty-two to get it. I'm already a year behind schedule, and they're about to call in a hazmat squad."

"Oh. Get to work, then."

"I guess."

They go to Summer's room and she indicates an overstuffed chair for Moony. He examines the boxed set of Tolkien's *Lord of the Rings* trilogy on her dresser. "Nice."

"It was my dad's. I think he secretly wanted to be Aragorn."

"Don't we all."

Dad took her to see *The Fellowship of the Ring* when she was too little. She got so upset when the Balrog pulled Gandalf into the abyss of Moria under the Bridge of Khazad-dûm, they had to leave the theater. And get chocolate ice cream. They watched it all the way through a couple of years later, though.

Moony sits. She holds out a glass of champagne.

"No thanks."

"How come?" She drinks down half of hers.

"Walking pharmaceutical lab. Throw in alcohol, I'll combust."

"Well then. More for me." She downs the rest. He's staring at her. "What?" she asks. "Everybody likes champagne." Her friend Grace drank it for breakfast. "Some university found links between champagne and cognitive health benefits."

"Keep it in your flask?" He raises one scarred eyebrow.

She looks at him a beat before answering. "No. I keep chicken bouillon in there." She pulls back the blackout curtains so they have enough light to see.

"Can you conjugate?"

"Of course. Don't look at me like that."

"Wonder how you can function well, is all."

"Lots of practice. I study *better* when I've had a drink." He does disapprove. He's wondering how much it all runs in the family. She sucks in her cheeks. If Moony *really* knew her, he'd probably march out of here. But she'll show him. She knows how to be a good student. She places his rejected full glass and her empty glass at the far edge of her bedside table and then plops down on the king-sized bed.

"Now can I ask you something?" she says, kicking her shoes off and sitting cross-legged.

He answers warily. "Okay."

"Why do you care?"

"Didn't say I did."

"Oh, fine. Feel free to pry into my personal life whenever you want, then."

Moony sets his jaw. "Need the tutoring income."

She chuckles. "Whatever you're charging, it's not enough."

SIXTEEN

Later the next evening, after a long day at school and a deep, fortifying shot of vodka, Summer marches into her mother's room. She has some questions.

Mom's seated in her gray marble bathroom, wrapped in an oversized terry-cloth bathrobe. She's stroking moisturizer upward on her thin chicken neck. Not someone Summer should be intimidated by.

"Oh, there you are," says Mom, as if she had called Summer in. "You know I'm leaving tomorrow, don't you?" Camus lies at her feet. He shows Summer his teeth. With his underbite, he's ridiculous, not menacing.

"Yep. You mentioned it."

"Winston's going, too. And I have two invitations to hear the poet laureate speak at the US ambassador's residence tomorrow evening. Since we won't be here, I thought you might like to use them."

"Okay." It's not exactly a big windfall, but she's surprised Mom thought of her. "Thanks." Mom's sure spending a lot of time with Winston lately. "Um, thanks for the shirts and jeans, too." Yesterday, Mom set her up with a personal shopper at one of the old *grands magasins* department stores. It was an exercise in frustration on so many levels, but she did find stuff afterward at the Gap across the street.

"Did you and Winston have a chance to chat?" Mom talks to Summer's reflection in the giant mirror as she smooths on liquid foundation.

"You could call it that. Why is he here again?" she says to the back of Mom's head.

"Trust business. He wants to know about your progress toward your diploma."

"I know. We discussed it. I keep telling you guys, every day, that I'm working and that things are fine." Despite everything, she doesn't really want to disappoint Mom again. But if things *aren't* fine, then it may not matter anyway.

"Darling," Mom says to the mirror, "he and I both are worried that if you forfeit the terms of your grandpa's will, these vultures will fight us even harder than they already are."

Vultures. "What happens if I . . . forfeit?"

"I believe the money's meant to go to an 'eliminate the whales' charity."

"No! Really?"

Mom chuckles without wrinkling her face. "No, not really. But some right-wing foundation."

Mom's trying to head her off. Summer demands, "And what about you?"

"What about me?"

"If I get the money, do you get any?" She puts her hands on her hips. That would sure explain why Mom gets so worked up about all this.

"No," Mom says with a prim expression. "My grandmama and your father left me very comfortable and I have my work, even though it's hardly lucrative. But you would certainly be able to take care of yourself." She chuckles. "And anyone else you could think of."

"Oh." That would be good, Summer thinks. She likes money and knows she's too wimpy to get by without it. Maybe that's all there is to it. Mom just wants her to take care of herself. She has been for years, emotionally anyway, if not financially. It's no secret that Adrienne never wanted to be a mom in the first place.

"How is it with Dr. Garnier?" Mom asks.

"Fine. She's, uh, well dressed. We were going to discuss Dad's death last session, but we didn't have time."

Mom doesn't bite. "Have you made some friends?"

"Yes. Loads of them."

Mom takes a sip from her drink, then backtracks. "I know you feel like we're riding you hard about your school and the will. I suppose we are. But it's a lot of money at stake. A lifetime of financial independence. What's being requested of you is not that difficult."

Summer bristles. "How do you know? How can you say that? Maybe not hard for you, but it is for me."

"Don't raise your voice. Why is it hard?" Mom asks evenly.

"I don't know. Studying is so . . . I can't focus. Anymore." Or care, she thinks. What's hard is to describe how she feels lately. If she could only use one word, it would be "gray." Or one phrase, *Trapped in a giant cobweb of blah.* Nothing is exciting. Not parties, not clubs, not movies or TV, not new shoes or a convertible. Not even Disneyland Paris.

Moony is a bright spot, but she's not even sure about that anymore. Explaining any of this to Mom is not worthwhile.

Mom resumes, "Dr. Garnier should be able to help you with that. But you've got to make a big effort here, Summer. To throw all that money away—a huge gift like that, would be like throwing away . . . your whole life." She gazes at Summer in the mirror.

"Why are there so many flipping strings attached? Why can't I just get my GED? Then an online degree or something?"

Mom says lightly, "Everything has strings attached, darling."

"Right." Mom's love and approval falls into that thousand-dollar category: Things with Strings Attached.

Summer reminds herself that Mom's mother ran off with a tennis pro, when poor Mom was only seven. And Aunt Liz was five. Another fascinating but verboten topic.

Mom continues but looks like she just sniffed an off wine. "Also because your grandfather was a very controlling man. He didn't want you to turn out like your dad."

"Jesus." Summer wishes for the thousandth time she had siblings to divert family attention. And the whole toxic thing between Dad and Grandpa. She didn't see Grandpa much, and doesn't really remember or was too young to understand it.

"There was so much antagonism between them that I'm sure in their next lives the two of them will be sent back as Siamese twins."

"*Conjoined*. And I don't get it."

Mom blinks at her reflection. "They'd have to learn to live with one another. Settle their bad karma."

"I didn't know you believed in reincarnation," Summer says.

"I'm just saying." Mom sighs. "Was there anything else?"

Yes, there is. She plunges ahead. "I wanted to ask you about Dad."

Mom's elbow juts in the air, holding the curling iron in her bangs. She shifts to see Summer at a better angle in the mirror, one thin eyebrow raised.

"How did he die? I mean I know his death certificate says brain hemorrhage. But what exactly happened? And why?" Their housekeeper had realized he was locked in the bathroom, she knows that much. Summer had been spending the night with a friend and was taken to the hospital before they took him off life support.

"Your father's drinking problem had gotten serious. He had alcohol-related complications."

"What complications?"

"Liver issues. Esophageal bleeding."

"What does that have to do with the stroke?"

"He had certainly been drinking that day." She pauses. "He . . . may have had a reaction to some meds he was taking. And he fell, too."

"So—wait. Did the stroke cause the fall?"

"We don't know."

"Then he went into a coma." Summer's feet are planted on the gray carpet, hands back on her hips.

"He did."

"And no one found him for a while."

"Yes." Mom bows her head. She had been at the country club the whole day. Scores of witnesses.

Summer presses, "So what are you saying?"

Mom closes her eyes. "His death was complicated." She sets the curling iron down, then turns to look at Summer in the flesh. "His depression, which he refused to deal with, affected everything. His drinking. How he took care of himself—or didn't."

Mom raises her eyebrows at Summer. Summer's own eyes in the mirror are wide with surprise. "He was depressed?"

"I thought you knew this." Mom frowns.

"I am not Sylvia the Psychic!" Summer explodes, throwing up her hands. "You're the only one who could tell me and this is the most time we've spent under the same roof for decades! Plus you never will discuss any of this." In truth, she had suspected that Dad was depressed, as a therapist at St. Jude's suggested, but it's still weird hearing it now. In the context of his death.

Mom forces her breath out her nose. "Wally wrestled with depression off and on since he was a teen." She pauses and looks at Summer pointedly. "It runs in his family."

"Wasn't he getting treatment?"

"Dr. Kong prescribed him antidepressants, but he wouldn't take them properly. And, there were his issues with Grandpa."

"Yeah, why was Grandpa so mean to Dad?"

"Mainly because your dad tried to stand up to him," Mom says with a sigh. "Grandpa stripped him of authority and all his shares in the company."

"Grandpa took Dad's shares in the company away?"

"Yes. With a bunch of expensive legal wrangling. And put them in trust for you."

"Those were Dad's?" It's a punch in the jaw. Summer sits down on the hydrangea-blue upholstered bench.

Mom shakes her head and says softly, "He just seemed to lose all energy and will."

"You could have saved him. You should have had his back!" Summer's voice quavers.

Mom glares at Summer in the mirror again. "I tried dozens of times to get him to help himself."

"I mean you should have been home. Found him sooner." Now Summer's voice cracks and she furiously blinks away the burning in her eyes.

"I'm sorry I wasn't." Frowning, Mom picks up a sleek silver case of blush, and brushes some on her cheekbone. "The tickets are on the front table."

Mom is not sorry. She packed Summer up and moved to Paris so fast, it blew Summer's hair back. But she's too tired and dispirited to generate any snarky comebacks.

"Have a nice trip, Mom."

SEVENTEEN

Summer and Moony stand in line outside the wall of the US ambassador's residence on the rue du Faubourg Saint-Honoré across from sleek haute couture and jewelry boutiques. Oversized luxury cars disgorge their multinational, expensively clad passengers. Students and bourgeois alike must go through security.

Moony's wearing a blue-striped button-down shirt and a forest-green sweater, grinning and bouncing like a kid. It makes her smile. She wasn't sure if he'd turn up or not and has to admit she would have been crushed if he hadn't.

Please don't let me mess this up, she thinks, standing as close to him as she can without being creepy.

"You're quiet today," says Moony.

"Am I? This is a long line."

"Everything okay?"

"Absolutely." She touches her nose ring.

"You look great," he says.

She smiles. She's wearing a skirt that minimizes her butt, and a pair of Mom's smooth leather boots. "You brought your passport, right?" she asks. "Not the Gulf one. The American one."

"Of course." He gives her a *How clueless do you think I am?* look.

A guard directs them into the compound courtyard and to another queue that winds into a small building. Summer takes the mint gum out of her mouth and sticks it in a thin, bullet-shaped trash can. She had a strong vodka and OJ before she left home and hopes there's no trace.

Moony asks, "How did the French test go?"

"*Super.*" This is an exaggeration, but she's sure she passed. "You're an excellent tutor."

"Thanks." The line has moved ahead and he steers her by the shoulder. She memorizes his touch. He's slow to remove his hand.

They slide their passports and the invitations to a uniformed guard behind a counter. "Zee names do not match zee invitations."

"Oh," says Summer. "They're my mom's. Adrienne Barnes. See? I'm Summer Barnes. It says 'and guest.' Moony"—she picks up Moony's passport—"Munir Butterfield Al Shukr—is my guest."

"*Pas possible.* Zee names must match."

"My mother was invited. She gave these to me."

A tall guard eyeing Moony's complexion and shaggy hair says, "Sir, could you step over here, please?"

"Sure," says Moony.

"What's the problem?" Summer demands, her whole head heating even though something inside her is sluggishly congealing. They search her backpack, pulling out the flask, opening it, sniffing it, and then putting it back in.

"We need to do a search. It will just take a moment." The guy nudges Moony through the metal detector. It shrills.

Moony explains in his clearest speech, "I have metal in my leg, hip, and arm." He points with his good hand. "And my shoe."

"Yes, sir. I just have to check." The guard makes Moony remove his fleece jacket, then roughly pats down his shirt and jeans.

"Through here, mademoiselle." Summer goes through the metal detector and stops on the other side. Somehow, the guy pushes against Moony's bad leg, causing it to buckle. Moony has to grab for the table edge to keep from falling.

"What the hell *is* this?" she explodes. "You heard him, he has metal in his *leg*. His bones are pinned *together* with it! He was crunched in a car accident." She feels like her dad is watching her. Refusing to let her back down.

"It's okay. Summer, please." Moony's expression is aghast.

"No, it's not okay. This is ridiculous." Moony shouldn't see her like this but she can't stop.

"I'll have to search you, too, ma'am."

The matron behind them mutters. The crowd does not appreciate this scene. Right on cue, a suited embassy type rushes in.

"What seems to be the problem?" the suit asks.

Molten anger threatens to blow the top of her head off like a new Arctic Sea volcano under the ice cap. With all her might, she makes herself say calmly, "My name is Summer Barnes. My mother was invited, Adrienne Barnes. This is my friend and he's being discriminated against. Will you please explain to these people that we're not terrorists?"

Moony's holding his head in his good hand.

She hears the shrillness in her voice. Here she goes again, ruining everything.

The suit studies their passports then says quietly, "Miss Barnes, Mr. Al Shukr, will you come with me please?" A guard hands her the backpack. Moony limps ahead of her.

The man leads them into a room inside the carriage house. Another suit sits at a desk. He introduces himself politely, looks at the invitations and documents, then scans the passports in a small device. He hands them back. "Sorry for any problem. I know your mother. Enjoy the evening."

"Thanks," mutters Summer.

Moony and Summer silently follow the line of people up the front stairs of the main mansion, into a large marble foyer, where some American poetry lady welcomes them. Five living rooms of various sizes, with twenty-foot ceilings, fan out from the foyer. They walk wordlessly through huge double doors into a turquoise, then pink, and a mint-green room, all lined with gold moldings, massive paintings, and French antique furniture. A long salon at the end has about sixty petite red velvet chairs lined up before a podium.

They sit near the back. The gilt molding on the walls is blinding.

"What?" she finally says. "I embarrassed you."

"Don't need anyone to fight my battles."

"But it was my battle, too. You're my guest. They humiliated us." The shrill edge to her voice is creeping back in.

Moony scowls at her. "Was normal security stuff."

"Fine."

"Why are you being so . . . What's wrong?"

"Nothing." Yeah, why is she being so?

People are holding flutes of champagne. She excuses herself to go find the source.

In the biggest salon, a crowd surrounds a long, linen-draped table covered with silver trays of canapés and glasses of champagne. Summer takes a glass and downs it, then sips another as she presses her nose against the cool glass of the oversized French doors. She stares out at the floodlit, perfectly manicured shrubs and the golf-green lawn that sweeps out from a wide terrace over prime Paris real estate.

Poor Moony. Someone needs to tell him that being her friend is rough duty.

Feeling better, she goes back to her seat. The ambassador, a mega-wealthy, graying ex-quarterback, is already introducing the poet laureate, a tall and gawky guy with tufts of sticking-up hair. He reads to the hushed room but she cannot follow him, though she tries her best.

All this red velvet is buzzing and jittering her head. Maybe from the adrenaline of her tantrum earlier. The crowd's weird energy is magnifying it. She can't not think about Dad's death. He was really messed up and he didn't even try to get better. Seems like he just drank more. And Grandpa used *her* as a pawn to make him worse.

Now everything is howling and freezing and stinging like she's standing outside in a blizzard. Wearing only a push-up bra and thong.

She's got to get out of here.

"Be right back," she says, but Moony doesn't even acknowledge her departure this time.

She heads for the bar, but zigzags through two new rooms before finding herself in a long corridor lined with oversized oil paintings. AMERICAN ARTISTS reads a plaque. Gentle applause from the reading sounds in the distance. She paces the length of it hoping for an exit. She can't leave Moony here, but she desperately needs to get outside. She can't breathe.

A cigarette will help.

A man in a dark suit strolls in with two glasses of bubbly and two cigarettes dangling between his fingers.

"Summer," he says.

It's Kurt.

EIGHTEEN

"What are you doing here?" Summer asks.

"I was invited."

"You know the ambassador?"

"Yeah. Great guy."

"You can't smoke inside. And I—I think it's strange that you're here." He looks fantastic in that suit—and more like twenty-something than her age—but she cannot talk to him right now.

"It's a pleasure to see you, too," he says, holding out a glass for her. His red tie features mini martini glasses and tiny cigars. "Although in my case, it really is."

He seems downright delighted, in fact, his face lit up like someone just gifted him a pony. "Oh, for chrissakes." She takes the champagne and drinks. He holds out the second cigarette so she takes it, too.

"Want to catch a movie?" he asks. "If we leave right now, we can make a seven o'clock show."

"No, I don't. I'm here with someone else." She takes a deep drag. "*You* sure get around."

He shrugs.

"So, do you work full-time? How old are you anyway? Did you already go to college?"

"Yes, old enough, and I've been to many schools."

"You and me both."

A suited security guy with shades and a squiggly wire behind his ear appears.

He says sadly, “Miss Barnes.” She doesn’t recognize *him,* and he doesn’t even look at Kurt who is suddenly interested in a John Singer Sargent portrait of a nineteenth-century ambassador’s wife farther down the gallery. A tiny part of her is glad this guy showed up.

“Absolutely no smoking in here. Would you please take it outside?” asks security. He points in the appropriate direction.

“What about him?” Summer demands, thumbing at Kurt.

“Excuse me?”

She turns. Kurt’s gone, slick as oil.

“Fine.” She stomps to the nearest door, grabs the handle and shakes. It’s locked.

“Miss Barnes? To your left.” He gestures. “Your other left.”

Outside in the courtyard, she smokes, chugs what’s left in her flask and paces. She cannot go back into the salon and sit still. The icy black weight of something terrible that’s going to happen is getting heavier and closer. It’s like she’s held it off for a long time, but now there’s nothing she can do to get out of its way.

Finally, people amble out. It’s over. Summer scans the crowd to find Moony, and to avoid Kurt. Moony limps out late looking sullen. She waves in relief and falls in step beside him.

“Thought you took off,” he says, not looking at her.

“I—I just came out here, and . . . smoked.”

“He was good,” Moony says coolly.

“I—” She wants to explain how she couldn’t stay in there anymore. That she feels unhinged—loose and lost as a polar bear pup drifting on an ice floe. She didn’t know Grandpa stripped Dad of his part of the company. And gave it to her. Of course Dad knew.

She’s been trying to get it all to blow away. Freeze and float off in the frigid air! But it won’t.

She can’t get into all this with Moony of course, but she could tell him about Kurt. How he keeps showing up. She was wrong before about being able to take care of herself and that it's not anyone's business.

But Moony is grim faced, and limping ahead of her, not waiting. She embarrassed him, left him alone, and there are plenty of other reasons, too. He doesn't want to talk to her at all. He hates her.

"He was Big Bird in a turtleneck," she mutters. "And his poetry sucks."

Moony climbs on a bus, and she hails a taxi. Her only friend and she's doing it again.

NINETEEN

The next day Summer does not go to school or even get up. When Ouaiba taps on her door midmorning, she calls from her bed, "*Je suis malade.*" She does feel sick, flu-ish, and a day off to rest is a solid idea.

At midday when she reawakens, she rethinks her decision. These are the kinds of choices that have not paid off well in the past. Cutting classes. Staying in her room. She feels ill, but it's a freaking hangover, not a virus. She can still salvage this. Just go late, turn in her paper, get her assignments. Apologize. Do her work. Try again tomorrow. Stop being a chicken liver.

James Brown sings in her head, *Get up offa that thing!* Beat, beat. *And dance 'til you feel better.*

Get up offa that thing! Beat, beat. *And try to relieve that pressure.*

She can get back on track. The *only* thing she needs to worry about is getting a high school diploma. Forget all these ridiculous male distractions or getting anywhere near their hands. Holding hands. What was she thinking?

Just. Do. Homework.

She walks to Place Victor-Hugo to get a taxi. She forgot to eat and her stomach is unhappy. She used to live to eat. Now she can hardly remember to.

A high-tech ice cream shop, walled inside and out with polished black marble, looks inviting. Some chocolate ice cream might hit the spot. She'll order one to go and then hail a cab.

She just turned in the history paper online that was due this morning, but needs to talk to the teacher about some extra credit or something. The paper is not her best effort, but it's done. Now she needs to show her face in her other classes. If only going there didn't feel like scaling Mt. Everest.

In the queue, she thinks about Moony and what she'll say to him. She will see him, because she will find him. And apologize for being so flaky last night. She must.

Although he'll probably roll his off-kilter eyes and walk away.

She sighs. Wise move.

A whiff of stale cologne, old beer, and cigarettes makes her turn. Kurt stands too close behind her.

"Fancy meeting you here," he says, white teeth gleaming.

"Ohmigod," she says. Part of her is horrified, part is thrilled. Her knees are weak. He takes her arm. That same warm iciness spreads from his touch.

"Let go!" she blurts out. People turn around and stare at her. He lets go, but looks hurt. Now she feels like an idiot. She's too touchy. No, she's not used to people touching her.

He speaks quietly. "I had an appointment on rue Copernic and saw you come in here. I thought a little ice cream might hit the spot."

She blinks. That's what she thought.

"What kind of appointment?"

"Business."

"You're following me."

His eyes widen in alarm. "Honestly, I'm not. I did follow you in here, but I thought you were following *me* at Les Puces. Maybe great minds think alike."

"Um. Sure."

"Will you at least sit down with me for a moment? To eat your ice cream?" His voice is bedroom low.

She doesn't answer. His pupils are oversized. Dilated. That means you're looking at something you like, right? Or you're high.

Or brain damaged.

"I'm such nice company. And you are—besides heart-stoppingly gorgeous—spunky and charming."

She snorts. There's no getting rid of him. Besides, no one has ever called her charming before. Certainly not gorgeous.

Or spunky, for that matter. "Okay, okay."

He sits at one of the small tables and she orders two single Belgian chocolate ice creams in a cup. She could bolt, and go to school like she planned. But honestly, what's the point? She's already late, another half hour won't make much difference. Besides, he's watching her from across the room, smiling, godlike. He's muscular, lean, and somehow tanned. Maybe from skiing or a recent weekend closer to the equator. His face is balanced perfectly between rugged and pretty-boy. He's wearing a satiny blue oxford shirt—that she'd like to run her fingers across—under a jacket and jeans. He absently pulls his hand through his unruly mane of hair.

She wonders why no one else is staring at him, wondering which celebrity he is. Probably because they're too cool in this neighborhood. People either seem to look right through him, or stare at him in alarm.

"Thanks," he says as she sits down across from him. "I'll get it next time."

He leans over the table and x-rays her with his eyes as he takes a bite of the rich dark ice cream. Then he holds the spoon in his lips and closes his eyes. She can't help staring. "Mmmm. Orgasmic," he murmurs.

She pokes her spoon in her cup then puts it, ice cream–smeared, into her mouth and sucks. Her blood is humming too fast through her veins now to eat. She wants to sit in his lap and kiss him. At least. She knows almost nothing about him but imagines her tongue tracing his cheek, down his throat to that smooth hollow—

"What's up with the crippled guy?" he demands severely.

"Huh?" She's snapped from her fantasy. "I—he's my friend."

"I don't think so." Now he laughs. "Not anymore. He's a waste of your time anyway."

"What? Look, if I want your take on things, I'll ask. Anyway, he's not 'crippled.' He's disabled. And not even."

"I'm starting to get jealous. You need to pay more attention to your true friends now, like me." He glances out the window, then gives her another sexy grin. "Hey, the sun's out and we must make hay."

"What?" He's so Jekyll and Hyde–like. The sun *isn't* out. And all she can think of is a "roll in the hay." She's also dying for a slug from her flask.

"Come with me," he says, standing. "I've got a great idea."

"I—I can't. I've got to go to sch—somewhere." How annoying that he assumes he's a friend. She can't keep up.

"Nonsense." He takes her by the elbow and leads her outside. It jolts her, but she follows. "You'll love this."

TWENTY

Summer insists on a taxi. En route to the surprise destination, she pulls out her flask and downs several glugs. "Whew. That's better," she says. "Thirsty?" She offers it to Kurt.

He takes a swig, then squints at her. "What *is* that?"

"Blueberry and vanilla bean vodka mixed. Plus a pinch of cinnamon. I like to think of it as a liquid muffin."

They sit side by side, just touching. He radiates heat and she feels it creeping into her. She scoots a centimeter closer to him, her thigh touching his long muscular one. They're headed toward the Seine.

He intertwines his fingers in hers. Cold and slick.

Woot.

She's holding hands in Paris.

Threads of icy numbness weave in and around her finger and hand bones. He's not quite as young as she thought. More like mid- or even late twenties.

It's hard to be relaxed because she's taking a risk. She knows nothing about him. Who is his family? Where did he grow up and go to school? But another part of her doesn't care. She's sitting beside him going she knows not where, trusting him, at least a little. Right? It feels like they've crossed a threshold somehow. Not to mention that she wants to climb into his lap. Not for a bedtime story.

The taxi crosses the Pont de l'Alma then stops on the Left Bank corner. Kurt gets out and taps his long fingers on the rim of the door while Summer pays the driver.

"What?" she says as she gets out. "No small change again?"

He shakes his head sadly. "No."

Nearby, La tour Eiffel towers above them. The wind whips cruelly here by the river. Heavy, bruised clouds blow over as she pulls her coat around her.

"So where now?" she asks looking up. "By the way, I've been to the Eiffel Tower. And it's still kind of a hike from here."

"Nope. We're not visiting the tower now. Follow me." He takes her by the hand and they cross to the other side of the avenue to a little pavilion. A small sign reads ÉGOUTS DE PARIS.

"Welcome to the Paris Sewers," he says.

"Oh. They let you go down into them?" Who would want to?

"*Évidemment*," he says. The French way to say *duh*. "Buy a ticket there."

"Just one?" she asks.

"I have lifetime privileges."

"Of course you do."

She does as instructed. Kurt leads her down the stairs. Sure enough, the stern woman who takes her ticket, does a double take at Kurt, then scowls and waves him through. Kurt winks at Summer.

It's damp, cold, and quiet. They walk along a dimly lit corridor. Multiple large pipes run along the low ceiling. They ignore the framed photos and explanations periodically hung along the wall and pass a tour group of old people gathered around an exhibit of posters in glass cases.

"This is kind of boring," she says.

"Patience." He squeezes her hand.

They turn into a wide intersection. The thunder of rushing water and the smell of rotten, ammonia-laced, slightly sweet, decaying raw sewage swallows her. It's overwhelming, even in the cold, like a punch in the nose.

"Ahhuuk."

"*Eau de merde*," Kurt says gaily.

She peers over the concrete wall into a wide chasm of foaming, brown-water rapids, leaning for a good look.

"Why is it closed off with wire?" she asks.

"To keep people out."

He doesn't mean just falling ones. The implication settles over her along with the stench.

"Look," he says, jiggling the wire. "It's loose here on the corner. One could push it back far enough . . ."

Things rush by in the water, too fast for her to identify. "Jeez. *Not* a good way to go," she says quickly, stepping back. Although if someone really wants to die, she thinks, what difference does it make?

"No?"

She looks at him. "What? You think it *is*?" Her stomach sloshes. "Why are we here again?"

"For your entertainment, edification, and enrichment."

"I don't feel too good." Her vision is white around the edges.

"You are pale. Buck up, *ma poule*."

The walls are closing in and she rocks side to side in her boots, reaching for something to steady herself against. She wishes Moony were here with her instead of Kurt. He takes her by the shoulders, then puts one hand on her hip bone. "Deep breath. What a disappointment. I thought you'd get a kick out of this."

"What on earth made you think that?" Her eyes are closed. She shivers involuntarily. "Wait. *You're* disappointed?"

He leans in close, pressing himself against her, and touches his tongue to her earlobe, then nibbles. Through her queasiness, it barely even registers. He whispers in her ear. "You're beautiful when you're nauseated. Such a shade of jade green."

The contents of her stomach may truly erupt. She shakes Kurt off and staggers back a step.

"Got to get out of here."

He says coldly, "There is nothing I abhor more than quitters. Chickens." He touches her cheek. "Remember that."

"Chickens don't like you either," she mutters. It's all she could come up with in her state. She forces herself forward and focuses on the arrows leading out. But she winds around several times past new rushing rivers of excrement as each corridor doubles back on itself. She returns over and over again to the main intersection, like in a feverish dream. Kurt must be behind her, but she keeps moving. Finally she recognizes the main gallery and a SORTIE sign points the way. She jogs through the visitor reception area, and up the stairs into the daylight.

Doubled over, she gulps in fresh air on the street corner, not caring that it's exhaust laden. She kneels on one knee to wait for her stomach to calm. If Moony didn't hate her, she could tell him about this. After ten or so minutes Kurt hasn't appeared. She walks back to the stairs and looks down.

He ditched her, the jerk. For her entertainment and enrichment. Please. A big buildup, expectations of something fun and romantic and then . . . lectures. And nausea.

She goes to the corner and waves for a taxi.

At least he makes school look good.

TWENTY-ONE

Over the next two days, Summer works to catch up at school, although she goes late and leaves early. She takes taxis, unable to override her trainophobia.

She cannot help but fantasize about Kurt. Undressing each other in a taxi. He's so hot, but she *is* out of her league with him. He could have any female he wants and yet he keeps making runs at her. Why? Because he's a jerk and probably a broke one. He must suspect she has access to money. "*Ma poule,*" he called her. *My hen*. Is that a normal term of endearment or does he knows she's a chicken princess?

They were certainly holding hands in Paris, but he's not at all what she had in mind. More like a boyfrenemy. Maybe it's her. For sure, she could handle him better if she were more experienced.

She avoids Moony at PAIS, cutting concert choir all together. She wants to talk to him, and to apologize, and almost texts him numerous times. But she cannot pull the trigger.

On Thursday, she turns in a big Environmental Studies lab, proud to have completed it. But then Mr. Hernandez hands back a trig test and Summer's is covered with red marks. He's requested an appointment with her.

Madame Lacroix springs a surprise French *dictée,* or an oral test, on them. She speaks slowly and clearly about actor Jean Dujardin and the film festival at Cannes. Summer writes down what she hears, definitely getting "Academy Award" right, but she's flailing and near tears. She studied all this, but her head is filled with Jell-O.

Cluck. Maybe drinking is killing too many brain cells.

Final exams are in less than two weeks. She must get her act together. Stop partying. Or more accurately, drinking alone. Which is uncool anyway. Stick to her study schedule. If she can just pass finals, she may be all right. Graduate by the skin of her beak.

On Friday, she goes into a ladies' restroom stall to drink a few slugs from her flask. Normally, she waits until after school as the rules here are clear and strict, and she's gotten expelled for less. But she's not going to be able to do what she must do today without it. Then she pops a Mento and marches into Concert Choir, head held high.

"Mademoiselle Barnes. You have decided to grace us with your presence," says Monsieur Blanche drily.

"I have," she agrees. She stuffs her sweaty hands in her pockets.

"It's been so long." For some reason, he likes her—the only faculty member who does. "We are preparing for the holiday concert on the seventeenth, as you may or may not remember." He holds out copies of sheet music. "'Feliz Navidad,' 'O Tannenbaum,' and 'Douce Nuit.'"

"How Euro. I mean, how nice," she says. There's no flipping way she'll show up for that. In her peripheral vision, Moony is trying not to smile, but failing, so she mirrors him. Widely. She takes her place and does her best to sing with the group. Moony keeps looking at her.

When class is over, Summer hangs back. Moony moves on, but waves at her.

Relief floods her.

But she has no energy left to deal with Mme. Laforge so she ditches her follow-up appointment to discuss colleges.

That evening, a Friday, she works on her English paper, smoking almost a whole pack of cigarettes. In her delayed-reaction way, she thinks quietly about Dad, too. He must have been depressed in a big way, from what she remembers. He gained weight, slept a lot, and sat around stony-faced, unresponsive to her, and to pretty much everything. At the time, she thought it was her fault. It's sad but it also explains a lot.

Yeah. She's got to watch out for it in herself. Genes and all that. History might repeat itself. She wonders if it would be worth it to get back on her last meds. She's doing okay, but she'll think about it.

Before she settles in to watch a documentary on mummification, she texts Moony with a fluttering stomach and clammy hands:

Sorry for everything.

She fiercely hopes that will cover it.

TWENTY-TWO

Saturday morning, Summer rises at the crack of 11:00 A.M. and eats Ouaiba's tasty French toast, *pain perdu,* with Canadian maple syrup from Monoprix. It reminds her of Saturday mornings at IHOP with Dad a thousand years ago.

Back in her room, her phone shows a missed call. Moony!

She calls him right back. "Hi," she says tentatively.

"Summer!"

"Um, saw that you called." She squeezes her phone-holding arm, until it hurts, then stops.

"Missed the prop meeting," he states.

"Oh, drat. Was that yesterday? Sorry. Won't happen again." He probably knows she's kidding.

There's a pause. "Never thanked you. For the culture."

"About that," she says. She sits, then falls back on her bed and stares at her ceiling. "I was really weird, even for me. I feel terrible about it."

"Enjoyed the poet."

Now she's squeezing her phone so tightly her fingers are bloodless. "But you were pissed off with me. Hooboy. Um, of course."

"Over it."

She closes her eyes and lets her breath out. Thank God, she thinks. Another chance. I won't blow it. She needs him and his friendship enough that it scares her. "What are you up to?"

"Marché Saint-Pierre. In the eighteenth."

"What's that?"

"Fabric market."

"*Why?*"

"Prop work."

"Are you there now?" she asks.

"Going." He pauses. "Come with?"

"Love to." Truer words were never spoken. She clicks off and hustles to get ready.

This time Moony's waiting for her, leaning on his cane, when she gets out of the taxi in front of the Métro. Traffic on the busy boulevard de Clichy zooms by them. They kiss hello. She wants to hug him, but settles for making sure her lips touch both his cheeks, rather than just puckering air. Then indulges herself in a sniff of his limey soap.

Don't be a perv, she reminds herself. She will be on her most balanced, sober, considerate, and responsible behavior today.

It's a rare sunny but cold day. A large bus full of Irish tourists (judging from the shamrock on the side) unloads down by the neon-outlined windmill of the Moulin Rouge. Even though Pigalle is full of sex shops and peep shows, it lacks the menace of the area outside the flea markets.

They pass an XXX store with packaged blow-up dolls and handcuffs hanging in the front window next to stacks of dusty DVDs featuring lots of female flesh. She pretends not to notice, as Moony's face is squinched into discomfort. Like he's worried she's never seen this stuff before. She appreciates his concern. Maybe he's pretty traditional, even conservative about sex.

"Come on," he says, veering up the hill that is Montmartre, passing small cheap souvenir and notion shops stocked with all colors of threads, zippers, ribbons, and trims. At the next block, he points. "Look."

At first she thinks he means the old-fashioned carousel across the street in a park. It's full of squealing kids. But then she gazes farther up the steep hill. Looming over them is a giant, white, multidomed church framed by bright blue sky and puffy clouds.

"Cool. Arkansas State Capitol crossed with the Taj Mahal," she quips.

"Sacré-Coeur. Built late 1800s. This way. Marché Saint-Pierre." He veers to the right along the bottom of the steep park toward narrow winding cobblestone streets.

Several big buildings ahead, hundreds of bolts of bright-colored fabrics line the sidewalks. Shoppers, not tourists, crowd this tight street—mostly women, many wearing head scarves and dragging small children behind them. The kids who are not whining and pointing at the carousel turn to gape at Moony as they pass. Summer sees him through their eyes, tall and commanding but tilted, limping, and imperfect. Interesting.

From the awning in front of one small shop hang gauzy, jewel-colored, gold-and-rhinestone–encrusted belly dancing outfits. Moony pauses to stare.

"What are you looking for anyway?" Summer asks, noting feather boas and fake gold chains as well. Maybe he has a thing for belly dancers. She smiles.

He clears his throat, and walks on. "Uh, cheap cotton, use as 'wallpaper,' maybe curtains."

"And why do you of all people get to be the one who comes out to search the city for this stuff?" The theater is full of able-bodied crew who should be running around instead of Moony. "What about what's-her-name, the Norwegian set designer?"

"New to Paris. Doesn't know where anything is. Anyway, rather be outside. They're building today. I'm no help with a hammer."

"But doesn't this tire you out?"

"No," he says sharply.

"Okay, okay. It tires *me* out. Why you can't admit that you might occasionally get a little tired is beyond me. I *love* to complain of fatigue."

They walk into a big three-story building, with worn wooden floors and old-fashioned, patterned opaque glass above the doors. The faint scent of hundred-year-old dust hovers. Up a set of creaky stairs, they find bolts of inexpensive cotton spread out on large wooden tables and Summer approves some small flowery prints, Victorian looking stuff, ninety-nine centimes a meter.

In his perfect, slow French, Moony asks a sales lady to cut many meters of two prints, and they stand in line to pay the cashier, who sits in an old-fashioned wood-and-glass booth.

Outside, he asks, "You been? Want to go up?" He gestures with his head toward the grandiose cathedral above.

She grimaces. "All those stairs? I'll have to have a cigarette first."

He rolls his eyes at her. "Come on."

They climb slowly, not talking much, and don't stop to rest until they're under an arch on the church's front steps. She's breathing harder than Moony when he nudges her to look out at the incredible view of all of Paris.

"Look," he says.

"Wow." She gazes in awe. "Your hometown."

"Napoleon's tomb. Les Invalides," he says, pointing at the distant landmarks illuminated by the afternoon sun. "La Tour Eiffel."

The Eiffel Tower looks like a little toy off to the southwest. She can't help but think about the sewers—the *égouts*—near it, but quickly pushes them from her mind. She *would* like a cigarette now, and a slug from her flask while she's at it, but will wait.

"Are Muslims allowed inside?" she asks, hooking her thumb behind them.

"Don't be ridiculous."

"Just teasing. Do you go to . . . mosque?" A busload of Asian tourists crowd up the stairs and push around them.

"Yeah, in Kuwait mostly."

"Do you pray five times a day?" She's sincerely interested. Maybe it makes life easier for him. Maybe it's the secret of his success.

"Sometimes. More like twice. And meditate. Visualize good health. Hybrid Islam, Christianity, New Age."

"Wow. You could offend huge numbers of people with that."

"But not God."

"Okay. Whatever lights your candle." How cool and not surprising that he's spiritual. And that he's totally forged his own irreverent path of reverence.

"You and religion?" he asks.

"Not on speaking terms."

"Ha. Care to elaborate?"

She kind of wishes she did have some sort of religion. Or maybe a guru. Or something. "My folks weren't religious. But my grandparents were and I spent enough time in Bible Belt churches to know it's a bunch of silly man-made rules and lame explanations of unexplainable shit to keep the masses—especially women—in line."

Moony grins. "How do you really feel?"

"I've learned to expect nothing from life," she says, with a toss of her head and a little more vehemence than she intended.

"Hmm," Moony says. "But what does life expect from you?"

She doesn't answer, but his question sticks in her mind like a melted Normandy caramel. Yeah, why is she here? If only she could find a reason.

Whatever it is, she's not going to waste this time with Moony worrying about it.

"Come on, let's go in," she says, standing. She gives him a hand up, successfully.

Inside, it's white and bright and as cathedral-like as she expected, although with cleaner more modern lines. A huge blue and gold mosaic of Jesus Christ himself hovers over the altar in the massive dome. He's flanked by assorted saints. Two large angels carved in bas-relief float above the congregation.

"Pretty impressive," she says, craning her neck back. "I have nothing against churches—or mosques—by the way. Just against religions."

"Mind sitting for a sec?" he asks. He's pale.

"'Course not," she says. They sit in two of the wooden, ladder-back chairs. It smells faintly of incense, Moony's limey shampoo, and their salty warmness from the climb. Maybe it was too much for him. She has got to pay closer attention, because he's never going to say anything until he's almost passed out. It was his suggestion to come up here, she reminds herself.

She won't ask if he's okay. So, surprising herself, she takes his good hand. It's warm and strong. And like she just plugged into . . .

An answer.

"It's beautiful in here," she says. "Totally worth the extreme climb. Thanks for inviting me."

And for being my friend, she adds silently. Say it! You big chicken. And don't let go of that hand.

She says softly, "And for being my friend."

Moony's smile practically blasts sunshine. Would that she could reflect it back to him. She tries.

It's the perfect time to tell him about Kurt. That she knows Kurt better than she let on at Les Puces. And that something about him scares her. She needs to hear what Moony will say.

But Moony says, "I have another operation."

"You do? I thought you were done."

"Christmas holidays."

"That sucks. What for?" A knot tightens in her middle.

"List is long." There's something different in his voice. Reticence or fear, maybe. "Complications. I . . ." He doesn't finish and sighs deeply.

"But you've had operations before, right? You know the drill."

"Yeah. Twenty-two."

"Jesus!"

"Yep. There he is."

She looks up. "Very funny. That's a truckload of surgeries. You know what they say though, 'twenty-third time's the charm.'"

"Heh. Yeah." He pauses and bows his head. "Sometimes wonder what the point is."

"Fixing you."

He gives her a *duh* look. "May never end, though."

"I really wonder how you do it," she says, glancing at the false bottom of his right sneaker. "All that you do. With your . . . gusto and, like, grace."

He shrugs. "Secret is . . . gummy bears."

"Imagine that." She could sit here forever, with Moony's hand in hers. It's amazing. Like Kentucky sings, "Looking for grace. I know her face."

He adds softly, "Just get . . . tired out sometimes."

"Well, *yeah*." She gently squeezes his hand. He squeezes back. "Are you scared?" she asks softly.

"No." He lets go and pushes his hair out of his face. "Just of clowns. Scare the crap outta me."

She broke their connection somehow and the loss of it aches. But she laughs. "That's how I feel about ventriloquists' dummies. But I'm not a big clown fan either. What can I do? Bring you flowers?"

He gives her another *duh* look. "Gummy bears."

"You got it."

TWENTY-THREE

Mom taps on Summer's door.

"Darling? It's almost two o'clock."

"Mmmf?" She sits up as Mom opens her door. "You're home."

"We got back late last night. Lovely trip. But we—I've been invited to Verbier for a few days."

"Huh?"

"It's my friend Françoise. Her husband just left her and the kids. For his twenty-two year-old mistress," she huffs. "So I thought I should be with her. I'll be back Wednesday."

"'Kay, I'm up." She rubs her eyes and looks around. Thankfully the vodka bottle is back in her armoire. "Whatever, Mom. It's fine."

"When was your last appointment with Dr. Garnier?"

Summer can't think. "Um, last week? I missed it because of school." She hasn't gone since the second one.

"I just haven't received a bill from her lately. And she tried to call me the other day."

"Uh, can we discuss this later? I'm not awake."

"Fine." Mom's heels *tip-tap* down the hall.

She should just tell the truth, that she doesn't really like Dr. Garnier and she doesn't want to go to a French shrink. But then Mom will insist on finding another one and on and on it will go. It's better this way.

She checks her phone for any messages. None.

Of course, she was wishing to see something from Moony. Best to make believe she wasn't. She should find out more about his operation, too.

The tablet, books, and notebooks on her desk tower menacingly.

She pulls on jeans and a sweatshirt and heads out to buy cigarettes.

At the neighborhood *tabac,* she orders an espresso and downs it. Outside gapes the entrance to the Métro. She used to love the trains. She needs to get over her trainophobia. She'll go back to her work after a brief excursion, some walking.

She counts breaths and steps as she descends and reads and recites the ads. Breathing in for a count of six, and out the same way, she makes it down to the first platform. A train pulls in right away, and, heart pounding, Summer steps on and beelines for a seat.

She's light-headed and concentrating so hard on her breathing, it takes her a while to notice the guy across from her. His khaki pants are alarmingly greasy. His long gray beard hangs woolly and wild and his paint-peelingly strong body odor hits her like a slap. He's talking to himself. That explains why she got a seat near him.

When he pulls out a screw top bottle of red wine, she holds up her flask.

"*Santé,*" he says and drinks, smiling at her. To her health.

"*À la tienne,*" she responds, reaching across the aisle to clink containers. And to yours.

Whatever his sad story, this man survives. He doesn't care what others think. His eyes have kindness in them, despite everything. He's cool and probably not afraid of trains. "Everyone should drink on the Métro," she says loudly. A regal African woman in a chartreuse rolled headdress frowns at her and the bum.

That wasn't so bad, she thinks as she gets off at Les Halles, the old food market area, now an urban park and underground mall. Above ground in the quickly failing daylight and light snow flurries, she sits on a concrete wall near the dark cathedral,

Saint-Eustache. She can make out a couple of unremarkable gargoyles, warding off evil. As if. Skateboarders on walkways zoom and dodge the sculptures, gaggles of Goths, *racaille,* and pigeons.

An old lady in a wheelchair with no coat or socks is parked by the entrance to the church. A thin blanket covers her that even from a distance Summer can tell is dirty. Poor lady must be so cold.

A lone tough kid, fourteen or fifteen, is skateboarding near the wheelchair and keeps looking at the old lady. Summer rises to head over, afraid that he's going to rob the woman. He jumps off his board right in front of the chair and peels off his gold down parka. The old lady pulls back in alarm. He holds the jacket out to her. It hangs there until she finally nods. He helps her put it on, then her bony hand pats him on the arm. The lady smiles and clasps her hands to her chest as the kid skates off coatless beneath a blazing orange sky.

A surge of sadness chokes Summer at this surprising act of kindness. Why? This old, poor lady . . . where does she live and who watches out for her? And the bum on the train. Life has to suck for him, too. But he drank to her health. He's unbowed.

How can they stand it? The cruelty and horribleness of the world. Of other people. And yet, that kid just gave the old woman his coat.

To keep her going.

She can't bear it.

Moony is kind to *her.* He puts up with her shit. He even seems to like being with her.

Kindness is like hope. It feeds hope.

Which just keeps us around to suffer more, she thinks, anger rising.

It's not worth it. Why does she keep trying so hard to force a life that will never work?

She stands and scans the crowd. This is supposedly a place to get drugs. She doesn't have the energy to pursue it but is open to the possibility.

As she pulls out her flask again and takes a deep draw, a tall guy in a black leather coat with his back to her catches her eye. He's talking to a young Goth guy and they're off by themselves.

Summer's pulse races. It's Kurt. His hair, height, and posture are unmistakable.

He has his arm draped around the guy's shoulder and they appear to be deep in heartfelt conversation.

And here he is again, in the middle of a metro area of over four million. What the hell?

Kurt and the guy walk away. She jumps up. Now she'll stalk *him*.

Maybe he's gay. She thinks of him nibbling her earlobe. Or at least bisexual. It would be a relief if he were gay, she realizes, and not trying to . . . hook up with her But she knows he is. Trying to possess her.

They skirt the church and the crowds, then walk up a pathway into a small grassy area. A thoroughfare runs beneath. She stands down on the street by a twenty-four-hour brasserie that is brightly lit and smells like sauerkraut and shellfish. People walk in and out. She slips around the corner, so she can watch from the shadows. It's deserted where Kurt and the guy are.

The two of them step over the low fence on the path and walk to a grassy edge. Darkness has descended, but streetlights from the road below illuminate them as they lean over to look down at diesel trucks and compact French cars rumbling underneath. The guy's shorter than Kurt and has no coat, just a thin black jacket, heavy black boots, and lots of chains. Kurt gestures at the street below. The guy shakes his head. Then Kurt pulls the guy's black spike-hair-framed face to him and kisses him on the lips.

The guy says, "*Je t'aime toujours, Michel.*"

I love you always, Michel? Maybe she misunderstood. The guy's expression is sort of desperate and sad. Maybe Kurt just wanders the city picking up people using different names. What a slime bag.

Kurt lights a cigarette, turns and heads down the path out of the park to the street. The guy stares after him. Kurt veers in Summer's direction. She dashes behind a parked van.

Okay, maybe it's just a friend.

He walks right past her, trailing cigarette smoke, back into the city streets. She leans against the side of the van and wills her breathing to slow.

A jarring screech of brakes and honking cars blares from the underpass. She springs back to the corner for a line of sight on the guy, but he's gone.

Her feet are frozen to the asphalt. Heaviness that can only be rapid-forming ice climbs through her legs and trunk. She didn't actually see it, but there was no place else to go. That guy had to have just stepped off the overpass. Because Kurt walked away from him? No, surely not, but something very weird is going on.

Even though she can't feel her feet, she sprints past the brasserie to the boulevard and the taxi stand. She leaps into the first one. As they speed off in the winter evening toward the other side of town, flashing blue lights pass them going the other way, trailing that sound of French sirens, *weee-ooo, weee-ooo, weee-ooo.*

TWENTY-FOUR

The apartment is dark and quiet when Summer gets back. Mom's gone. In her room, Summer pours a tall vodka and gulps it down. The guy was there. He disappeared over a big commotion on the street, right below where he'd been standing two seconds before. And then sirens. There was nowhere else he could have gone, but down.

By choice.

"What is *wrong* with this city?" she bellows. "Why is everybody offing themselves?"

And Kurt was there.

Why has he been twice now near the scene of—She takes another deep quaff of vodka. He couldn't have known that she would be at Les Halles. She didn't know herself. It was random.

It was like she was drawn there. Pulled like a magnet.

Just stop.

She's being ridiculous. Overactive imagination.

Everything's fine.

While she's at it she fills her flask and takes a few slugs. The alcohol burns, then soothes and unclenches her. Antifreeze.

There's only a little left in the bottle so she bottoms up, too, for good luck. The vodka is helping. Her dear bosom friend, Wodka. She should make a documentary about it. Now she'll settle down.

She goes into the bathroom to pee, and then afterward, checks herself in the full-length mirror in her room. Her skin looks kind of blue. She *is* a little thinner—are those not ribs?—same big butt. She startles when she hears a loud buzz.

Huh? The outside intercom. She jogs unevenly down the hall that's tilting just a bit. Through the viewfinder she sees Moony. Yay! Oh, phlegm, she completely forgot he was coming for tutoring. She wouldn't have drunk so much. Shit on a stick. But it's wonderful he's here. She can handle it.

She buzzes him in the building, then fumbles with the lock that's all sticky, throws open the door, and leans hard against the hall wall. Takes forever for the prehistoric iron cage elevator to arrive.

"So glad to seeeee you!" She throws her arms around Moony and kisses him moistly on each cheek.

Moony looks surprised, then says evenly, "You're hammered."

She starts to say something but burps instead. "'Scuse me." It is hitting her kind of hard and fast, but she's not so far gone that she's not worried what Moony will think. 'Cause she really likes him. A lot! She giggles.

He blinks slowly. She takes a breath and says, "Noo, not that much." She tries hard not to slur her words, but she feels them sliding out from between her teeth and tongue in misshapen, elongated ways. "Jusss a little. Shoulda had it in grape juice." She's consumed at least a quarter bottle of some funky Romanian vodka. All at once. Even for her that's a lot. "Grape*fruit* juice."

Moony sighs and puts his coat back on. "I'll come back tomorrow," he says slowly and clearly.

"Nooooo." She grabs him by the shirt. "Dohn leave. Please. Whooaa." She loses her balance and crashes into him. "Sorry." He helps right her, but he looks so grumpy.

"That Goth guy. Jumped off the overpass. *Jumped*, Moony. I liiiike you so. Much. But I'm scared a . . . know whad I mean?" she says, throwing her arms around him. "How 'bout a hug?" He hugs her back, to her drunken surprise. He's also trying to help hold her level.

They tilt, and then crumple to the floor. He winces.

"Ohhh shit. You okay?"

"Fine," he coughs, but she realizes she's glommed on to his weak arm and shoulder. She lets go and sprawls back onto the Persian carpet where it's surprisingly comfortable.

"Some tea," he says. He pulls himself up by holding on to the gilded marble console.

She tries in vain to focus on him. The foyer is tilting fully now, starting to spin. "Wish you coulda met my dad. I'm jus' like him . . ."

He puts his hand on his hip and stares down at her. "Summer," he says firmly. "Get up." He gives her his left hand. "Hot tea."

Her roiling stomach demands her attention. "Ohhhh. Notta hampy capper."

"I need to go."

"NOOO!" she bellows. About the only thing she can now focus on is that she doesn't want him to leave. And that something is really wrong. "Pleeez staaay." She rolls over and pushes herself to her hands and knees, but then crashes sideways to the floor. "Huh." She tries again, then realizes molten vodka is coming up the pike. "Bleehhhh uhhh gonna be sick . . ."

And then she is. All over Mom's precious carpet and the parquet floor.

"Wooo." Still on her hands and knees, she holds still, to make sure nothing else is coming. There isn't anything else. "Splashage," she observes.

Moony appears with some paper towels and a dish towel. "I feel bedder," she assures him, although it's an exaggeration. "Moony, Moooony, no, dohn clean up I'll do later. Ouaiba'll help."

Camus trots down the hall to sniff the barf, his nail tips tapping on the parquet floor. "Outta here, *rat* dog," she yells. He shows his underbite and then retreats.

Meanwhile Moony spreads the paper towels over the mess and wipes her face. Then he holds out his good hand.

She takes it and he pulls up all her weight, throws his arm around her, and pushes her down the hall toward her room. "Where is Ouaiba?" he demands.

"Up stairs . . . six floor. Intercom thingy—" she says, pointing up.

He practically carries her into her room and plops her onto her bed. He takes her shoes off, then puts the metal waste basket beside her. He also puts her toothbrush glass full of water on the bedside table, but she doesn't see that until she wakes up hours later.

Miraculously the mess is cleaned up when she staggers out of her room at 4:30 A.M. Although that intricate, pale carpet will never be the same.

Summer feels like a giant dried dog turd with a mouth and stomach full of charcoal briquettes and a tight crown of barbed wire. She completely deserves the pain. Welcomes it. She knocked Moony down because she couldn't stand up straight. Then she puked all over him. "Stupid stupid stupid stupid stupid," she mutters, her eyes and fists clenched tight. "Oh. My. God." Why on earth did she pound down so much vodka? She of all people knows how to hold her liquor.

Despite the hour, she texts him:

My EXTREME bad. I'm so so sorry. Thanks for being such a good friend.

No reply.

She shuffles into the living room and grabs Mom's vodka. She only needs a tiny bit. Hair of the dog and all that. She freezes. The floor in the hall creaked. Then she remembers Mom is gone. Whew.

The pounding in her temples is at a disco tempo, the sickness in her stomach is swelling. She closes her eyes. No. She's got to stop this. She is so not in control of this party. As much as she'd like to think she is. She clanks the bottle down.

In the kitchen she opens a blue French sports drink, Allez Oop, and takes a few swigs. Then, head throbbing, she goes back and gets the bottle of vodka after all. This is an emergency. She measures in a modest half shot. She's *hydrating*. She chugs half the sports drink and then pours in just a little more vodka. The alcohol enters her bloodstream fast, like a warm hug. She can breathe again.

A box of Doliprane sachets—French Tylenol powders—sits on Mom's bathroom counter. She dumps the flowers out of a small silver vase, pours in fresh water, two powders, and chugs.

She sits on the couch in the dark living room, looking out at the moon rising above the Eiffel Tower, and the other city lights. She could sit there for a long time.

Being still is best.

Camus *trip-trops* across the wood floor. He looks at her then jumps up onto the couch. She pats her lap. "Really? Come on, then, it's okay. I won't bite," she says. "Long as you don't."

He jumps into her lap. Curls up, solid and warm. She strokes him, smiling at the fact that they could possibly be friends. He likes her better since she barfed.

They supposedly bring in lap dogs at old age homes to let the patients pet because it lowers their blood pressure. Carrying Camus, she gets her music and puts on earphones. The sweet low melodies and gospel backup singers of Kentucky Morris's latest, "Itemize My Demise," fill her brain.

Say you didn't ask for this, turns out you did.

She closes her eyes and scratches Camus's ears.

What does Camus think about being alive? A dog's world has limits and as far as she knows, there's no existential questioning, despite his name. And when you think about other creatures, like insects or viruses, it's even more true. They don't understand what's beyond them. Could we explain the concept of near-death experiences or nuclear fission to a beetle? To Camus? But that doesn't mean they don't wonder. Or feel sad. Like Camus staring at the moon out the window. But he's thinking, *What the heck is that? Something to eat?* He just wants to survive.

So what's beyond human comprehension, and our five senses? Probably a lot. This isn't all there is, right?

Sometimes it feels like Dad might be watching over her. At odd times, it's like he just floated into the room. That would be cool, only he had a hard time watching out for her while he was alive so she's not so sure it's such a hot idea now.

The vast majority of humans believe, *feel,* that there is something beyond this life. Something greater than us.

They can't *all* be stupid.

One thing's for sure: Humans are not in control. They like to think so. Mom thinks that. But they aren't.

Do any dogs ever *not* want to survive? A sick one maybe.

Maybe she's sick. Something could be seriously wrong. She probably needs help.

She first got fixated on Pandora when she was twelve. Right after Dad died, come to think of it. That's why she could relate to all that pain and evil Pandora let into the world. It was right where she lived. The spirit of hope—illustrated as a wispy little fairy trapped in the box—unsettled her deeply. At the time, it seemed like hope was left behind for humans as a sort of torture. To keep them suffering all those ills, and basically to prevent them from just giving up. It was so annoying.

It still is.

Kurt hugged that guy.

Oh my god, *she* hugged poor Moony and knocked them both to the floor. She winces.

Ha. It's okay. He'll forgive her.

Eyes closed, she drops her chin to her collarbone. No, he won't. He knows you for what you truly are now. Just like Grace and Conner and Katie. Katie, back in ninth and tenth grade, was a straight shooter, an athlete, then redefined herself as Justin's girlfriend. They lost touch when Summer got kicked out of Hockaday. She and her best bud Conner had a big blowup near the end of her career at Verde Valley. But Grace from senior year at St. Jude's was a lush, a slacker, and a traitor, and even she couldn't handle Summer's partying and whatever—unpredictability. For sure, now Moony's had more than enough.

She blinks and gulps a swig of vodka to loosen the tightness in her throat. She has a sobering vision of it igniting and burning her head and neck from the inside out, like a wildfire. The icebergs will crush it out, though.

Here's where the rubber meets the road. Yet more vodka, Summer? It's for her extreme headache, but this has to stop.

Strangely, as she strokes the warm dog curled in her lap, the slightest hope flickers within.

There's only one thing that really matters. She must do everything within her power to keep Moony's friendship and respect.

Well, after last night, maybe just his friendship.

TWENTY-FIVE

Two hours later, it's still Monday morning, and even though death by firing squad would be a welcome relief from this hangover, Summer showers, braids her hair, pulls on a sky-blue T-shirt under a blue-gray sweater that sets off her skin, puts on lip-gloss, drinks coffee, and calls a taxi to arrive at school on time. Her homeroom teacher does a double take when she sees her. Summer marches into first period English Lit and even though paying full attention is not an option, she sits ramrod straight and pretends to.

Then she rushes to Moony's locker, sure he'll stop by. She spots him down the hall, walking slowly with Jackie, his skinny, highlighted, bejeweled, French-Lebanese friend. In fact, he's leaning sideways, listening attentively to Jackie-the-selfish-cow's animated monologue.

Summer pulls herself into the science lab behind her, hides behind the door, and strains to hear Jackie's conversation. They move into her line of sight through the cracked door, and Jackie stands on her tiptoes to give Moony a tender kiss, for chrissakes. The two walk off in opposite directions.

Summer covers her face with her hands. She deserved to see that.

She trails Moony to Concert Choir, then, at the last moment, she ditches it. Bawk, bawk, bawk, she thinks. She also skips lunch as even the smell of food will likely make her toss her tortillas all over again. By the end of the day, she can barely walk or chew gum or form sentences she's so depleted. But she gets on Moony's bus and sits near the front. He's already in back with a couple of soccer players and doesn't seem to notice her.

Her only hope.

Forty minutes later when he limps up the aisle at his stop, she jumps up, wiping her slick hands against her jeans, and gets off behind him.

"Moony!" she calls. "Wait."

He turns. Dammit, he's scowling at her.

She takes a deep breath. "I want to apologize for booting all over you."

"*Was* a lot of upchuck." The faintest of smiles pulls at his lips.

"I'm really, really sorry. I forgot you were coming, I didn't mean to drink so much, I hadn't eaten really, and I—"

"Poetry reading?"

"What about it?" She's twisting her intertwined fingers.

"A pattern."

"I know, I know. I know. I've been partying a lot lately. And I'm a shit friend. Will you please just come have a coffee with me? My treat."

He pauses, looks pained, then pushes his hair out of his face as his jaw muscle flexes. "Okay. Therapy appointment in thirty."

They walk in silence the half block to the market street near his apartment, rue de Lévis. It's already dark, and harsh yellow lights illuminate a few rough working guys swilling beers in Moony's neighborhood café. The congenial *patron,* who has a long fringe of gray hair around a mostly bald head, knows Moony and calls out a greeting. Summer orders two espressos at the counter. The espresso machine hisses at her.

At the small table, Moony says, "So. Alcohol's a problem?"

Summer hedges, "It probably has the potential to be, but last night was just an unfortunate, perfect storm kind of thing. Honest." For the briefest of seconds, she thinks about telling him what she saw at Les Halles. But she can't. Too raw and crazy. Besides, she knows how to cut back. She could stop all together, but she *likes* drinking. She needs it. "I'm so sorry. I swear to you it won't happen again."

"Ever been to an AA meeting?" he asks.

Her mouth drops open. "Alcoholics Anonymous? Are you joking? That's for drunks! I mean, old people who are drunk all the time. I've been drunk, um, once."

Moony rolls his eyes.

She runs a finger along a crack in the Formica tabletop and takes a deep breath. His disapproving look is annoying. Don't get mad, she warns herself. Say why. "Moony, your friendship means a *lot*. I don't want to lose it."

She glances at him. He's stirring his espresso around and around with the little spoon.

"*Worried* about you," he finally says. "And can't deal with this."

Summer doesn't know how to respond. "I—I'm fine. And I won't do it again."

"Don't mind partying. But . . . drinking so much. Alone. Why?"

"It's fun." She grins.

He's stone faced. "Why?" he repeats. "With your dad's history."

"It's more that if I *don't* drink . . ."

"What?" She doesn't respond. "What?" he insists and something in his voice makes her strive for honesty.

She squeezes her hands into fists. "It will . . . overpower me."

"What do you mean?"

"Because I'm not strong like you."

He shakes his head. "What will overpower?"

She thinks of Kurt nibbling her earlobe, then swats it away. "Oh, the blizzards and wildfires in my head mostly." She laughs in a too-high voice.

He looks perplexed.

She makes a funny face but knows she's trying too hard to make this all light.

Moony sighs.

She gets it! She tires him out. He's not sure she's worth his time and all the energy she demands. She knows she's not the only person in the world with problems. It's just that right now, the avalanche or falling glacier—no, the Balrog of Morgoth—is so giant and so close, breathing fire and cracking that whip of flame, pulling Gandalf into the abyss ahead of her, there's no room for anything else but trying to escape it. She knows she can't do it alone.

She knows she can't do it much longer.

"Look. You're absolutely right." Moony's strong but he's already carrying so much. He can't carry her, too. "I have been overindulging. And I have to get my act together." She pulls her flask from her backpack, then walks outside by the door and with a dramatic flourish pours what's left (not much) into the gutter. She sits back down. "That's it. First day of the rest of my life."

Moony fishes something from his backpack, then places four euro coins on the table. "Thanks," he says, standing. She can't read his expression. He's not mad, but he's shut down on her.

"Wait a minute. I said my treat. You didn't even drink it anyway."

"I gotta go," he says, shaking his head, eyes closed.

Her only friend limps away. Over the Bridge of Khazad-dûm.

"Can't fool me. I can tell you're really beginning to like me!" she calls. He's almost out the door when she says, "Ha! Joke's on you. I've got *two* flasks."

She doesn't really, but thank heavens all that vodka is waiting in her armoire. Tomorrow will be the first day of the rest of her life. Right now she's gonna order a brandy.

TWENTY-SIX

Summer takes a taxi home. She sits in the stuffed chair in her room and stares unseeingly out the dark window. Losing Moony as a friend cannot be crystalized away. It's her own fault for thinking she could convince him to be her friend. How many times does she have to spit out the word "hopeless"? She can't read or study, can't eat, isn't sleepy. She finally gets up to pee because she's disinclined to wet herself, but huddles in bed without washing or brushing her teeth. She doesn't sleep.

Summer cuts school the next day. With tremendous effort, she rises midday and eats a bowl of lentils that Ouaiba fixes, then sits at the kitchen table and tries valiantly to study. It's all that's left, all that she has to hang on to. But everything she reads, she must reread. Then again. And again. And again.

She needs some Adderall.

Why is she even bothering?

A notice in the folded *International Herald Tribune* on the table catches her eye.

FEELING DOWN? NEED TO TALK TO SOMEONE? SOS SUICIDE HOTLINE.

A Paris number is printed in bold beneath.

Summer doodles little triangles by the number and wonders who would answer if she called. Some old person probably. Would they speak *good* English? *Excusez-moi? Jumping* on *a bridge?* And if a person *were* feeling like jumping off a bridge, what would they say to them? What on earth could they say? It's good that they have it, though. Seems like there's a big market for it here.

That evening she's doubly tired, but so *not* sleepy. She checks her phone again.

Nothing.

She remembers Dr. Garnier's advice. She bundles up and heads out for a short walk. First she pours vodka into her flask. She didn't drink all day, a record for her. And she really needs just a couple of small sips now. If she can maintain control over the amount, she'll be fine.

She heads up avenue Victor-Hugo to Étoile and then just keeps going, all the way down the Champs-Élysées. She's strolling alongside six lanes of choked traffic, through crowds of Christmas shoppers and lovers, tourists, and prides of unsupervised, edgy young teens. She walks under sprays of red and white lights, past brightly lit *très cher* jewelers, the Renault show room, small and large movie theaters, brasseries, fast-food places, banks, and overpriced clothing, luggage, and souvenir shops. As in a bad dream, she keeps going, along stretches of dark park, past the huge fortress of the American embassy through the trees, all the way to Place de la Concorde. She's still not ready to stop. In the Jardin des Tuileries, she shuffles along a lighted path and passes two cops on bikes. The Louvre sprawls before her.

She crumples onto a bench, looking at a wall between her and the river, with the brightly lit I. M. Pei pyramid off to her left, and the Petit Arc de Triomphe to her right. She's so tired, she's numb.

It's quite a sight, the pyramid. The Tuileries in the dark is incredibly romantic. It would be so spectacular to have someone here to share it with. To warm her frozen hands. She forgot gloves.

Inside her coat pocket, she fingers Kurt's card and her flask. She unstoppers the latter and takes several big swallows.

If you're ever up for a movie or something, call me.

She pulls out the card. It's engraved on heavy dove-gray stock with black type:

Konrad Vondur de la Rivière
Hôtel Napoléon III
Place de la Concorde
Paris
06.50.33.88.66

Not a business card, more of a calling card; 06 is the prefix for cell phones. If he's American he must have Euro parents with a name like that. And *living* at the super fancy Hôtel Napoléon? Jeez. He's definitely not broke. It's just a few blocks away. If he's "home." Okay, he's . . . mysterious, and yes, a little unsettling. But he fires up one kind of warmth in her anyway.

She knows it's childish, but if Moony hates her, then why not?

Before she can talk herself out of it, she taps Kurt's number into her phone. He answers on the first ring.

"*Allô?*"

"I, uh, ahh, Kurt?"

"Summer," he says happily.

"Uh. Hi."

"*Quelle surprise.*"

"I hope you don't mind me calling."

"Are you kidding? I'm glad you've recovered from *les égouts*. When I came out, I saw you driving away in the taxi. I was a little worried, but knew you'd be fine. You are, aren't you?"

"Yeah. Of course. It was an interesting experience." If he was worried about her being sick or mad why didn't he try to find out?

"Where are you?" he asks.

"I'm in the Tuileries. I was, um, just thinking about getting something, like, to drink and . . . I thought of you." There. She said it.

"Love to," he says, fast as lightning. "Meet me at Café Marly in ten minutes."

"Oh. Right. In the Louvre."

"Summer?"

"Yeah?"

"I'm so glad you called." He clicks off.

She takes another deep swig from her flask. That was kind of romantic, wasn't it?

In the bustling café, she sits at a table in the back and orders two Bloody Marys. The waiter says, "Someone is joining mademoiselle?"

"*Mais, oui,*" she says. She has more energy now. Or maybe it's agitation.

And in he walks. He's wearing a high-tech black ski jacket instead of his longer coat, blue oxford shirt and black cashmere sweater, jeans, and—she notes—Wellingtons. Olive-green rubber boots.

"Puddle jumping?" she asks him as he kisses her hello. His unusual scent is ripe tonight. Sulfur-ish.

"You'll see," he says, sitting. "You look ravishing." He stares at her. If looks could eat, he would be gobbling her. "Ah, *pour moi*? How very nice." He lifts his glass. "To . . . explorations and decisions."

"Sure." Summer clinks glasses with him. "So how are you?"

"Very well. And you? Settling in?"

"Um, I guess so."

He narrows his dark eyes. "It's aesthetically pleasing, as advertised, but a cold and heartless city, don't you think?"

She runs her finger around the rim of her glass. "Now that you mention it, yeah."

"I do have a treat for you tonight. An unusual outing. I think you'll get a kick out of it."

"Let's see. How could you possibly top the sewers? The city morgue?"

"No. Much more lively."

"Nascar racing?"

"No, more intimate than that." He's laughing.

"Nude mud wrestling?" She's feeling downright loose and light. Sexy and funny. Thin and beautiful. Healthy and alluring.

"Ha. Drink up. Let's go."

"But you just got here." She drains her glass.

He smiles. "Waste not want not. It's time."

TWENTY-SEVEN

Kurt takes Summer by the hand and leads her from the crowded restaurant into the night. "It's not too far if you're up for a stroll," he says as they pass the Hollywood-lit pyramid.

They head toward the nearby Seine.

"Okay," she says, although she's already been strolling so long she has blisters.

He *is* a sweet, kind guy, she thinks. Maybe she should have called him sooner. It's exactly as she pictured it. She's holding hands with a hot guy, strolling by Parisian landmarks. But his hand is cold, more like gripping a frozen chicken breast.

They walk in silence until they reach the Pont des Arts, a wooden pedestrian bridge. Should she warn this guy that she's . . . not in a great place for a relationship? Don't be absurd, she thinks.

And don't think about the Goth guy.

A little voice in her head repeats *Goth guy* about three more times before it crackles into diamond dust and floats away.

Floodlights on each bank illuminate the bridge and to a lesser extent the river. On the other side, crowded, old stone buildings perch atop the steep wall above the quay. They pause midway and look upriver at the lights of the Île de la Cité. Summer zips her jacket. It's colder over the water.

"Cigarette?" asks Kurt.

"Thanks."

The Seine is high and fast moving from all the recent rain. It swirls and eddies beneath them, black and oily.

"Spectacular," Kurt says. "Flowing like time. Cold. Patient. Romantic." He squeezes her hand. "Easy to slip into."

Summer wonders how it would feel and look from ten feet below the surface: floating along in the icy current, arms outstretched, wavy streetlights faintly visible through the darkness above. All quiet. It's not a frightening thought, rather somehow a soothing one. They watch the river for several minutes, as her giddiness from the café subsides. She thinks of sitting with Moony on his egg yolk–yellow rain poncho.

She cranes her head back for stars. Slabs of darkness, high clouds, move across the sky. The faint light of one lone star struggles to pierce the haze of city lights. If she could just reach out for that sucker, and then vaporize from the heat of it, she would go happily. Right now, she thinks.

"What are you thinking?" Kurt asks. He flicks his cigarette butt into the water and pulls her close.

"How I would like to touch a star. Become a star."

"Awesome. Free at last."

"Hmmm."

"No more pain or despair. *The stars go waltzing out in blue and red / And arbitrary blackness gallops in.*"

"Right," she says softly. "My life would flash in front of my eyes. I've always wondered how that works."

"Would you miss much about it?"

She thinks a moment. "I guess not." Moony's warm hand in hers at Sacré-Coeur, pulsing with connection and caring. She squeezes her eyes shut against the image.

Kurt takes her by the shoulders and she shivers. He leans in close. "The world is overwhelmingly difficult for you, isn't it?"

She doesn't answer. It's a dumb question. Her pulse is racing. She loses herself in his dark eyes that pull her to his exquisite face.

They kiss. On the lips, one time.

It's hardly electric. It vacuums away energy, into the void of which rushes deep sadness and longing for . . . she doesn't know what. Not sex.

A hollowness expands within. Like deep space. Cold and dark and movement-less.

Absolute zero.

Her whole body, and beyond. It's so quiet it's almost peaceful.

But not quite. A few cosmic rays from some distant, collapsed star still register.

She steps back. "Uh, thanks for meeting up with me," she murmurs. "I *was* having a low moment. I think I'm better now." She doesn't want to kiss him again.

"Everything is going to be fine." He pulls her back to hug her and she smells his garlic-sulfer muskiness. Then he gently intertwines his fingers with hers.

Our first kiss, she thinks. Not what she expected.

He fishes something from his pocket and shows it to her. A padlock. Then he turns it over. Written in black marker is "Kurt ♥ Summer."

"For my locker?" she asks, not caring whether he knows she has one or not. "Gosh, very thoughtful, but I don't even use it."

"No. As a symbol of my commitment to you." He jams it between the metal links of the fence spanning the bridge. Others already hang there. He locks it with the little key, then tosses the key into the air. Arcing, and tumbling, it catches a glint of floodlight before it's swallowed by the darkness. A faint *plonk* sounds from below.

"Whoa." Summer likes the idea of the gesture, but it unsettles her. She is attracted to him but doesn't exactly like him. Does he like her? For real? He's moved things forward a little fast. What if she isn't ready? Is there no going back?

Or forward?

"Does this mean we're, like, together? Going out?"

"Yes," he says, still observing the river. "It does."

"How about that." It feels anticlimactic. Meaning*less*.

He pulls her by the arm. "Come on."

On the Left Bank, they turn down narrow side *rues* until she is completely confused. Finally they stop on a dark, quiet street in front of a high wall and door.

A French guy walks up, dressed in dark jeans and a fleece jacket with a small backpack slung over his shoulder. He has on a knit ski cap, with long curly hair jutting out from beneath. Even in the dark, his face is pale and sharp. He looks at Summer questioningly.

"*Bonsoir,* mademoiselle," he says.

"*Bonsoir,* monsieur," she says, like she knows who he is. He embraces Kurt in a kind of strange French un-ghetto clutch and clasp, then punches in the door code. No one introduces themselves. "Follow me," he says with an accent, as he opens the heavy door and motions them in behind him, finger to his lips.

Summer whispers to Kurt, "You go first." They cross a stone courtyard. Straight ahead, through large double doors, half glass, they see a marbled lobby. But they veer right to a smaller wooden door. The guy punches in a number on a second code pad. It opens to narrow steps going down to the *caves,* or basement storage rooms. Summer takes Kurt's gloved hand as the guy pulls out a flashlight and turns it on.

They descend. On the basement level another big metal door blocks the way, and for this, the guy has an old-fashioned skeleton key. "*Tiens,*" he says, handing Summer the light while he fits the key into the lock. The door swings open. They step into a dirt-floored corridor that winds back past many locked storage *caves.* It's dank, musty, and black as the inside of a tomb. Wisps of cobwebs brush Summer's face.

At the very end of the *couloir* they stop before yet another locked door and the guy opens it, too, with a key. They follow him into a small storage room, past an empty, floor-to-ceiling iron wine rack and some dust-coated cane chairs. At the back wall, the flashlight beam reveals a narrow, downward-sloping opening behind an iron grate.

"No way!" she says. Meaning that she has no intention of going in there. Kurt's face is illuminated enough to see his disapproval.

"Shhhh," says the guy. He pulls the grate back and lowers it to the dirt floor.

He and Kurt crouch down and slip in. There's no light and she has no choice but to follow them. Inside the tunnel, which is about five feet by four feet, their breathing and steps echo. Her back aches from crouching over. Something scurries by.

After what seems like forever, they come to an even smaller opening and Summer must climb down metal ladder steps in the side of a slimy, dripping wall. Then they drop to their hands and knees and slide through an even lower tunnel, which is wet and smells like fertilized mud. "Oh crap, oh crap," she mutters. She's afraid she's going to lose it and start screaming.

Finally they emerge, one by one, into a concrete-walled "gallery" where they can stand. Her knees are weak and she can still hear the beat of her pulse in her ears. They go left and now make good time, occasionally passing under a shaft through which flows cool air. There are about two or three inches of water and Summer's leather boots and jeans are soaked up to her knees. The whole front of her is. Fortunately, the temperature is actually a little warmer down here than outside.

Finally, voices, sound and light appear ahead. They come into a wide limestone-walled space where about thirty people lounge. Most of them have a light of some sort, or a hard hat, a flashlight, some candles. Summer notes many wine and liquor bottles, and of course, cigarette smoke.

To her left, a small chamber opens and through it, she can see what looks like a four-foot-high wall made of small, round, loose stones. The guy shines the flashlight on them. Hardly stones, it's a neat stack of hundreds of human thigh bones, the round, bulbous ends facing out. Several jawless skulls are arranged artistically in the piles at intervals.

"Ohmigod," she says.

The catacombs. They're in the freaking catacombs underneath the city: 186 mazelike miles of quarries mined in the Middle Ages for rock to build Paris. In the late 1700s as the cemeteries were filling up, they began storing bones down here. Or so her mini-guidebook says.

She looks at Kurt, ever grinning. "You and your subterranean outings. What is it with underground spots?"

Kurt doesn't answer. Summer sits down and someone passes her a bottle of vodka.

TWENTY-EIGHT

Almost everyone is French. Or at least speaking French. There is one guy who appears to be about fifteen, but other than that, the underworld is peopled with twenty- and thirty-somethings. *Cataphiles,* ha. People who love the catacombs.

"Come here often?" she says to the bearded guy next to her.

"*Pardon?*"

"Do you"—she points at him—"come here"—she points to the bones—"often?" She throws up her hands.

"*Je m'excuse mais je ne comprends pas,*" he says. He doesn't understand English.

"*Est-ce que . . . tu viens ici . . . souvent?*" she tries.

"*Non.*" His girlfriend pulls his attention back to her.

"Fine. Cheers," she says, and drinks.

Summer wishes Moony were here. He would get a kick out of this. Maybe. Even if he hated it, she still wishes he were here. Fat chance of him ever doing anything with her again, though.

To not be a total mooch, she passes her flask around but keeps an eye on it. Kurt has wandered off to talk to someone on the other side of the large space, which both annoys and relieves her.

She studies the skulls and the patterns they make in the stacked bones, breathing in the dampness and cigarette and candle smoke, eavesdropping but hearing very little that's comprehensible, and wondering what she's doing here. This is a date. Right? And being out in this secret—romantic place?—in Paris with Kurt, this is fun, right?

The guy who brought them walks by, his thin jaw set. He doesn't notice her and heads out the way they came in. There appear to be several corridors off this area. The catacombs are supposedly labyrinthine.

"Bye," she says. Now where's he going? And what's his story in the first place? He's a druggie, for sure.

She wants to find a way out of here, too. The dampness makes her shiver. If she went back the way they came—and that thought stops her cold—those doors might be locked from the other side. Then what? She takes a deep breath to tamp down the panic that just got lit.

Kurt catches her eye, then resumes talking to some lady.

But why panic? She's right where she needs to be. No one would ever find her if she crawled into one of these alcoves and curled up next to some bones and went to sleep. And didn't wake up.

But she would. And she would be hungry.

She smiles. She could gnaw on some bones.

She could chug enough alcohol to poison herself if all the cataphiles chipped in. Summer sighs. With her mighty tolerance, there might not be enough down here. She needs something sure.

It's a shame that guns are so hard to get in France.

"No way," she says to no one, hearing the opening notes of a track. "Kentucky Morris. 'Why R U Here.' From The Pain Circumference Tour." She needs to turn Moony on to Kentucky because she's caught him listening to some weird goofy Euro stuff.

A Brit with the boombox nearby announces, "Followed his Sweet Darkness Tour."

"Outstanding," says Summer. "Any friend of Kentucky's is a friend of mine."

Just then, a stampede sounds down distant corridors. Everyone freezes. Followed by a loud pop and a hiss. The chamber floods with thick smoke made puke yellow by the lights. Yelling and the sound of heavy running bounce off the walls. A big guy in camouflage and a black ski mask materializes right before Summer. He bellows something. She can make out another masked guy floating in and out of the fog near him.

The first one shakes his fist at her, sputtering in French.

"Too many freaks," she mutters. "Not enough circuses."

"Lie down!" yells her neighbor, already prone. "Bloody Skins."

Coughing, she does as she's told. It's all so surreal; she's had enough to drink, plus she's already emerged unscathed from the cramped bowels of Paris. She's not that frightened.

The predators work efficiently, going through every bag and pocket down there. It seems like there are more of them than partiers.

A guy with an olive-green ski mask on his face goes through her backpack, right at her head. He roughly pats her down. The guy takes the rest of the cash in her jacket, her Swiss Army knife, and her dad's silver flask.

"NO!" she screams and scrambles to get up. He kicks her hard in the ribs with his steel-toed boots. An explosion of red fills her body and she curls up in the dust.

Groaning softly, she opens her eyes, and the guy stretched out next to her warns, "Shhh."

Another girl cries out, and Summer closes her eyes and curls her body up tighter, as her side throbs purple pain.

Then . . . from down past the pile of bones, three screeching whistles echo off the stone floors and walls. Footsteps run out. No one on the ground moves.

"*Halte, police! Arrêtez là!*"

"*Les cataflics, à l'heure,*" someone mumbles nearby. *Flics* are cops. "*À l'heure*" is "on time." Thank goodness.

TWENTY-NINE

Hazy flashlight beams bounce around the space, and foot stomps echo down the catacomb corridors after the Skins. Summer pulls herself up and brushes off. Through the smoke, white helmets and dark uniforms appear. She coughs and wipes her face. Others do, too. Where's Kurt?

Someone pulls her by the upper arm. "Come on!" says her British friend quietly. "Best to avoid these wankers."

Blood pounds in Summer's head and the pain in her ribs makes her nauseous. Yeah, all she needs is to get dragged to the city jail. It's against the law to be down here. Seriously, where the hell is Kurt?

She ducks behind the guy as they scurry past the stacked leg bones down a corridor. Darkness quickly envelops them, as the lights, smoke, and commotion of the party scene recede. She whispers, "Know where you're going?" She could be making a big mistake, but it doesn't really matter. She hears at least two other footsteps crunching on gravel behind them and she doubts they're cops.

"Yeah, vaguely. Name's Richard. I've got a torch here somewhere." He pulls a small flashlight from his jacket and illuminates their way. "It's not too far. If we don't get lost."

"Whatever," says Summer, clutching her middle. "I'm Summer."

"*Lead me out of the dark, up that path past the mark . . .*" He recites Kentucky lyrics.

"I know, right?"

Very soon, they enter another dimly lit gallery. They pass a stooped, stick-legged old man in a red fuzzy coat walking his long-haired Dachshund. Richard warns him in French that *les flics,* not to mention the Skins, are ahead, so he turns around. Two other guys catch up with them.

After hiking in single file for what feels like hours, they come to an open door and several flights of concrete steps lit with fluorescent lights. Climbing makes Summer's lungs and ribs burn and her head spin. They emerge from the side of a building onto a dark street, in god knows what part of Paris. It's so late, it's early. The two guys and the old man disperse. Summer and Richard wait at a taxi stand across from a run-down Vietnamese restaurant.

Summer pushes the call button and sits down on the curb. Maybe Kurt got arrested.

"Are you all right?" Richard asks.

"I'm fine," she says, strangely grateful for the throbbing in her side that's been keeping her out of her tortured brain.

"What were you doing down there by yourself?" he asks.

"A guy led us down there, but he left," says Summer. "I came with a friend."

"Where is she?"

"He. No idea. Might have been injured." Then she mutters, "Or he's a massive jerk." They're all *involved* now, and he ditched her? Again?

She has two twenty-euro bills in an inside zippered pocket in her backpack that the shitheads didn't find. And amazingly her phone is there, too. She gives one of the twenties to her new friend since all his money was "nicked." He sends her off in the first cab that comes.

The next day Summer doesn't get up. Doesn't go to school. Her hangover is crushing and she's exhausted and hardly slept thanks to her injury. When she finally pulls herself from bed, it's almost dark outside. She winces from the pain under her arm and to the left of her left boob. It's red and violet. A rib or two may be cracked. And they got Dad's beautiful flask! Her eyes tear up.

She wants to leave here. Go back to the US. Stay with Aunt Liz or maybe even rent her own apartment. Something small and cozy, with solar panels. She would totally miss Moony, but she could invite him to visit.

She hates Paris. Why is she even here? Whose incredibly stupid idea was this?

Oh, yeah. Mom.

She's heard nothing from Kurt. He's probably fine. Obviously, he's not concerned about whether she's fine or not. Unfortunately, his fascinated stare, the strange negative electricity of him, his smell, and their freaking padlock on the Pont des Arts are all superglued in her brain. But even at her most crush-conquered, there's something slick and jaded about him. He ditches her at the worst possible time.

"Mom?" She should be home now. Summer shuffles down to her room. Maybe in San Francisco she'll just get a GED. Then figure out college.

Mom's packing, about to go to the airport again. Her rosy perfume lingers in the air. She zippers her leather roller bag with determination.

"I got a call from the dean of students this morning," Mom says coldly. "In the middle of a meeting."

"Mr. Evans? He and I are best buds." But Summer knows she's busted.

"I told him you were sick."

"I was. Thanks."

"You have five *unexcused* absences in four weeks. The limit is four excused per semester. You lied to the school, told them I knew. He also said you were flunking five out of six of your classes."

"Which one am I not flunking?" Being treated like a ten-year-old sucks, but she deserves it.

"Concert Choir."

"There must be some mistake," Summer says, grinning. "I never go to that class."

Mom not only doesn't smile, her lip quivers. She says, "You're eighteen years old. You can obviously do whatever you want. If you fail this term, and don't graduate"—her voice cracks and she shakes her head—"what are we going to do? I really don't know what to do anymore."

Summer stiffens. Oh, crap. Mom's pulled strings, paid lots of bills, and just wants her to do her part. What Mom thinks is best for her. "I'm pretty much up-to-date now in all my classes. I would have turned in a bunch of stuff today if I hadn't been sick. I'll—I'll take care of it tomorrow."

"The terms of the will are very clear. You must finish the semester and get your diploma now." Mom takes a big drag and blows the smoke out in a thin white stream as she stares out the tall double window. Like steam screeching out of a kettle.

Dabbing at her eyes with a tissue, Mom asks evenly, "What do you plan to do with your life if you lose the money? Live with me?"

Summer pauses. "No." She doesn't plan to do anything. She bows her head.

There it is. Schoolwork and her inheritance, let alone a plan for young adulthood, have all felt like a waste of time because she knows she won't be around to suffer it.

Mom says, "Instead of going to Jonesboro, maybe you should stay here through the year. We could enroll you at ACP." The American College of Paris. Mom sighs and rubs her eyebrows. "Then transfer to some San Francisco college or wherever the hell you want. But first, you have to graduate. This is not a problem for millions of other kids and I know you know how to do it." She pulls the handle up on her bag with a violent *thunk*. "I'll see you day after tomorrow. Go study, for god's sake."

She *clip-clops* out. Summer locks herself in her room and lies down gingerly on her bed. She comes from a long line of runners-away.

Mom's right, of course, and she doesn't know the half of it. She *can't* run away again. Why is this ice rut of hers so deep and difficult to break out of? It's more like a luge run. She has to deal. Buckle down. She could really lose all that money, be forced to watch it go into the bank account of some hardcore, good ol' boy, right-wing charity. That would suck.

Maybe she should confide in Kurt. He might have some ideas to help her out. Mom would love Kurt, if Summer introduced them. He's so presentable—looks, fancy Euro family, probably educated.

No. That's a good example of a bad choice and one she's made too many times already. With his help, she's going to blow up majorly, *again*. By hanging out with him and calling him, she's encouraged him way too much.

She can't confide in him, she has to *stay away* from him.

Get a grip. This is where the rubber *really* meets the road, girlfriend.

She needs to talk to Moony.

THIRTY

Summer sits on her bed. That little fairy Hope kickboxes all her sore rib bones. She texts Moony after composing and deleting her message several times.

Are you speaking to me? If not, I understand.

She hopes with a burning, aching pain, like thawing frozen extremities, that he will forgive her. Again. She didn't argue with her other friends once they got fed up with her.

Moony expects the most from her. And even though she disappoints him like everyone else, maybe he hasn't given up yet. Fingers crossed. Anyway, she'll keep asking him.

Five minutes later he replies:

I am. But home sick today.

She pumps the air with her fist, falls back on her pillow and breathes out in relief and frustration. Another chance, thank heavens. But Moony's sick! Through the fog of her own problems, she hasn't focused on him. His physical health makes her more anxious than she already is.

Sorry! Get well quick. Check with you later.

Summer goes to school the next morning, but doesn't see Moony. Afraid he's still sick, she texts him.

I'm at school. Are you here?
Yep. I'll catch you later.

She collects all her assignments, talks to her French teacher in bad French, and turns in an English Lit essay, even though it's weak. She learns she missed a major math project and has to make it up before finals. She goes to the library at lunch and tries to concentrate on trigonometry, sneaking only one gulp from her half-liter plastic Evian water bottle-cum-flask.

That afternoon, several kids surround Moony at his locker, so she waits and approaches him after they leave. His face is pale and haggard, and he coughs from deep in his lungs.

"Gosh, that sounds good." She gently touches him on the arm and almost asks if he's okay, then stops herself. She's going to have to find out about his health some other way since he won't talk to her about it.

He answers anyway, "I'm okay. You?" He's squinting at her. "You look . . . tired."

"*I* look tired? I'm great," she says, managing a cheerful smile. Too bad she went the low-hygiene, absolutely-no-makeup route this morning. "Really, fine. But wondering why you sound like a tubercular street person."

Moony's face goes stony.

Summer says quickly, "I'm really in need of academic bolstering. Trig. Tomorrow. Help." She does need his help—desperately—but to ask just occurred to her. She hopes she doesn't sound opportunistic.

He relaxes into a smile. "No sweat. Trig, huh?"

"Yeah, I know. You aced it years ago."

"After school?"

"No rehearsal, right?"

"Not today. And Miranda canned you. Three no-shows. Sorry."

"Oh, crap. That's terrible. Guess that's the way it goes."

"Can tell you're broken up."

She smiles, then says in all seriousness, "But I am sorry to let you down."

He puts his good hand on her shoulder. "Thanks. You ruined my credibility."

"Really?" She's alarmed.

"No." He gives her a weak smile. "Meet me at my locker after seventh."

After last period they head across the wide courtyard toward the lower school. Moony invites Summer to ride home to his apartment with his mom. She's honored, but is a little worried about meeting Ms. Butterfield.

They walk in amiable silence. She wants to tell him about the catacombs, still so painfully fresh in her mind. And Kurt. That she's keeping him mostly a secret from Moony gnaws hard at her. Where to start?

Moony stops, convulsed with coughing, and she pounds him on the back. He shakes his head in an *I'm all right* kind of way, or maybe it means *Thanks but don't say anything.* Then they enter the lower school.

Ms. Butterfield's third-grade classroom is bright and cheery, festooned with colored construction-paper chains, student artwork, plants, and posters. Moony's mom has shoulder-length brown hair framing a gently plump, fair-skinned face and blue eyes. She's putting on her coat and smiles hugely when she sees Moony. It fades when she notices Summer.

"Mom, this is my friend Summer, coming over for tutoring. Summer, my ma, Karen Butterfield."

They shake hands. Summer's smiling too big and stops.

In the parking lot, Summer squeezes into the back of

Ms. Butterfield's compact hatchback, ignoring the pain from her ribs. It's tight but she realizes proudly it would have been worse at her old weight. She feels Moony's mom's appraising and disapproving gaze in the rearview mirror and can't keep from wiggling her nose ring. Moony's mom peels out of the parking lot.

"Summer, what brought you to Paris?" she asks at a red light, her tone revealing that she already knows full well.

"Um, Air France."

Moony laughs, then coughs, but Ms. Butterfield is not amused. Summer watches her in the mirror.

"Just kidding," says Summer. Don't be defensive, she tells herself. "My mother lives here most of the year."

"Where were you before?"

"At St. Jude's School."

"But you just arrived. In the middle of the semester." Moony must have told her.

"Yep. I was expelled."

"What for? If you don't mind my asking."

"Mom," says Moony, frowning.

She sighs. "You don't have to answer that."

"No, it's okay," says Summer. "For substance abuse infringement." She doesn't mention it was the third time at the fourth school in five years.

"That'll do it," Ms. Butterfield says. But she seems satisfied and launches into a story about a third-grader who wanted to know what "tempted by the fruit of another" meant, and they all laugh. Summer knows she got off easy and crosses her fingers after the fact.

Ms. Butterfield parks and they walk half a block down a market street that smells like fresh-baked baguettes. Fruit and vegetable hawkers, blue-coveralled Frenchmen, bleat out the day's specials. This afternoon, at least at one stall, it's haricots verts.

Moony's building is off a side street, and only four stories high instead of the usual six. He punches in the code, and they climb the narrow staircase to the top floor since they won't all fit into the miniscule elevator. Summer has to catch her breath. Moony does, too, and he looks mad about it.

Inside, it smells faintly of lavender air freshener and burnt toast. Moony and his mom remove their shoes, so Summer takes her boots off and leaves them next to the shoe rack by the door.

The small apartment is lined with windows and skylights. A scratchy living room couch sits on dark red and blue Oriental rugs, and a brass Arabic coffeepot perches on the shelves lined with books. In one corner of the room is a heap of crutches of all sizes, and contraptions—probably leg braces.

"Work in my room," he says. "Snack?"

"Whatever you're having," Summer says. "Bathroom?"

Moony shows her, and Summer pulls out her water bottle as soon as the door is closed, and pours all the vodka into the toilet.

THIRTY-ONE

"Welcome to the inner sanctum," says Moony, leaving the door to the hallway partially open. A single bed with a dark-green-and-white-striped spread is tucked into the corner of his small room. An armoire fills the other corner. A brass lamp glows. Everything is in military order.

His desk and bookshelf take up the other end of the space. On a shelf sits a photo of Moony when he was about eight, before his accident. A perfect little boy with large new front teeth stands beside a man in a white Arabian headdress with the black cord coiled around his crown.

"Your dad," Summer says, leaning closer to study it. The man looks intelligently through wire-rimmed glasses with a hint of mischief in his eyes, and probably a good sense of humor. He grins into the camera, gripping and clearly proud of his handsome, big-toothed son.

"That's him." Moony offers her some pistachios.

"Thanks. What do you call the headdress?"

Moony leans in over her just as she straightens up. His head dodges hers as their faces come within inches and her breast brushes his shoulder. "Sorry," he says. "A *ghutrah*. In the Gulf."

Summer steps back. "*Gu-tra.* Cool," she says. Is her breath okay? "Lawrence of Arabia–like." She *really* should have worn one of her new tops and put on some zit cover-up, at least.

Moony shakes his head. "Lawrence of Arabia was an imperialist interloper." He crunches some cracked pistachios.

"Whatever you say. Do you see your dad very often?" She eats a couple, too.

"Not really. We talk, he sends YouTube links, money."

"Is he rich?"

Moony smiles. "No. But not poor. Works for the Ministry of the Interior." He pauses. "Go to Kuwait every year, usually Christmas break. Not this year."

"Why?" She backs up against the armoire.

"Operation."

She grabs her opening. "So what kind of operation are you having?"

"It's boring."

"Not to me."

He plops down stiffly in his desk chair that's only a couple of feet from the bed and frowns. Says nothing.

"But it would be good if he were here for it, wouldn't it? Won't he come visit you?" She hears that she's talking all fast.

"Can't this time."

"Oh."

"Not crazy about his second wife. Treats me like a freak."

Her mouth falls open. How could *anyone* treat Moony like a freak? "That's ridiculous! I'd like to gore her with my tusks."

"Ha!" he says, then coughs.

Balancing on the narrow bookshelf crammed with books is a red felt board paved with Cub Scout patches, a signed baseball, a photo of the Paris-St. Germain soccer team, and a model of some molecule. And dozens and dozens of medication boxes and bottles. He presses two pills out of a blister pack as she stares, then swallows them without water.

"Meds," he explains needlessly. "Have a seat." He indicates the bed. "You're pacing."

A small photo of a full-faced, pretty but serious-looking

twenty-something woman with glasses sits behind a yellow model Ferrari. A slight mustache shades her upper lip.

"Is she a relative?" Summer asks, sitting and crossing her legs.

"No. Old friend."

"Hmm. An older woman."

"Maybe. Time to work."

Textbooks are lined up on his desk, along with his computer, calculator, stacks of notebooks, and index cards. Blue and red flyers from his part-time Web site design and computer trouble-shooting business, are stacked in the corner.

She pulls out the trig book and winces from the pain in her side. Moony looks at her funny.

"Sore rib," she says.

He sits beside her on his bed and explains the chapter the test was on, drawing rough equations. He makes it easy. He smells like spring breezy soap, and . . . golden wheat. While he leans over their work and talks, she tries not to get distracted by his close warmth and how incredibly cute he is. How smart and patient. His brown eyes study her hair, and her neck, and her hands with the nails bitten to the quick, which she then folds into fists. He prolongs any closeness, pulling away slowly.

"What are you, like first or second in the senior class?" she asks, after successfully completing three problems for him and getting rewarded with gummy bears.

"Second."

"What do you want to be when you grow up?" Summer asks.

"Help kids with rehabilitation." Side by side, now their shoulders press together.

"A juvenile prison guard?" She grins. Body contact is so awesome. It's weird she almost never touches anyone. With the unsettling exception recently of Kurt.

He laughs. "Physical rehabilitation. They'll know if I can do it, anyone can."

"Perfect."

"I'm up for full scholarship," he says. "University of Missouri." His knee bumps hers and doesn't leave.

"Moony, that's fantastic! Congratulations." She pats him on the back.

"Don't have it yet. Will let you know."

"I certainly hope so," she says.

"You?"

"What?"

"Said you have to finish college by twenty-two. Then what?"

She scoots back on the bed. "I haven't given it a lot of thought. I need to. Um, I guess I can do whatever I want."

"Chicken business?"

"No way. Couldn't even if I wanted to. It was sold."

"So . . . ?" He waits. "Interested in . . . ?"

She pulls her knees up. "I don't know." She's not going to say studying death across cultures. She snorts. A deathologist.

He nods, like that's okay with him. He moves to his desk chair. "Truth or dare."

"Goody. Truth," says Summer.

"How many boarding schools have you gone to?"

"Uh, four," she says. "Not counting PAIS."

"Since ninth grade?"

"Since eighth grade. Truth for you?"

"Yep."

"Who's the lady in the photo?"

"My favorite nurse."

"That is so sweet." Summer could sit on her and squash her, too.

"My turn. Why five schools?"

She hugs her knees. "I was asked not to come back the next year, or I was kicked out."

"Why?" he asks again.

"That counts as a separate question. But I'll answer it. Getting caught with alcohol or drugs, failing grades, or all of the above."

"Had a drink recently?" He raises that scarred eyebrow.

She hesitates, but decides against arguing with him about the rules of the game. "Define recently." She glances at him. "Okay, scratch that. One gulp at lunch."

He can't hide his concern. "At school?"

"Um, yeah."

Moony beams his good eye at Summer. "You don't need help with trig," he announces.

"What? Yes, I do."

"You need help with drinking."

THIRTY-TWO

Moony's bright brown eyes are like the searchlights on the top of the Eiffel Tower. He knows how Summer is doing at school. He only knows the tip of the iceberg as far as her enthusiasm for brain-altering substances goes, although she did splash barf on his shoes.

His tidy room warms. Summer doesn't mind lying to Mom. Or to herself. But she can't to Moony. And strangely, she doesn't mind him saying she needs help, despite the fact that her cheeks are radiating heat. She takes a breath. "You think?" She tries to sound sarcastic, but it doesn't work.

"Do you *want* help?" is the next question, all relaxed and easy. He touches the underside of her wrist. For a half-Arab kid, he has real American directness.

She shifts, crossing and uncrossing her legs as the bed squeaks. "What are you? Saint Moony, peer counselor?"

He waits patiently.

"I suppose it's a, uh . . . possibility," she says, smoothing the green stripes on his bedspread.

She's snowed scores of teachers, counselors, and doctors. But what does she think? Like a tire someone's let the air out of, the puffed-up-ness of her pride softens.

Help. Help. Help. She repeats it over and over in her mind until it loses its meaning, and becomes some mysterious Dutch participle.

What does it mean exactly? Allowing someone who cares to do things that support her. Moony already is. Maybe allowing someone to get close. Moony already is. Pretty much, anyway.

Admitting the lies she tells herself? Yeah. Most likely.

If she *doesn't* get it, and soon, it will cost her a fortune.

Literally.

She sighs. Hard to get worked up about that.

Getting out of the deep, dark rut she's been in for so long would be freaking hard. But what about making choices for herself and what *she* wants, instead of what everyone else wants? That might be worth working for.

What does she want?

Moony's friendship. She glances into his eyes.

That's really all.

He's watching her. She curls a page of her notebook in a tight little roll and clears her throat. "Yes. Yes, I think I do."

Pandora alights in her mind again. The illustrated bedraggled little fairy Hope left in the box. Who keeps humans around to suffer all those ills. But maybe it's not a wimpy little fairy like she always thought. Maybe it's one of those killer fairies with blinding strength. Hope with some horsepower behind her might be just what she needs.

Now Moony leans forward and takes her hand. His touch is warm and so right and reassuring her throat tightens. He doesn't let go.

"What about an AA meeting?" he asks, looking toward his bookcase.

She pulls her hand back. "What about it?"

"In English. Sometimes at the American church."

He swivels in his desk chair to his computer and types fast with his good hand. Two seconds later he has the Paris Alcoholics Anonymous Web site, which lists all the meetings, in English, every day, all over the city.

"One there tomorrow night," he says. "19:00."

"Let me get this straight," says Summer. "You're saying you would come with me." She gnaws her pinky nail. "Because I have no interest in going by myself."

"Yes."

She stands abruptly, then sits again. "Well. I . . . um, okay then. We could check it out. If it's horrible, we can leave, right?"

"Pick you up at 18:30."

"Six thirty. Crap. Okay."

Ms. Butterfield invites Summer to stay for dinner and to call her "Karen," which Summer accepts. It's lasagna, Moony's favorite from Picard, the frozen food store, along with a lamb's lettuce salad and Oranginas. Summer makes a big effort to eat and to hold up her end of the dinnertime conversation about Mars exploration, REM sleep, autism, and French labor law. Not one mention of someone's appearance, something they did wrong, what school they went to or their pedigree or lack thereof, intrudes. It's all interesting and normal, and Moony and his mom seem to enjoy each other's company. She wonders what she would be like if she'd grown up with Karen as her mother.

Karen has a generous glass of red wine but doesn't offer them any. When Karen gets up and Moony's not looking, Summer seriously contemplates taking a quick glug. Jesus, she thinks. That's truly pathetic.

When Moony double-cheek kisses Summer good-bye, he pulls her in for an extra-long hug. She involuntarily goes stiff and feels his shoulder blade jutting against her hand at a strange angle, like he has a metal can opener glued under his shirt. A desire to pull away and run out the door flits through her tense muscles. He holds her gently and then she relaxes against him and rests her cheek on his broad shoulder. Breathes in his wheaty-ness and the yum smell of that lime shampoo, his body so warm and solid against hers.

It feels like home. She and Moony twinned, a zygotic cell just split, at the center of Paris, and the world, and the universe.

The buff fairy Hope break-dances in her heart, with acrobatic leaps and rolls. She can be all right. She can get her life on track. Moony's got her back.

The world seems so right, she takes the uncrowded Métro, without incident other than shallow breathing. She proudly walks to Mom's apartment in the drizzle. Her damp hair flaps her face.

There she is again, the corner prostitute. Wearing a short vinyl skirt, a crocheted yellow and pink muffler, and gripping a black umbrella. Summer crosses the street in order to walk by her.

This time Summer says, "*Salut.*" Her attempt at *Hey, what's up*. She doesn't slow down and tries to sound casual.

Then she realizes it isn't the same woman. And this one's obviously thinking, *Cut the crap ugly-ass, honky rich-girl American. Who do you think you are?* In French, of course.

Summer studies the sidewalk and picks up her pace.

She leans heavily against the teak panels in her building's coffin-sized elevator as it ascends. What is it about bums and prostitutes? Dad became a bum, more or less. He just had enough money to stay off the streets. What about the ladies, though? Why does she think and worry about them?

Having money warps and separates people. So does having none. The Buddha was a rich prince who gave up everything material, and then found enlightenment. And purpose. Jesus hung out with prostitutes and lepers. He certainly had direction.

She could give all the money away if she gets her inheritance. Or most of it. What would that woman she just passed do with a million dollars? Or maybe it's too late for her now. What would she have done if she and Summer were switched at birth? She might be a flipping Busybody Without Borders.

Then she gets it. That's the only thing that separates her from the streets, and probably having to sell herself to survive, is money. What else could she do? Show up every day for work at a fast-food place? Drive a UPS truck? Telephone sales? Hardly. So far, she can't even handle high school. If a pimp supplied her with enough alcohol and drugs, she'd be good to go.

Where are these hookers from? Probably not even France. Probably sold by their families, and held against their will. They have to do what they're doing to survive.

What's hard to imagine is wanting to survive that bad.

THIRTY-THREE

The next day, Friday, during lunch, Summer trudges over to the lower school to Karen's classroom. The wet-wool smell of kids' coats hanging near the door and traces of lemon-scented bleach envelop her. She closes her eyes and she's in her old elementary school hallway in Little Rock, standing with Dad, showing him her tempera portrait of their cat, Alma. It hangs for all to see. Dad holds her hand and beams at her, proud.

She hasn't drawn or painted anything since ninth grade, and she used to do it a lot. Maybe she should again.

Summer raps on the door and sticks her head in. The third-graders are all bent over their desks writing furiously. Whoa—nothing more sobering than two-dozen eight-year-olds. What happens if they all decide to riot at the same time?

Karen looks up and smiles warily at Summer. Abandoning the pile of papers she's marking, she comes out into the hall.

"Hi," she says.

"Hi," Summer says. "Isn't it lunchtime for them?"

"They already had it."

"Are they taking a test?" Their concentration is so intense.

"No, they're writing stories."

"Oh. That's good." Summer focuses on the scuffed toes of her boots.

"My lesson plan is probably not why you came by," Karen prompts her.

"Uh, I wanted to thank you for dinner."

"You're most welcome," she says. "I hope you'll join us again."

"Yeah, for sure." There's another pause. "I wanted to ask, what's up with Moony's—uh, Munir's operation? Is he all right?"

Karen leans into the classroom, and satisfied the kids are behaving, turns back. "Nothing that unusual. But he's been having a hard time lately."

"What's wrong?" Summer asks.

"What isn't? There were so many fractures, so much internal organ damage."

"Is his . . . life in danger?"

Karen takes a deep breath in through her nose and crosses her arms. "No more than it ever has been, although any operation has risks. He's just worn out. Feeling weaker. And that makes him—us—a little nervous."

"What about that cough?"

"Oh, that's just a bronchial infection. I shouldn't say 'just,' but relatively speaking it's not a big concern."

"Good. Is he in pain? From like, other stuff?"

She grimaces like *she*'s in pain. "He's amazed all the medical personnel he's ever come in contact with," she says. "His ability to walk and function as well as he does is a miracle. They put his chances of surviving that accident at less than five percent."

"Wow."

"But he has so many complications, so many problems. And yes, he deals with pain pretty much constantly." She stares at the green and red construction paper holly bunches on the bulletin board across the hall, sighs, then looks back at Summer. "He just won't give in to it," she says with admiration. "I've been trying to get him to slow down for years. It's the only reason I agreed to that stupid scooter. It's a lot easier for him than public transportation."

"He has a scooter?"

"His dad recently sent the money for it," she says with her jaw set. "He spreads himself too thin for an able-bodied kid, let alone someone with his health problems." She pauses. "You should see what *you* can do with him."

"Are you kidding? I can't tell him anything."

Karen chuckles. "Anyway, we're hoping this next operation will relieve some of his latest complications, and some pain."

Maybe it has to do with his bowels or something. If it were a hip replacement or heart reconstruction, they would just say so.

Karen moves toward the door. "I need to get back in there." She pauses, then says, "Want to come in and say hi to the kids?"

Summer widens her eyes in panic.

"They love Munir."

"Of course they do." Summer nods. "Okay. Just for a moment. You're not going anywhere, right?"

Karen's already in front of the twenty-some-odd desks. "Class? Time's up. Pencils down."

The children oblige.

"I'd like you to say hello to our guest, Miss Barnes."

"Um, Summer's fine."

"Hi, Miss Barnes," say the kids mostly in unison.

A girl with pigtails shoots her hand up.

"Yes, Anna?"

"Are you a teacher?" she asks Summer.

"No, I'm a student here. In the high school." All eyes are on her. It's unnerving but they're filled with wonder and interest and excitement. She hopes it's contagious.

"Is it hard?"

Summer laughs. "Funny you should ask. It's a little hard lately because I wasn't doing my homework. If you miss learning something one day, it makes things harder the next day. Right?"

An African-American girl with braids waves her hand. Karen nods at her.

"Like you can't do division if you don't do multiplication."

"Exactly," says Summer.

Another boy raises his hand and blurts out, "Ms. Butterfield, can I read my story? Can I? Can I?" He wears a school bus–yellow polo shirt.

Karen says, "How about the first paragraph, Jack? Remember we talked about paragraphs yesterday."

"Okay!" He stands, smiles shyly at Summer, then recites, "'The Robot Hamster.' One night I heard loud noises coming from the basement." He pauses. "But we don't have a basement."

"Oooh," and "Yeah!" yell all the kids.

"Thank you, Jack."

"That is awesome," says Summer. She can't stop grinning.

Karen holds up her finger and the class goes silent. "Maybe Miss Barnes can come back another day."

"I'd love to," says Summer. "Bye, kids. Thank you." The kids' voices, their enthusiasm, the bright colors—she has a shocking sensation of floating *with* the current. Not flailing, or drowning. What would it be like to be in charge of a room full of these creatures? A flipping circus. But cool.

Karen follows her into the hall.

"Well," Summer says, "that was way better than I expected."

"Do you have younger siblings?" Karen asks.

"No siblings." Not for lack of wishing for them though.

"You're a natural," Karen tells her. She clears her throat. "Uh, Summer?"

"Yes?"

"Your friendship means a lot to Munir. Things that mean a lot to him, mean a lot to me." She grins awkwardly.

Summer nods. "It means a lot to me, too." Karen has no idea.

THIRTY-FOUR

Friday night, as promised, Moony chauffeurs Summer to the American church in the seventh. He picks her up on his green Vespa that's specially rigged so he can do more with his left hand and foot. He makes her wear his new, sleek black helmet, and he wears a scuffed, old white one. She rides behind, leaning into him. He accelerates over cobblestones and weaves like a madman in and out of the Renaults, Peugeots, Citroëns, pedestrians, green garbage trucks, and buses. Summer's legs are shaky when they finally arrive.

"Holy crap. After that, I really need a drink," she says. She hasn't had any alcohol since her one gulp in the PAIS bathroom yesterday, and does not feel well.

He grins.

"Stop smiling. You're a closet sadist. Okay, what am I supposed to do?" she asks. It's not just the ride that's making her shaky. "It *is* in English, right? Do I have to say why I'm here or how much I drink or something?"

"Yep. Saw a movie. Use first names. Then just listen."

"Hi, I'm Razorback. I'm an alcoholic?"

"Hi, Razorback," he says in a falsetto.

She tries not to smile.

The AA meeting is upstairs in a large room with creaky wooden floors. She and Moony are holding their helmets. An older woman in a blue blazer comes over to greet them. "Hi, I'm Lila. Are you visiting?"

"Yes," Moony says.

"Welcome to Paris, then. Help yourself to coffee and cookies."

"I'm *not* a tourist. I live here," huffs Summer. Moony quickly steers her over to the coffee, then they sit down.

Summer nibbles a butter cookie, hoping it will help her stomach. Dad never attended an AA meeting, and the whole setup sounds a little fishy.

The room fills until there are about thirty attendees. They start on time, but people keep coming in: twenty-year-olds, eighty-year-olds, businessmen, tourists, a mother with a baby, middle-aged women, fashionistas, druggie types. Lila leads the meeting. They go around the room and everyone says, "Hi, my name is ______. I'm an alcoholic." Then as Moony demonstrated, everyone else responds, "Hi, ______!"

Moony says slower than everyone else, "Hi, my name is Moony. I'm here to learn."

"Hi, Moony!" everyone choruses.

Lila says, "Wonderful. This is an open meeting and all are welcome." She glances at Summer. "And all that is needed for a closed meeting is a desire to stop drinking."

Summer says, "Hi, my name is Summer." After an awkward pause, she says, "Period."

People say out of unison and a little halfheartedly, "Hi, Summer."

"Liked me better," he whispers to her.

"Shut up and learn," she whispers back.

Summer concentrates on listening, and twirls her nose ring. They talk about steps, serenity, "focus on the drinking, not the thinking," "just for today," and of course, "one day at a time." Then people share long-winded stories or whatever their current thoughts are. Some have thick accents, mostly French, one Russian, and are difficult to understand.

It lasts an interminable hour and Summer squirms. It's boring and she doesn't have a problem like these people do, or at least not one she can't handle herself. At one point, Moony reaches over and takes her sweaty hand. She'll just enjoy the time with him.

Finally, everyone stands up, hold hands, and says the serenity prayer. It's over. People linger and chat.

"That's it?" Summer says. "Aren't they going to tell me how to stop drinking?"

Lila, nearby and moving chairs, says, "You just do. Then you come here to keep on not drinking."

"Just stop. Just like that."

"Take the first step. Admit that you're 'powerless over alcohol and that your life has become unmanageable.'"

"Well, what if it hasn't?" Summer asks. Moony looks up at the ceiling.

Lila shrugs, lugging a chair to the back. "*Tant mieux.*"

"So much the better'?" Summer asks Moony.

He sighs. "Yeah."

Lila comes back for another chair and says, "There's a youth AA meeting over in the first, also on Friday evenings. You might visit them."

Summer pulls Moony out the door behind her. "I've got to get out of here."

They get on his scooter under the glow of a streetlight. "No offense," Summer says, "but just give me a ride over to the bus stop by the Métro."

"Okay, you insist." He starts the motor.

"If I can completely stop drinking, then I'm not powerless, right?" she says into his ear. "So I'll stop. No question it'll help me get my schoolwork done. Among other things."

"That's great," he says.

She pauses. "Thank you," she says softly. "For coming with me." His generosity floors her.

He turns his head around. At the same moment she leans forward. Their helmets clunk and their noses brush. They both freeze.

Then he kisses her on the lips.

THIRTY-FIVE

Summer kisses Moony back, tentatively at first. She's drawn in, then carried off in what's deep and warm as a tropical river that she feels in every watery cell of her being. Through their lips flows a time-lapse video of hot springs bubbling up through soft earth, vast verdant wildernesses budding, growing, and coloring through seasons, under rainstorms of drama, moon phases of heartache, with one sun truth shining above it all:

Despite the fact that she's a huge pain in the ass, Moony likes her.

Maybe even loves her.

THIRTY-SIX

Summer is safe and strong and capable when she's with Moony. When her lips are connected to his, she's—

Her eyes pop open.

She's not strong or capable. Or safe. She's a freaking black hole and no one should connect to her. Talk about being in a bad place for a relationship.

Then Kurt's cold kiss jolts her with mega-guilt.

Summer pulls away from Moony's lips. She cannot do this. She was just kissing Kurt and Moony knows nothing about him.

But it was so different, so empty, with Kurt. He has some unhealthy force over her and gains strength from her weakness.

Summer hesitates; Moony does, too. Their faces hover a few centimeters apart. She breathes in the smell of his clean skin, the old leather from the helmet strap. Cookie breath. He's so *right*.

She leans back slowly.

And she's so wrong.

Moony turns around and puts the scooter in gear. Summer holds on to him with one arm and grips the seat edge with the other. They fly across the river to the Métro entrance. She straps her helmet to the back with his bungee cord, and says, "Thanks again. See you." She doesn't look him in the eye, even though he's watching her closely. Instead of standing right there at the bus stop, she runs over to and down the Métro stairs.

Yes, her heart is thudding, she's hyperventilating, and it feels like she's going to die, but she doesn't care.

Echoes of that woman witness's scream from when the lady was killed at Étoile station fill her head as she rumbles along beneath Paris, staring at the grit and old chewing gum on the filthy floors. She tries to make sense of the evening. Her blood buzzes, her stomach roils, she can't breathe. What should she do? Pretend it didn't happen? She's acting like a thirteen-year-old, she knows. On top of everything else. She groans aloud. The noise of the train, the lights, the people crowding near her, it all feels like a glacier chunk is about to crash down on top of her.

She wishes they hadn't just kissed!

No, she's glad. It's the one true thing that's ever happened.

But she'll ruin it for sure.

Ice tinkling in glasses tells Summer that Mom is back and sitting in the living room with someone. She smooths her hair and tries to collect herself.

"Hi, dear," Mom calls. "Come on in."

"Howdy, Summer. How ya been, darlin'?" Wild Winston stands. "Happy Friday the thirteenth."

Summer rolls her eyes, but gives him a peck on the cheek. "I thought you left," she says.

"Well, I had business in Frankfurt last week."

Summer goes to the table where all the bottles are on a shiny silver tray, and makes herself a Perrier. She squeezes a lime slice into it. It tastes shockingly weak. Blech. But clean.

Winston says, "I visited your school on Wednesday."

"You did?" Summer spins around. Crap!

"You weren't there."

"I was sick."

"I talked to the head of the school, the dean of students, and the college counselor." He swills a swig of scotch.

"Yeah? And?" She plonks the crystal glass down and crosses her arms over her chest. He is not her parent. Or her boss. He's a freaking employee, wannabe boyfriend, and she hasn't liked him since she was six and he talked to her like she was a chubby, useless idiot.

"Summer, darlin', you understand what's at stake here, right?"

"Yes."

"You've got to pass this semester. Graduate. And then you've got to enroll in college as soon as possible. Time's wasting." He smiles as if to reassure her that he's on her side.

She's grinding her teeth and stops. "I know. I'm working on it."

"I understand you got off to a good start, but that you're already up the creek in most of your classes."

Mom says, "They said you're still not passing your classes."

Summer thrusts out her chin. "I *said* I'm working on it." They're both looking at her hard, trying to read her, trying to figure out why she can't accomplish this seemingly simple task. "This school is hard. They demand a lot. Coming in the middle of the semester may have seemed like a good idea, but I'm having to learn everything they've already done the two months I wasn't here."

"I understand that. But no one can do it for you. You're a very intelligent girl," he says.

Summer wishes the compliment were true. "I have a tutor. My friend Moony. I've turned in all my work. I'm preparing for finals. I will graduate."

Winston looks at Mom and she shrugs. He says, "The terms of the will are ironclad. Your grandpa saw to that."

"So everyone keeps reminding me," she mumbles.

Winston ignores her. "And as the executor I have to confirm that you are following them. You gotta help me here a little, darlin'."

If he calls her "darlin'" again she's going to leap over the coffee table and jam her fingers up his nose.

She sighs. Autopilot responses. Everyone's trying to get to "yes" here. "Look, I just came back from an Alcoholics Anonymous meeting. Moony went with me. I've, um, stopped drinking. That will help me concentrate full time on my studies. I've got it under control." She holds out the glass of Perrier as proof.

Mom's eyes open wide. Winston's surprised, too. "I didn't realize you had a drinking problem," he says.

"I guess it's gotten worse lately," says Summer.

"I—That's great, sweetheart," says Mom. She looks like she's trying to calculate a long row of numbers. "Why didn't you—Good for you."

"That's great," Winston echoes.

"Is there anything else?" Summer asks. She wishes Winston wouldn't keep hanging around. He's so annoying. And Mom went away with him. What is up with that?

"Keep up the good work," says Wild Winston.

I flipping intend to, thinks Summer. But not for you.

For Moony.

She *could* deserve him one day. By all that is good, she will deserve him.

Then she'll kiss him.

THIRTY-SEVEN

Summer sits at the desk in her room, chewing her nails, and with great focus completes a French assignment. What is Moony doing? What's he thinking? She reads as much of Dante's *Inferno* as she can stand, which isn't much. Smoke is practically coming out of her ears from the mental effort as she tries to finish reading the assignment on flea-ridden medieval France. She struggles to keep the taste of Moony's lips on hers from constantly interrupting her thoughts. If she could just hug him daily—like at his apartment, forget about herself against his body, in his arms—she could do anything. Even become the girl he deserves.

She could also *really* use a drink. But she absolutely will not. Just for today.

Later, after she's written the first draft of an essay, she eats a yogurt in the kitchen, then goes to Mom's room. Her mother's smoking in bed propped up against her upholstered headboard, reading reports of some kind. Camus is curled at her side asleep.

Summer knocks on the open door.

The usual half-full glass of vodka and grapefruit juice sits on her bedside table, on top of a *Paris Match* magazine. *Les Guignols de l'info*, the French *Colbert Report* with puppets, plays soundlessly on her TV.

"What is it, dear?"

The old Limoges porcelain lamp painted with a silly Bo Peep shepherdess illuminates a small overnight bag open and half-packed on the floor.

It reminds Summer of the time when she was in second grade and Mom tried to teach her French. They went around the room in the house in Little Rock naming things like *la table, la lampe*. Easy ones. That shepherdess lamp was there.

Mom read her *The Three Bears*. *Les Trois Petits Ours*. She lets it roll out of her mouth the way Mom taught her. "Lay twah petee-toors."

"Excuse me?"

Summer didn't mean to say that out loud. She smiles and leans against the doorjamb. "You really shouldn't smoke in bed." Mom only started smoking again since Summer arrived to live with her.

"It's my last one. Is that what you came in here to tell me?" Mom puts the bound report down. "I didn't know you were drinking . . . so much. I'm proud you've taken it into your own hands."

"Thanks." Summer sends a silent thanks to Ouaiba, too, for not ratting her out.

"I've already put the liquor away. Is there anything else I can do? To help?"

"It's fine. I know it's up to me, and uh, I have to learn. How to not drink."

But Mom *can* help. By clearing up something Summer's been wondering about for years. "I wanted to ask you. You met Dad in your business, right?"

Mom folds her arms. "Yes. When your grandfather hired my firm." She ran a public relations company contracted by Barnes Chicken back in the nineties when the public realized how much the company exploited their employees, not to mention the poultry.

Summer asks, "When did Winston come into the picture?" If he's going to be hanging around she deserves to know the truth.

Mom squirms weakly like a worm on a fishhook. "I don't think that's any of your business."

Summer has her answer. Mom hooked up with Wild Winston before Dad died. Winston is *still* simpering around even though he and Mom are supposedly history.

"No wonder you left Dad on the bathroom floor."

Mom stubs her cigarette out like there's a big spider underneath it. "I could let you continue living in the dream world you've built around your father," she says with cold steeliness.

"I haven't built a dream world around him."

"It's time you knew what really happened." Mom pauses and glares at Summer. "He killed himself."

THIRTY-EIGHT

Summer takes a step back and glares at Mom. "I've heard this from you before. Dad didn't take care of himself, drank too much, yadda, yadda, and so on."

"No." Mom doesn't take her eyes from Summer. "I mean he committed suicide."

Summer flinches.

Stiffens. Flash-freezes.

She creaks and crackles from the inside out.

The silence between them condenses.

"I'll be damned," Summer finally says. It's something Dad might have said. "I knew it. I *knew* it. Why did you never tell me? Why the hell are you only now telling me this?" Her voice sounds strangely cold and calm to her own ears.

"Because your grandfather swore us to secrecy. He was mortified that his son killed himself."

"You mean everyone lied about it? Was there ever even a stroke at all?"

"I believe there was a brain hemorrhage from falling. Only a couple of people knew the true story." Mom sighs and rubs her eyes. "I'm ashamed I've kept it this long. In his usual dictatorial way, your grandfather made sure that the public never learned the truth. He had the state government, police, media, everybody in his pocket, so he generally got his way." Mom shakes her head. "Your father died of an intentional overdose of narcotics. And alcohol, and a fall. It *was* complicated. But he killed himself. And he was thwarted by that old son of a bitch even in his final act of defiance."

The room is tilting. Act of defiance? Summer steadies herself against the wall. "Because he knew about you and Winston."

"No," Mom says calmly. "I wasn't 'involved' with Winston before your father died, by the way. Wally was depressed and alcoholic. A very ill and difficult man who refused all help. But I did not betray him." She gets out of bed and walks to Summer, holds out her arms. "I'm sorry, sweetheart. I know how much he meant to you. He loved you very much."

"Don't touch me."

Mom lowers her arms and sniffs. "You do need to know this. Depression runs in that family."

"And I'm just like him!" Summer cries. With stiff ice legs, she strides down the hall and locks herself in her room. She ignores the knock at the door.

"Sweetheart!" Mom says through the door. "You are not like him! Not like that! Please, open the door."

Summer says nothing and waits for Mom to go away. There's a long silence then, "Summer, listen to me. I love you. I know you. You are your own person. You have your own strength."

So much like him indeed. Summer opens one of two vodka bottles still in her armoire, pours some in an empty Evian bottle, then the rest in a glass and downs it. Good thing she hadn't thrown them out yet.

THIRTY-NINE

Summer leaves the apartment. It's near midnight and she wanders along the boulevard as cars speed by and their wheels hum annoying high frequencies over the cobblestones. Just step off the curb.

She digs her hands deep in her pockets against the cold. Snow flurries zig and zag at odd angles through yellowish streetlight beams.

She really wants to look behind her, but won't. She knows a sixty-mile-per-hour avalanche full of boulders and ice chunks and uprooted, cartwheeling trees is roaring down upon her.

She wants to scream. Hell yes, they should have told her. A long time ago. So many dark secrets and such an effort to keep her ignorant.

Her father. How could he? If he loved her. Leave her—*on purpose*—like that. She wants to kick him. *He* was supposed to have her back.

Dad left her unprotected and alone. She knows he didn't *feel* like he had a choice. But he *did*.

Yet underneath all that churning frozen froth, the big puzzle pieces slide together, like glaciers. She knew it somewhere deep inside. And she completely understands why he wanted to do what he did.

The anniversary, December 17, is in four days.

Once when she was eleven, she waited outside of her dad's study. She wanted to show him her excellent report card. He'd been in there, it seemed, for weeks. She had to screw up her courage to knock. He was just sitting in his reading chair with his head in his hands in the dark. "Dad?"

He didn't answer. Or move.

"Dad?" she said louder, but shakier. She fought to keep herself from running out.

He put out his hand, at first she thought to shoo her away. But he motioned her closer. He pulled her into a tight, desperate hug. His cheeks were wet with tears. Then he said, "Baby, remember. Don't back down."

Summer turns into a side street and passes a bakery. An old Irish pub beckons next door. She slips inside.

The copper-haired bartender wears a black and white rugby shirt. He smiles. "*Bonsoir*, mademoiselle."

"Top of the evening."

"What can I get you?" he says with an Aussie accent.

Summer thinks of Moony's lips against hers. His hand in hers at the meeting. That hug. She *will* stop drinking, just not tonight. It's already ruined, not-drinking-wise, anyway. "Irish whiskey?"

"You're eighteen?" For hard liquor.

"I am." She'd be glad to show him her Arkansas driver's license.

But he doesn't ask for it. "Neat?"

"Why not? Make that a double."

He pours and she downs it. "One more," she says. "To savor."

"Rough day?"

"The usual. But thanks." When she starts telling a bartender her problems, she'll know she's in real trouble.

He obliges. Summer pays then sits at a window table. A South African rugby game is on and a lone patron watches it, gripping his pint of Guinness. She realizes someone is sitting at the bar, very near where she was just standing. An older guy in a longish black coat and hat. As if feeling her stare, he turns around.

Of course. Kurt is here. The world's biggest jerk. She can't believe his nerve.

Bringing his drink, he walks over. "Mind if I sit down?"

She stands. "Free country. Mind if I leave?"

He laughs.

She downs the rest of her whiskey and walks out. She's pretty sure France is a free country.

"Good night," calls the bartender. Kurt doesn't follow.

Once outside in the damp, cold darkness, she cannot help spinning around to look in the window. Sure enough, Kurt's watching her.

He comes out before she can decide what to do.

"You look breathtaking this evening."

She knows he's full of crap. "How'd you get a drink without me to pay for it?"

He grins. "It was on the house."

"You're a total jerk and I don't want to talk to you." Her feet won't march away though.

"But you are." He reaches out for her upper arm, but stops short. He gazes into her eyes. "Summer. I am so sorry about the fiasco in the catacombs. I couldn't find you afterward and my phone was stolen."

He dragged her into the sewers and deserted her amid human bones piled beneath the city of Paris. She was assaulted and almost arrested. He's narcissistic, probably sociopathic. But his eyes are boring into hers with such love and longing. He traces his cold finger down her cheek. He's so beautiful she has to look down.

She hugs her sore ribs. "Along with my favorite flask."

"I saw you just as you were getting in the taxi. So I knew you were okay," he continues. "I just got back from London."

"I was fine," she grumbles. See? she tells herself. He's sorry. There's an explanation. But he must have gotten a new cell phone. Although how would he get her number?

"May I make it up to you?"

He pulls her to him, kisses both her cheeks, nuzzles her throat, and holds her. Her cold anger softens and melts, as her mind goes blank. Her physical attraction to him clouds her thinking. Plain and simple. He's a freaking electromagnet who smells like he spilled an entire bottle of good cologne on his jacket. Yet the strong smell of, like, something decaying permeates the notes of spice and grass. She's going to have to say something about his hygiene habits.

She pulls away. "How did you find me?"

He looks at her a beat, almost as if he can't believe her question. He shrugs. "I've been thinking about you. A lot. A few blocks back, I veered down this way. I've never been on this street before and I decided to go in there to check it out."

"Woooh, psychic." Not likely.

Maybe he was in there already and she found *him*.

"Come on," he says, taking her hand. "This is my lucky day."

FORTY

Summer and Kurt walk in comfortable silence. Holding hands in Paris! She's not only forgiven him, she's ready to flipping get engaged.

No, not really. She is along for the ride, though. Like when someone drives dangerously fast. What do they have to do before you say something? Or before you scream at them to stop and let you out. For now, momentum carries her and she's cool with going along.

She doesn't have the energy to fight it.

They descend into the Métro. She feeds the turnstile a ticket and he elegantly vaults it. She shakes her head in disbelief. The ticket office window is right there, but the man inside doesn't even look up. Kurt shoots her a triumphant smile. Her pulse and breathing have accelerated, being down here. But it's like she's on autopilot.

Below, the train squeals to a stop and the doors open. They get on.

Kurt takes the one open seat. "Thanks for the seat," she says, but he pulls her onto his lap and wraps an arm around her middle. The physical contact makes her draw in her breath. She leans back into him and he caresses her neck with his chin. Then beneath her coat collar and sweater and shirt, he strokes the scar at the base of her neck.

"Cut it out," she says, getting up. From her Evian bottle she swallows a slug of vodka.

They get off. He pulls her by the hand and jogs down a long corridor to another line. In the shadows of the glaring lights, Kurt looks over thirty.

"What *is* the rush?" She's sucking wind.

He grabs her hand again and they ride the escalator to the platform below. Only a few people wait for the train.

Kurt raises his chin in the slightest acknowledgment of a Romany woman sitting against the wall in a corner, a sleeping baby in her arms, and a dingy, long wine-colored skirt spread around her. She looks at him with a penetrating expression for a couple of beats then turns her head away.

"Don't tell me. You know her, too?" Summer asks.

He smiles mysteriously.

"Drink?" he asks, holding out his hand. Summer pulls out her plastic half-liter bottle.

"To decisions," he says, grinning. "And peace . . . of mind."

"Yeah, *santé*." They each drink. "Where are we going now?"

"It's a surprise."

Kurt leans out to look down the tunnel from the edge of the platform. He holds out his hand. Summer hesitates. He's way too close to the edge. But he's playing some sort of game here.

"Don't be afraid," he says. "I've got you." Like at Outward Bound camp—or group therapy. A trust exercise.

"Which reminds me: Last time I listened to you I was beaten and robbed," she says.

He peers into her eyes. "That was out of my control. You don't know the full story and you never asked what happened to me, did you?"

"No."

"Just trust me."

"Fine." She takes his hand. He pulls her to the lip of the concrete platform. Their toes hang over. She thinks of sparkly ruby slippers, then feels Kurt grip her firmly as they hear the faint rumblings of the train leaving the next station.

"*The light of your love . . .*"

"*Chases the fear away,*" she finishes. Thanks, Kentucky.

Summer holds her breath and struggles to keep her balance above the gravel and the crumpled newspaper inserts and soda cans. Which rail is the high-voltage one? Has to be the far one. If she fell in, and stayed close to this side, she could climb out. As long as she beat the train.

The train's rumbling amplifies. She steps one foot back.

"NO," Kurt barks, then says softly, "Wait until the last moment." He grips her hand. "Stay where you are. There's a gap. The train won't hit your toes. Just don't lean forward." Her head would get knocked off, she figures matter-of-factly, if she leaned forward.

Last spring, at St. Jude's, boarding school number four, she went up to the school tower alone. She sat on the ledge, her feet dangling, and one of the kids below had yelled up to her, "Do it! Jump!" She had not been thinking about leaping, exactly, rather about her recent humiliation with the debate team cocaptain-who-shall-not-be-named, and the betrayal of her friend Grace, and her impending flunking of senior year, meaning she had to stay at this hellhole school yet another semester or more. Among other things. She contemplated it at that moment—to fly away, but then didn't want to give those a-holes below the pleasure, even though it was tempting to aim for one of them.

People shuffle to be in place to board the train that is now visible in the tunnel. They shoot her wary or disapproving looks. The noise crescendos and the rush of stale, warm air ahead of the lead car blows across her face. The train bursts through the tunnel at the other end, screaming toward them. She closes her eyes, her whole body electrified.

Not the third-rail-fried way.

"See?" he says. "Adrenaline rush." He laughs.

Brakes screech as the train slows.

A firm hand grabs Summer's upper arm. "Mademoiselle!" a man snaps, jerking her backward a second before it passes her. He rattles something off about danger and stupidity. It wouldn't have hit, or even touched her. Only come very close.

She looks at Kurt. He's laughing. She grins but is shaking. She wonders why he just did that. A trust exercise. Ridiculous. A rush, yes. It didn't make her feel more alive, though, it made her feel completely apart. Like she was watching herself from behind.

A low-heeled black shoe on the tracks.

The first time she saw Kurt, he said, "A deliverance."

Kurt is easy. Being with him is exciting, or at least unpredictable. No thought or work required. He wants her just as she is. He takes command. She can follow his lead.

She loves Moony but to become the girl he deserves is impossible.

FORTY-ONE

Summer gets out of bed Saturday midday. She didn't sleep much but it's time to escape the twisted tendrils of sheet and duvet before they strangle her.

She's hungover, exhausted, and last night is foggy and unreal. Did she really go to an AA meeting? Did Mom really tell her that her dad offed himself? Then she played chicken in the Métro with Kurt?

For chrissakes.

Moony.

Did she really kiss him?

Yes.

That kiss glimmers like a ruby lying amid the pile of stinking fish guts and coal and rusted car parts that was last night. Like a ruby-throated hummingbird in her rib cage. A gift for that kick-boxing fairy.

Okay, enough lame metaphors. Deserving him will be a freaking long and winding road.

Thank god, it's a new day.

She finds her plastic water bottle and empties the vodka into the toilet. Again. Followed by the rest of the bottle that's in her closet. And the other full one.

She had a bad night, but this is a new start. As she pulls on her clothes she studies the framed photo on her dresser of her dad. He's about her age, in a University of Arkansas Razorback baseball uniform holding a bat. He grins boyishly, rosy cheeked. Handsome.

He coached her Little League softball team when she was seven. One humid spring evening, a girl hit a homer when the bases were loaded. All those kids came running in and Dad was jumping up and down by home plate, so excited, high-fiving the kids. Then he hugged her and her mom.

He was healthy once. He taught her to swim and play tennis. He stopped drinking for a long time, too. They read and watched the whole *Lord of the Rings* series together twice and three times, respectively. They'd sneak off together regularly to get cheeseburgers and blue Icees that they both loved and Mom forbade.

She wonders what happened to him, how depression set in, the choices he made. Things probably piled up on him like they have on her. And he probably tried really hard to get his shit together. Like she's trying.

Summer plops on her bed and opens the history reading on her tablet.

Those kids in Moony's mom's classroom had such life in their eyes. They aren't old enough to be all jaded and tired. She hopes anyway.

What's interesting is that when she's with kids, she feels like things will be okay.

It's always a fair exchange, too. She teaches them how to float and then do the breaststroke; they give back in respect and real growth and laughter. Like that kid who was dying to share the Robot Hamster story with her. She smiles. When she makes an effort, they make one back. That's more than she can say for most people.

Kids usually like her, too.

Why?

Maybe because they are less discerning? That would be kind of hard to swallow. Older people know better, that she's a poor excuse for a human being.

But no, when she was a little, she was very picky. She didn't like adults who patronized or dismissed her. Like Wild Winston. Kids are judgmental, too. They're totally perceptive and they don't like people who try to bullshit or talk down to them. They want adults to be "real" with them, confident and respectful, and help them figure out how to navigate this hard and sad world. And they love to laugh.

Ha. She could be their example of what *not* to do.

She needs to be around kids more.

She needs to contemplate this further. Maybe talk to Karen.

Summer glances at the time, and refocuses on reading and taking notes on Charlemagne. But now Moony's face as he gazed into her eyes in his room keeps interfering. He kissed her, so the next move is up to her. She should call him before she loses the nerve. He probably won't call her, and she so doesn't want things to be awkward between them. Then she can study in peace.

"Hey," she says when he answers.

"S'up?" he replies. He sounds neither happy nor unhappy to hear from her. Maybe he's trying to be neutral, or maybe he's mad about that kiss.

Maybe he's sorry.

Her stomach sinks. "Nothing much."

There's a long pause. She wants to blurt out, *It was freaking hard to call you and you're destroying me with enthusiasm here.* But instead she says, "Um, thanks for going with me last night. This really is the first day of the rest of my life."

"Good!" He does say this enthusiastically and it relaxes her a little. "And no prob."

She hears talking in the background. "Where are you?"

"Home."

"Are you in the middle of something?"

"Uncle's here."

"American?"

"From Kuwait."

"Oh. Nice."

He says quietly, "Have to take him to the Louvre. Then dinner. You?"

"Nothing much here." Another pause. "I guess I'm going to study."

"Later, then." He says it so fast, like he can't wait to get off. It super-chills her.

She chokes out, "Okay. Good. Have fun."

Disappointment weighs and pokes her like a chain mail T-shirt. As she could have predicted, they're pretending nothing happened. Or he's really sorry he kissed her.

As he should be.

No, she's relieved. It is much better this way.

She pours herself an OJ in the kitchen, and seriously considers adding vodka. Good thing she poured all hers out. She's just taking a sip when the house phone rings. She jumps.

"Hello?" she answers.

"Summer? It's Kurt."

She gulps. "Oh. Hey. What's up?" She tries to sound casual. Her heartbeat is what's up.

"I can't stop thinking about you. I really need to be with you. Will you come see a movie with me?" he asks.

She doubts he can't stop thinking about her, but what the heck. She's glad.

She hesitates two seconds. "Sure."

"I'll meet you in front of the Gaumont Ambassade. On the Champs. Seven o'clock? Several movies are showing then. We can choose."

"Great. See you there. Um, thanks for calling," she adds lamely. She needs a break. A movie will distract her fine. There's no harm in it and if Moony's going to ignore her, then it's all she can do.

A much-needed spurt of energy fuels her hasty change into a gauzy white blouse and a pair of her new skinny jeans. She spritzes on some of Mom's Dior perfume, combs her hair, and brushes her teeth. She smears a little barely pink lip gloss on her lips.

It's not that far, so she walks while the moon rises over the city, disappearing and reappearing beneath drifting, heavy clouds. She mouths the words of a Kentucky song. *Don't deny the depth of the darkness, oh, nooo.*

The multiplex movie theater is surrounded by wall-to-wall people, and cars and elaborate tangles of Christmas lights pack the long Champs-Elysées. A huge queue snakes out from the ticket booths for the eight movies showing. She sees Kurt from a block away. He stands out, standing in line.

His back is to her, his thick hair gleaming. He holds a cigarette. The collar on his black coat is turned up. And the soft red scarf around his neck flaps in the bracing wind. He turns as she approaches and smiles broadly.

"Hi," she says.

He flicks his cigarette on the sidewalk and embraces her with a leisurely kiss on each cheek. Only a hint of that cologne attempts to mask his strong, unwashed, bitterly sour odor. Does he notice her Dior?

"I have a present for you." He pulls a newspaper-wrapped package from his coat pocket and hands it to her.

"What is it?" she asks.

He doesn't answer. She tears off the newspaper to reveal a sterling silver flask, older and more ornate than Dad's. Beautiful.

"I can't accept this."

"Of course you can. It's my fault you lost the other one."

"That's true." It looks exactly like one that caught her eye at Les Puces.

"*Je t'en prie.*"

"Wow. I don't know what to say." So much for refusing expensive gifts from gentlemen.

"A tiny token of my affection for you."

Now all the times she's paid for them and all the times he disappeared mean nothing. No one's ever given her such a thoughtful gift before.

"Thanks." She gives him a hug. The flask sloshes. "Anything in it?"

"Open it and see."

"Oh. I kind of . . ." She trails off, then says almost inaudibly, "I'm not drinking."

Kurt laughs heartily. "You were last night."

"You don't have to be quite so amused."

"It's very good cognac. One sip won't hurt."

One day at a time. She can't very well not drink from this gorgeous gift. She pushes Moony from her thoughts. A little won't hurt. The key is keeping it to a little.

"'I can resist anything but temptation,'" she quotes, opening the stopper top and taking a slug of strong, smooth cognac. It tastes like heaven. "Aaaah."

"Oscar Wilde," says Kurt.

"Yep. He's in Père Lachaise, you know. This is so excellent. Care for some?"

He takes a pull then hands it back. The bourgeois couple in line ahead give her disdainful looks. Summer takes one more sip, savors the burn, then puts the flask in her jacket pocket.

"I thought we might see the *Chainsaw Chicks* movie," he says. "It's so deliciously depraved."

"You're kidding, right?"

"Nope."

"I, uh, those are kind of sick." That's the *only* film up on the marquee that she has no desire to see. She would rather watch an incomprehensible French movie. She can't believe they are even showing that here.

"You can close your eyes in the rough parts. It gets easier. This one is very well done and it's *version original.*" In English.

Small hard lines that she's never noticed crinkle his eyes. He could be a lot older than she thought, which gives her a sort of woozy feeling. That and *Chainsaw Chicks*. She takes another draw of cognac.

But he laces his fingers in her gloved hand. Old guys go for younger women, even if they're homely. Maybe that explains things. But how old is he? Thirties? Maybe it only shows now because he's been up all night or something.

"Fine," she says. "Have it your way." Her excitement from before has morphed into abdominal dragonflies. Mutant ones on meth. Yet her thick fatigue makes it so hard to think.

He makes a show of pulling out a smooth black Italian leather wallet to pay. Then makes a show of finding it empty, so Summer pulls out a twenty. She gets the French popcorn *sucré* and a diet Coke and he gets nothing. She does like standing beside him. *Hey, look, everybody! I'm on a date with a hot guy.*

The theater is only half full and smells like stale popcorn, but they sit in the very back with empty seats on either side. He's still holding her hand like he thinks she's going to bolt. It has crossed her mind. But she pulls away to open her new flask and pours as much cognac into her "Coca Light" as will fit and chugs. Then he puts his arm around her shoulders.

It's nice to be physically close and she can't help but relax a little. His gesture is protective and she likes it.

The movie starts. Blood's spurting and body parts are flying as the too-loud sound system fills the space with screams before the opening credits stop rolling. She turns her head into his shoulder, kind of used to his odor. He pats her and chuckles.

"Thanks for coming to this with me," he says.

"Hmm."

A little later, there's a sort of sexy scene with the crazy guy and a young hitchhiker. It's only a matter of minutes though before she's history, and Kurt's hand migrates around her back, through her armpit, onto her right breast. He caresses it gently, then firmly. His other hand crawls between her legs.

She pulls away from him. "Cut it out." Now she's sorry to be watching this horrible movie with him. She puts her arms in her coat, knocking over the box of popcorn.

"Don't fight me," he says. Her arms are still half stuck in her coat. He massages the scar tissue on her neck and pulls her back in her chair, with strength she can't fight. He touches her between her legs again, but softly.

Physical desire shoots through every blood vein in her body.

Kurt whispers warmly in her ear, "I want you more than life itself." Next thing she knows, he's manipulating his hand inside her jeans. She's breathing hard. He's caught her off guard. A theater full of people wouldn't stop her from making a scene, but during this feature no one would notice anyway. Maybe he figured that.

He whispers, "You are so hot for me."

She squeezes her legs and gets a hand free. She grabs his to stop him. He relaxes and strokes her cheek and hair. Then gently, teasingly works his fingers back into her pants. She would yell or punch him, but she can't.

She doesn't want to.

"Ah, Summer, I will have you," he breathes. He pulls her head to him and kisses her, flicking her tongue with his. He sucks the breath out of her. The room's on fire. His fingers work her over. He knows exactly what he's doing.

But he stops.

She's panting, shaking, like a coiled live wire.

The screams on the screen fill her head. She can't look at the screen or at Kurt, who still has one arm clenched around her. She's half waiting for him to put her hand on his crotch. His turn. But he doesn't. He just sits there calmly, and as far as she can tell, he hasn't gotten worked up about any of this at all. She doesn't turn him on?

He whispers, "No, you don't. You disgust me."

She doubles over, as if she's been hit. An icy wave of fear washes over her. She buttons her jeans, grabs her backpack, and stands up.

"Urgent appointment?" he asks.

"You're an asshole," she hisses. "Get out of my way."

He smiles.

FORTY-TWO

Summer double bolts the doors of the empty apartment then texts Moony with shaking thumbs:

Please please call when ur free

Using Mom's easy-to-find liquor, she makes a tall vodka with a splash of orange juice and downs it. She makes another, sits in the living room in the dark, nurses it, smokes, and waits. Camus trots in and sits on her lap. Summer barely notices. About twenty-five minutes later, Moony texts:

Still on family duty. What's up?
Need to talk.
OK, hang on.

A few interminable minutes later, her phone sings.

"Summer? You okay?"

There's a long pause. "Moony. Thangs for calling. Yeah I'm okay, but . . . I—jus . . ." She can tell she's slurring. She confesses, "I've been drinking."

"Figured," he says evenly.

"Something happened," she blurts out.

"What?"

"Oh, Moony, iss—it, I caan't—"

"Anybody with you?"

"Nope."

"Okay. Coming over."

The next morning, Summer wakes on the long living room couch, covered with a blanket and one of her pillows under her head. Camus sleeps at her feet. She has no idea what happened. She probably passed out. Someone covered her up. It had to have been Moony. Or Ouaiba. Who let Moony in when he arrived and she didn't answer. She cringes at the thought of Kurt, feels sick actually, and at the huge mess she is, and how her life is so effed up. Totally and completely. Let's see. Is there anyone she's not letting down?

The dog walks across her abdomen and licks her chin.

"Thanks for that, Camus." She rubs his head and he licks her hand. They're fast friends these days. But somehow his affection makes her feel even worse. Dogs are loyal regardless of what a shit you are.

What day is it? Sunday, and Mom will be back this evening. It's Ouaiba's day off and Camus needs to go out. She's still dressed and staggers to the elevator, the dog in her arms, to take him to the courtyard to pee.

When she comes back, there's a text from Moony.

Coffee?

Where?

Café au Coin.

OK. There in 30.

Her head and whole body hurt, and Moony will be highly annoyed with her, but seeing him is the only thing that matters.

FORTY-THREE

Café au Coin is the dodgy one on the market street near Moony's apartment where Summer went before. But she's glad to go over to his neighborhood, the seventeenth, and so grabs a taxi. After all, she made him come all the way to her house late at night and then passed out on him. She has to talk to him. She has to tell him.

The market street is bustling and all the stalls are piled with leafy green and beta-carotene-rich produce that hurts to look at. It's still before noon and it's raining lightly. Summer enters the café, says, "*Bonjour,* monsieur," to the proprietor, and sits at a table. She needs something in her stomach and orders a croissant and a café crème.

Moony walks in slowly with his cane, pale—and stern looking.

Summer jumps up and hugs him, noting the startled look on his face.

"I passed out, huh? You buzzed Ouaiba?"

"Yes, Sherlock." He's *trying* to look mad, though.

"I'm so sorry, Moony. That you came all that way. Thank you."

"So what happened?" He falls awkwardly onto his chair, leaning heavily on his cane.

"What happened to *you*? Why the cane now?" She sits down.

"Doctor's orders. Fell. It's stupid."

"Oh, Moony." She huffs in frustration. He needs to talk to her as much as she needs to talk to him. Why won't he? She knows the answer, though.

The proprietor comes over to exchange greetings and see what Moony wants. He gets an orange juice, then sighs deeply.

"May need *another* operation after Christmas one. Body's . . . straining. After everything." Summer reaches out to touch his hand, but Moony pulls it back.

She says gently, "Dude. You need to slow down." He's already mad. So what if he gets madder?

"Tell me," he demands. "What's going on?"

She puts her hands in her lap. "I've been—upset . . . there's something really . . . it's hard . . ." Why can't she just say *There's this pervert who has scary control over me and I need your help?*

Moony interrupts, looking distressed, "Summer. About that kiss."

"Ohmigod. That's not it!"

He looks down. "No, I want to say . . . took advantage of the situation. Not the time or place."

"It's cool." She twists her fingers under the table. It was a fine time and place, she thinks.

"Also, I'm here for you . . . if you ever . . . want me. *But,*" he says, "happy to just be your friend." He lets his breath out.

She lets her breath out and nods at her cup. He's so brave. "Thank you. It means everything to me, Moony. That you're here. But honest to God, it's not that. I—I'm . . ." She stares at the Formica tabletop and loses her train of thought. She puts her head in her hands as if that might shake her aching brain into action. "I'm so tired of all this. Life. Here. I mean. I can't keep on."

"You drank. Big deal. Start over."

"No, but yeah, but I—I couldn't even make it one day."

"Don't give up," he says, frowning slightly. He takes her hand in his left and looks at her intently. "Something's really wrong. Tell me what happened."

"It's hard to talk about. But you're the only person in the world

I can tell." He gently squeezes her hand. She takes a deep breath and says what she must. "It involves a guy."

He lets go of her as a flash of pain dulls his eyes. Seeing it stabs her in the gut. Then Moony's brows lower. "Who?" he says.

"I wanted to tell you . . . a while ago. I just couldn't."

"Not that guy you saw at Les Puces?" he asks.

"It's no one you know," she hedges. "No one from school. He's, uh, older."

"What happened?"

Summer swallows. The words she needs aren't there.

Moony leans forward and says intently, "Did he . . . do something?"

"Yes! Well, not exactly." Her face goes hot. She fidgets with an unlit cigarette. "But he, I guess, sort of . . . But I didn't say no, or fight him. He sort of forced me, in a movie theater, just . . . but also caught me by surprise, and . . ." She pauses, then her eyes fill.

Moony's eyes narrow. "What's his name?"

"Kurt de la something something."

The scar between Moony's dark eyebrows crinkles. "What an evil asshole."

"Thank you," she says, putting sugar in her coffee and stirring. "I needed to say it. I feel much better talking about it and thank you for listening. I'm just confused. I don't even *like* him, swear to god, but he has this . . . hold—that's what scares me." She glances at Moony.

He frowns like he's trying to figure something out. "Don't see him again. Anyone hurts you, disrespects you, should be banned. And punished."

"I haven't seen this side of you."

"Can still kick butt. With walking implements."

She smiles. Moony bashing Kurt with a crutch.

"I'm serious."

"I know you are. I love you for it." He looks at her quickly. "It's funny," she says, "when I was little, I had, like, girlie fantasies about a handsome knight saving me from dark dungeons. You are kind of knightlike." He is. He's noble, and courageous, and fights for what's right.

"No, knight-*lite*." An uneven smile spreads across his face. "Mine were . . . battling evil doctors with ray guns. To protect Nurse Sophie."

"That's who that picture was of! In your room," she says. "Nurse Sophie."

Moony's cheeks pink.

"She had a mustache," Summer can't help pointing out.

He juts his chin forward. "It was a pure love."

"I imagine."

"You're jealous."

She concedes. "You're right. Totally. I don't know why you haven't dumped me as a friend. But I thank Allah you haven't."

He flashes that boyish grin, and takes her hand again.

Summer puts the unlit cigarette back in the pack. "I so need a drink," she announces.

Moony stares at his lap and huffs.

"But I won't. For the next five minutes anyway. And I appreciate your not saying anything about last night. I'll get firmly back on the wagon after I get through this. With, like, seat belts and harnesses and all. Everything's truly and deeply effed-up and I just have to deal. I *will* deal, okay?"

Moony says, "It *is* that guy, isn't it?"

"Who?" she asks, knowing full well.

"The dodgy Egyptian football guy. From the flea markets." Now he's really frowning.

"Egyptian?" Kurt's not Egyptian, is he?

"Summer. Stay. Away. From him."

"I know. You're right." That's the simple solution, she thinks. But she's already tried that and didn't do so well.

"Want to come over?" asks Moony.

"Yes." She rubs her eyes. "But all my work and stuff is at the apartment, and I have to get busy. My first final is tomorrow. Call me?" She's so glad she told him.

He nods but looks disappointed. They kiss cheeks a little awkwardly, and part.

In the taxi on the way home, Summer vows to cut off all contact with Kurt. Not answer his phone calls. Walk the other way if she sees him. Never talk to him again. If only he didn't have that knack of showing up and being so persuasive. He said she disgusts him. Keep that in mind, cupcake. That he's a bad influence on her is an understatement. She glances around the street when they stop.

Nope, not here. But if he were, she's not sure she would succeed in ignoring him. Even after all he's done to her. It's easy to say now, that she'll avoid him, but it doesn't seem to work.

She's got to get away. Time and distance between them is the answer.

As she enters their apartment building, Kurt's leaning against the corner of the building across the street.

FORTY-FOUR

Summer rests heavily against the elevator wall as it ascends. Kentucky sings into her earbuds, *Said this love affair is crowded, either darkness goes or I do.* Her phone vibrates, displaying Kurt's number. She silences and ignores it.

Once inside she takes her phone out of her coat pocket. Three texts from Kurt read:

Call me.
I really need to see you.
I really, terribly, need to see you. To talk to you. Please.

She closes her eyes. Part of her wants to answer. What if it's something truly important? But three of them piled up there one after the other remind her he's a creeper.

Fine. She'll turn off the phone and keep it off.

Escaping Kurt is critical. She underestimated him.

She's got to do it for Moony, too. It would be impossible to explain, but she can't focus on him, or even be around him now. If she can get free of Kurt's corrosive, poisonous influence, then she can concentrate on Moony.

Summer shuffles into Mom's marble bathroom, takes a deep breath and says, "Um, I need to buy an airline ticket."

Mom's putting on makeup. The steamy air smells like rosemary and eucalyptus spa shower gel. Mom sets the mascara wand on the edge of the dressing table and turns to look at Summer standing in the doorway.

"To where?"

"To San Francisco. I thought I'd call Aunt Liz."

Her eyes pop wide. "For when?"

"As soon as finals are over. Like Saturday."

"You've talked to her already?"

"No, I'm asking you first." It's not that Mom and Liz don't get along, but they aren't really that close. If Summer had a sister, she would talk to her all the time.

"Christmas is a week and a half away. I told you we're going skiing! With the Menendezes. And I was hoping to celebrate your graduation with a little get-together first."

"I really have to leave here." Summer's twisting her hands and stops.

"And what will you do in California?" Mom purses her lips.

"I don't know. Maybe some volunteer work. With like, kids. Aunt Liz will have some ideas."

"You want to spend Christmas with her. And leave me here alone."

"No, not that. I . . . I . . . It's complicated."

"Try me."

Summer hesitates. "I—I think I won't last until Christmas here."

"What on earth do you mean?" Mom squints at Summer with her jaw set. "Are you flunking out after all?

"No!" Summer takes another deep breath. Just tell Mom the truth. "I don't know. I'm worried. Maybe. There's . . . it's a guy, here, actually, that's messing me up."

"A guy? Do you mean your handicapped friend?"

"No! I met him . . . not at school."

"How do you mean he's messing you up?"

"Like, he always wants to drink. I'm not drinking now. I'm in a . . . sort of fragile place." Her voice squeaks. She's plucking at her throat.

"That doesn't mean you have to leave." Mom frowns with a modicum of concern. "Sounds like it would be a very good idea not to see this person."

Summer rubs her forehead, trying to loosen the piercing tightness. "I can't avoid him."

"Don't be ridiculous. You can always avoid someone." Mom pauses. "I think this is about running away. Summer, you can't keep changing location every few months, by force or choice. You must stay here and deal with your life." She narrows her eyes. "And graduate."

Mom's right. She does want to run away. But she has to make Mom understand that it's for a very good reason. Summer shakes her head. "But, I don't think I—" She pauses, then says softly, "Mom, graduating will be moot if I'm not around to inherit."

"What do you mean 'not around'?" Mom demands.

"I mean . . ." Summer stares at the marble floor, pulling her fingers one by one. "I don't know. Just in case I'm, like . . ." Summer looks Mom in the eyes, silently pleading for her to understand. ". . . hit by a truck or something."

"I give up." Mom waves her manicured nails.

No such luck.

"Ask Dr. Garnier about it. And I certainly hope you told her about your father. But right now, I don't have time for this nonsense. I am so tired of it! This is how it *always* is with you. You're given opportunity after opportunity—on a silver platter no less, yet you refuse to do anything. To live your life. When I think of those African village girls who would die for your opportunities." She looks at her watch. "I've got to be in Neuilly in twenty minutes, and then Geneva tomorrow, for the week. We'll talk about it later."

Summer knew this would be an exercise in futility. She about-faces and slumps out.

"Summer?"

"Yes?"

Mom breathes in through her nose. "I am sorry about the way I told you about your father. It wasn't the right time or place."

Summer keeps a neutral face. She won't acknowledge the apology, and since Moony said the same thing, it's the second time in one day she's heard that. But she appreciates it.

Back in her room, with a credit card, Summer buys an e-ticket on Air France for a flight to San Francisco early on Saturday the twenty-first, in six days. Somehow, she'll get through this next, last week of school, honor Dad's anniversary by passing her two finals on the seventeenth, and then grab her passport and just *partir.* Her big suitcase is in the *cave* in the basement. She doesn't want to go down there, it creeps her out and who knows who could be lurking. So she empties an old duffel bag filled with tennis racquets, packs a few things, and puts it under her bed. Then she sits down and tries to study.

FORTY-FIVE

On Monday, Summer drags herself out of bed and calls a taxi to take her to school for her European History final exam. Other than a brief, "Hope you're feeling OK. Good luck on finals," text to reassure Moony, she keeps her phone turned off. When she sees the questions, she knows she'll probably flunk it. Just like a bad dream. She may pass her trigonometry test, thanks to Moony.

As Summer is leaving, she passes by her English class and the teacher sees her.

"Summer?" She motions her in. "You were absent when I handed back the Dante papers. I have yours here. Do you check your PAIS e-mails?" She hands it to Summer.

"I guess not enough." Summer tries to smile at her teacher. "Hmm. 'D plus,'" she reads aloud.

Ms. Chang tilts her head. "You had some interesting observations, but it was supposed to be three times that length for starters. I'm afraid you're failing this course. There's still the final on Thursday. Do you want to discuss it?"

"Uh, not really. Not at all in fact," Summer says, crumpling the red-marked paper. "Gotta run, thank you, Ms. Chang." Run. That's a laugh. She can barely lift each foot.

Okay, maybe she won't be able to salvage the semester.

That familiar cold in her middle sinks heavily all the way through her. She did try. More than she has for years, for sure. Just not enough. Time or effort. She'll have to deal with all that when she gets to the US. She can figure out another way to graduate, and then to get into some university somewhere. To make Mom happy anyway.

She trudges out of the room and clips a girl in the hall, causing her to drop a big leather bag. It's skinny, beautiful Jacqueline.

"Summer!" she says.

"Hi, sorry. Just escaping Ms. Chang."

"What?" Jackie's wearing a yellow wool jacket with white fringe and a short black wool skirt. She has big, bright gold hoops in her pierced ears.

"Take your earbuds out," Summer mouths and points.

Jackie does. "I never see you around." She slings the bag back over her shoulder.

"Uh, yeah."

"Aren't you a Kentucky Morris groupie? Sad news about him, huh?"

"What?"

"Haven't you heard?" Her eyes are wide with dismay.

"Heard what?"

"He died last night. Hanged himself while in Bangkok. The Triage the Darkness Tour. He left a suicide song and everything."

"You're—you're joking."

"No, I wish."

Summer clutches her middle and bows. "Oh, no."

The avalanche has slammed over her. It's swirling and hurling her, and there's not enough air.

"Are you okay?"

If the brilliant, talented, successful, and beloved Kentucky doesn't think life is worth living, then what is she supposed to do? Like in cartoons when Wile E. Coyote gets frozen, one little tap breaks him into a thousand pieces.

"Shattered," she says.

"Yeah, I know, right? Hard to believe that someone with so

much going for them would take their own life," says Jackie, twirling her hair around her finger.

Summer mumbles, "Actually it's not." If people knew the truth, they would say that about Dad. People said it about the star high school basketball player in Little Rock who shot himself. Almost everybody who commits suicide *had so much going for them.*

"Well, I know what happened. To cause him to do it. They say he just broke up with Lou Lou Banal."

Summer contemplates scuff marks on the waxed floor then looks up. "It's not just one thing. He's been thinking about it for a long time." She pauses as bits of his lyrics play in her head. "A long time."

Jackie blinks at Summer, pauses two beats. "I wanted to talk to you."

"Now?"

"About Moony." Jackie's heavy perfume curls around Summer's head, making her sniff.

"Okay."

"You and Moony have been hanging out, outside of school some."

"Yeah?" Summer flicks at her backpack strap. Kentucky's song "Come and Go with Me" is playing in her mind and it's hard to concentrate. Where's Jackie headed with this?

"He likes you a lot, you know," Jackie says in a soft voice.

"Uh . . ."

"Do you like him?" Jackie fastens her large brown eyes on Summer's. It's so third grade.

"Of course I like him. He's . . . my best friend." People are filing around them in the hall, so they step closer to the lockers.

Jackie tosses her long shiny hair behind her. "I mean, you know, like, physically."

"Did he ask you to ask me?" Summer demands. No way Moony would. Jackie's being nosy. But Jackie's looking out for him, too.

"You know him. He would never do that. He talks about you a lot. I just know."

They stand there a few seconds while Summer doesn't answer. She loves him, and yes, she does want him. She'd be so psyched to believe that what Jackie says is true. But it makes everything worse. Even if he hasn't yet figured it out, she knows: she's the most terrible thing that could possibly happen to him.

"So, do you?" she asks.

"No," Summer says, touching her nose ring and closing her eyes. She hugs her notebook against her chest. "I do love him." Jackie frowns like she thinks Summer's lying. "It's not because he's . . . not perfect! It's complicated and none of your business." Now Jackie gives her a snotty, disdainful look. "What, do you want to jump his bones?" Summer demands, which she immediately regrets.

Jackie says coolly, "I already have."

Summer opens her mouth but nothing comes out.

Jackie smiles. "It didn't work out, but I care very much for him."

"Oh, good for you." Summer hates her.

Jackie narrows her eyes. "Don't you dare lead him on, or even think about messing with his heart." Then she pivots and marches away in her high-heeled boots.

"Or what?" Summer whispers.

FORTY-SIX

At home in her room that night, Summer tries to watch a movie. Thank god Mom's gone because she doesn't want to talk to or see anyone. She's so exhausted, yet it's hard to sit still. Moony keeps popping into her head, how Jackie said he loves and wants her. How *she* wants Moony, but how she can only deeply disappoint him.

She also can't stop thinking about Kentucky Morris. She loves him, too. His music is mournful, sometimes angry or even just a tad whiny, but it transmits so clearly and beautifully to her that she's not the only one. That he knows how she feels. And struggles. She cannot fathom that he checked out. Hanged himself. And abandoned her!

She does understand why he wanted to, though. Totally.

Then the truth of his decision hits home. He's a brilliant guy. He hasn't deserted her, he figured out the answer.

And led the way.

She's not had anything to drink all day. She could just pour herself one modest shot of Mom's Russian vodka. The desire is wrapped around her like a flipping two-hundred-pound chimpanzee.

She tries to ignore it for five minutes at a time, but then it sticks its long monkey fingers in her ears and mouth.

The front doorbell rings. Summer startles. She checks the clock.

It's almost midnight. Maybe it's a neighbor with an emergency. No one from outside could get into the building.

The apartment is dark and too cold, and she drapes her duvet around her.

The bell rings again, more insistent.

Summer's pulse quickens. She tiptoes to the door and squints through the peephole.

It's Kurt. Holding flowers.

"Hi," she hears.

She backs away, her vision narrowing.

"Summer," he says. "I know you're there."

"Go away!" she yells through the thick, painted wood.

"I feel terrible about our misunderstanding on Saturday. I've got something for you. I came directly here from the airport. Just flew in from Bangkok."

Misunderstanding.

"Come on. Please open the door."

She stands there for a dozen heartbeats. Can she run down to the other end of the apartment and barricade herself in her room? Call the police and explain her problem in French?

"What do you want?"

"I just want to be with you. You are the light of my soul. Please," he repeats plaintively.

"You don't have a soul," she mutters. "And it's, like, way too late to be making social visits."

"Summer. Open the door and let me in."

Not by the hair of my chinny-chin-chin, she thinks with no trace of humor.

"I'll wait," he says. "I'm very patient."

"Fine. Knock yourself out." She turns to go.

"It's not me you should be worried about, *ma belle poule*," says Kurt. "It's you."

She breathes in sharply. He knows.

"You know as well as I do that *you* are the one to be afraid of. *I* have the answer to all your problems."

Summer leans her forehead against the smooth enameled door. Somehow Kurt understands what's been in her mind for such a long time she can't even remember when it started. What she's been thinking about constantly lately. No, not thinking. Underneath thought.

Feeling.

Believing.

And for so long, denying.

The answer to all her problems.

She has nothing to lose. She closes her eyes and opens the door.

He hands her a truncated bouquet of tight chrysanthemum buds, dark red. He kisses her on both cheeks, as she lets the duvet drop to the floor. The scent of rotten garbage and a pale hint of cologne surround her. "I could use a drink," he says.

Seeing his face reminds her of the last time she was with him. "W-what was that all about?" she demands, putting her hands on her hips, looking as pissed off as she can. "*Chainsaw Chicks*."

"We've grown close. I want to be closer still. And you need to understand who's in charge."

"You're *not* in charge," Summer says.

"We'll see." He smiles. "I know what you want. You do, too."

She looks down at the stained Persian carpet.

"My love," he says, lifting her chin and gazing soulfully into her eyes. "Other than holding your hand, I won't touch you again."

The horrible thing is, she's not sure she doesn't want him to.

"Without your permission," he adds.

She also knows he's lying. "God knows I need a drink now," she says. "You're impossible to deal with sober."

"I'll have whatever you're having." He takes off his leather jacket and tosses it on a chair in the foyer. He wears a loud red-and-black-checked shirt and a black tie.

Summer turns on a lamp in the main salon, grabs two brandy

snifters and pours generous cognacs. The bottle says it's twenty-five years old, but she already drank that and replaced it with more affordable stuff from Monoprix. Who can tell the difference?

"So to what do I owe this visit?" she asks, sitting on the couch across from him.

"I just missed you. Cheers. To decisions." He's on the opposite couch and holds his glass up.

"Cheers," she says. She takes a big swig and immediately feels better. "Can I bum a cigarette?"

"Of course." He pulls a pack of Gauloises out of his breast pocket and lights two. "Thanks." She takes a deep drag.

He sips from his glass and makes a face. "No offense. This is shit cognac."

Summer shrugs. "So what's the answer to all my problems?"

"Me."

"Ha. You said you had a present for me."

He pats the spot next to him on the couch. Summer comes over but stays standing. From his jacket pocket he pulls a photocopied copy of an *Arkansas Democrat* newspaper clipping and hands it to her.

She holds it under the lamp. Grandpa and Dad stare back at her from the late nineties. She's never seen this picture.

"Where did you get this?" She stubs her cigarette out in a silver ashtray.

"Off the Internet. I copied it at the American Library."

SR. & JR. WALDO BARNES, CHICKEN KING AND CROWNED PRINCE, the headline reads, PURCHASE JIMMY RON SAUSAGE AND DAISY DAIRY FARMS FOR LARGEST FOOD CONGLOMERATE IN THE SOUTH. Grandpa is grinning and Dad looks young and sullen.

"There were articles in all the major media," says Kurt, "including *The Wall Street Journal*. No picture there, just a drawing of your grandpa's large head."

"My dad looks . . . melancholy, doesn't he?"

"What a terrific word. He was."

"How do you know?"

"I knew your dad. You're so much like him." He blinks like a reptile.

"He killed himself, you know," she says, as she takes another slug of cognac. "How could you possibly know my dad?"

"I'm older than I look," he says, smiling. "I told you. I know a lot of people."

She puts her hand to her cheek. "You were in the hospital that night, weren't you?"

"Briefly. Outside his room. You and I made eye contact."

An early snowflake. An encounter, a thought that she froze and blew away. She suspected, even then, the truth about Dad. "So why are you hanging out with me?"

"I love you."

She chokes on her drink. "Oh, right!"

"Like a fat child loves chocolate ice cream." He's referring to her, of course.

She gets up to refresh her cognac. The light goes out. Next thing she knows he's all over her like white on rice. Black on tar.

He kisses her, long and deep and hard. She can't breathe. "You *are* mine," he whispers, clutching her tightly. His strength is frightening.

"I guess," she says, gasping, trying to pry herself from his claw-like grip.

"You guess?"

"Well, what does that mean exactly? Let go of me a minute. Please." To her surprise, he does. So unpredictable.

"Truth or dare?" he asks.

"Are you serious?"

He nods eagerly and bounces down on the couch next to her. "Choose."

"Uh, truth?"

"Ask me who you are," he commands.

"What? That's not how it works."

"Just do it," he growls.

"Who am I?" she whispers.

"You know why you're alone, don't you?"

"Wait. That's another question. I—"

"You're worthless. An accident on earth."

The room goes still.

"A spoiled, lazy, hate-and-anger-filled loser. We all wonder why you get so mad at everyone else, when it's yourself you should be mad at."

She says nothing.

"No one, not even your mother, not even your ridiculously upbeat crippled friend, can love you. You're an embarrassing burden to your family. Have been, even before you pulled that pot of Chef Boyardee on your chubby head."

She nods. She's been a disappointment as long as she can remember. It's weird, incredible even, how he knows and will say out loud the deep down truth. That everyone tries to pretend isn't so. It's strangely freeing.

"You already know that all the money in the world won't make you worth something."

"I know."

"Now it's time you take 'Dare.' You can make it all go away." He snaps his fingers. "Just like that. Like your dad did."

"Do you think . . . he'd want that?" she asks.

"Dearest Summer," he says and caresses her cheek. "He did love you, more than anything. Of course he would want that. What's best for you. Don't forget. Things will never, *ever* get better. Ending it now is best."

Summer nods.

"And you'll leave the world a better place without you."

"Yeah."

"Your little friend. You'll destroy him, you know. Can *you* imagine loving you?"

She shakes her head. "No."

"And, can you stand this forever?"

"I can't stand it for another day."

"You finally fully understand it's hopeless, don't you? All the fresh starts in the world won't make a difference. That idea about working with children? Ridiculous. What a terrible, negative influence you would be."

"I know."

"So come with me."

"I was going to San Francisco," she mumbles.

"To get *away* from me. But you stupid, stupid girl, you know that's not possible."

She asks almost inaudibly, "So, where will we go?"

"Can't tell you. It's a surprise." He takes her hand in his and whispers in her ear, "Trust me?"

He stares at her that way he does. So earnest, so deep into her soul. She is the question. He is the answer.

"I will love you forever. And you're ready. To take the next step. The *big* one."

The dense weight of all that has been building up, piling on her, since the beginning of time, has led to this night. "I guess it's been coming for a while," she admits.

His voice softens and he touches her cheek. "Deciding is one thing. But the hardest part is carrying through. I am here for you, my love. Let's seal the deal with a kiss."

"Kiss" being an inadequate metaphor. Like a striking rattlesnake, he yanks her to him. His shocking strength overwhelms her. She's smothered and blinded, lost, heart thudding, struggling. She wanted this, right? She holds on, as he almost squeezes the life out of her, suddenly so much larger than she. A jolt of pain from her catacomb-hurt-rib and the big purple and yellow bruise there radiates throughout her body as he pushes her roughly to the floor and tears at her jeans.

Wait, she thinks, what about safe sex?

Ha! It doesn't matter.

Later she pulls herself across the dark room, drawn to the pale silver light coming in the giant French window. She presses her cheek against the thick silk curtains, held back with braided cord and tassels.

The Eiffel Tower is doing its sparkler thing across the river while the searchlight on top sweeps the entire dark city, over and over. Looking for what? Lost souls. It's the saddest thing she's ever seen.

Even though she thought she did, she doesn't want to eat snails by candlelight or hold hands through museums filled with Impressionist art. She certainly doesn't want to go to *school.*

And she doesn't deserve or want her grandpa's fortune. Not even a little bit. Never did.

"Must be midnight," she mumbles. All those snowflakes. They didn't blow away. They piled up and froze solid all the way through her. Summer, the giant ice statue. It's hard to function when you're an ice statue. It's impossible once you've shattered.

He's behind her. She turns around. He gently takes her face in his hand. "I have your word?"

She opens her mouth, then closes it. Opens it again. "What?"

"Don't play coy," he growls. "What do you think I want your word on?"

"Suicide," she whispers.

"Bingo!"

"Yes," she says, closing her eyes. "But not tonight. Tomorrow." He is in charge, but at least she can do it her own way.

The front door slams and Kurt is gone.

FORTY-SEVEN

Summer gets up very late the next day. Tuesday, December 17.

Dad's anniversary.

Even though she didn't sleep much, she feels more energetic than she has in a long time. Some of the icebergs that have been pressing her down, have . . . shrunk a little. Climate change. She knows what she needs to do.

She finally has purpose.

After her shower, she looks at her body in the mirror while drying herself off. Soon, it won't exist anymore. What a relief.

In the kitchen Ouaiba is cutting up fruit. "*Bonjour,* mademoiselle," she says. "*Pas d'école?*" She apparently gave up worrying about Summer's sleep habits and trying to get her to eat weeks ago.

"No school," Summer confirms. It's her own personal holiday: Last Day on Earth.

She drinks some OJ and glances at the back page of the *International Herald Tribune.* Next to a classified ad thanking Saint Jude, the SOS headline catches Summer's eye. FEELING DOWN? NEED TO TALK TO SOMEONE? Then at the bottom, FEELING SUICIDAL? The telephone number hasn't changed.

"Ouaiba?"

"*Oui?*"

"*J'ai besoin de* . . . wire cutters." Summer holds her two fingers up and opens them like scissors.

"*Des ciseaux?*"

"No, stronger. *Plus fort.* For wire. *Pour fil? Corde? Métalique?*"

"*Ah, bon?*" She's perplexed.

"*Pour un projet d'école,*" Summer lies. What kind of school assignment would require wire cutters she'll leave to Ouaiba's imagination. Summer does not want kind, tolerant Ouaiba complicit in her plans in any way. She could probably get in trouble later. Summer will have to cover that in her note. "Where can I get them?" Maybe there's a toolbox around here somewhere.

Ouaiba nods. She knows where some might be.

The house phone rings and Summer ignores it. But she checks for the blinking red voicemail light afterward just in case. There's an old message from Dr. Garnier that Summer skips. Next, it's Madame Simone again, the eleventh- and twelfth-grade counselor. She's been calling for two weeks. Then, Mr. Evans, the dean of students. Now she's really in serious trouble. Missed exam this morning, meeting with her mom, expulsion, blah, blah, blah. Summer erases the messages without listening to them. She's sorry to have caused them all the hassle.

It doesn't matter. Soon, she'll no longer exist. A quietness has settled inside that is completely unfamiliar, and already, almost . . . relief.

Except for Moony.

Summer hasn't checked her own phone since early the previous day. And she didn't see him at school yesterday. She turns on her cell. She can leave it on now.

Three texts, five missed calls, and one voicemail. All from Moony.

Oh, and one from Dr. Garnier that Summer deletes.

At the sound of Moony's voice on the one message he left, her throat constricts. What will she do about him? What will she do without him? She wonders if she'll be able to see him—like, once she's gone. Watch him. Watch over him, even. During his operation.

Probably not.

He's in class now, but she texts him:

Sorry, phone was off. All's well.

He immediately texts back:

Where r u?
Home.
Coming to school?
Not today.
Can I come by after exam?

She hesitates. Nothing could be better than to see him, to throw herself at him and never let go, actually.

He might mess up her resolve, but she texts back:

Sure.

Her resolve is firm. She wants to thank Moony and say good-bye without alarming him. He's already worried about her. More than anything, she doesn't want to hurt him. He doesn't know it yet, but he will be infinitely better off once she's gone.

In her room, Summer checks through all of her stuff like someone else going through it after the fact. She writes a short note to Aunt Liz that says, "I love you. Please don't be mad or sad," and puts it in an envelope in her underwear drawer. She unpacks the duffel bag under her bed, and uses it to take all the empty liquor bottles from her drawers and closet down to the green recycling bin in the courtyard. When she comes back up, there's a gray plastic bag on her bed. From a hardware chain store. Summer pulls out what looks like pliers. Good. Wire cutters.

The intercom buzzes. She runs down the hall to answer it.

"Moony!" Summer says. "I'll be right down."

FORTY-EIGHT

"Sorry I was MIA there. My cell phone was off," Summer says as she kisses Moony's cheeks hello. Those dragonflies are jousting in her middle. Just pretend like everything's . . . normal.

He holds her by the shoulder and studies her face. "You're okay?"

"Yes." She looks down. "I'm fine."

"Been worried."

"How were exams?" She wiggles her nose ring.

"Hunky. Not taking them?" He asks like this is a perfectly reasonable decision to make. His face is pale and shadowed under his eyes.

"No, I was going to, but the voices told me to stay home and clean my weapons."

Moony's eyebrows shoot up.

"Ha. Sorry. Just joking. Want to go get something to eat? I'll fill you in."

He's using the cane and moves slowly. They walk to a Moroccan restaurant two blocks away and sit in a low, peacock-blue silk-cushioned booth. The smell of roasting meat, saffron, and cardamom surrounds them. Moony's back is to the window. Car lights and Christmas strands blink on the street over his shoulder.

They chat about unimportant things. She's going to put him at ease if it kills her. He's watching her every move.

Moony orders the lamb tahini and mint tea and Summer orders

couscous and sparkling water. Moony asks, "One day at a time?" A nice way of asking, *Are you sober?*

"Yeah," she says. For you. "Today's the first day of the rest of my life." It's also the last. He looks at her funny, so she adds quickly, "Thanks for going to that meeting with me. I should go back." Ain't that the truth.

"You're quiet," he says, looking puzzled. She feels like she's been talking a lot. "Seem different."

I'm committed, she thinks. Sadly to someone else. But it's for you.

The waiter places a bowl of raw veggies and olives in front of them.

Moony pops an olive into his mouth.

Outside, a man in a fedora walks by the restaurant, pauses and looks in. It's Kurt. He winks at her over Moony's shoulder, points at his watch, then walks on.

Summer smiles. It's kind of funny. That Kurt's not nearly as scary to her as Moony.

She must do what she came here to do. "So, what I wanted to talk to you about is . . . that I'm leaving."

Moony blinks. "When?"

"Um, Saturday."

His face falls. "Thought you weren't going to."

"Moony, I've got to."

"Back to the US?"

"Yeah," she fibs.

"Where?"

"San Francisco."

He leans forward. "Because of that guy?"

Summer blinks and curls the corner of her napkin in her lap. "I—No. Because I just want to go home." She should ask him why he called Kurt Egyptian.

Moony looks at her questioningly, with pain in his eyes. He sees through her!

He says, "No gummy bears?"

"Oh, crap! After your operation." He's going in the hospital in another week. The day after Christmas and five days after she supposedly "flies" to SF. High-voltage guilt zaps her. Can't she at least wait until after his surgery is over? Especially one he's dreading?

But it's impossible. That's next week. The sooner she removes herself from the world, and his life, the better. Tonight is the night.

She doesn't know what to say. Lie some more: *I'll send you some?* Tell the truth: *No, I'll be dead?* She must be so careful not to alarm him. No one else will give a fig when she croaks. But he will. She cannot have Moony feeling guilty when he finds out. It's the *only* thing she's worried about.

"I'm so sorry I won't be here for your operation," she says carefully. He's been here for her, totally and completely and at great cost to himself. "I *have* to . . . leave. Now." One day he'll understand.

He says somberly, "I'll miss you." He picks up a carrot stick and points it at her. "Chickening out on me."

She's digging her nails into her palms under the table. "I will miss you, more than you know, Moony. Please, please say you'll forgive me." What a terrible, shitty friend she has been.

"But you're here through the week," he says, looking sad and old. She sure seems to have a way of aging her friends. "And what about exams?"

It's Tuesday. Four more days until Saturday. She should have said she's leaving sooner. Because she is. "Uh, yeah. There are those." She crosses her fingers beneath the table.

"You'll come back, visit your mom, right?"

"Sure." She presses her nose ring, closing her eyes. This sucks so much. Lying to the only person that matters. Could she just tell him the truth?

No. It's too late.

"No scholarship," he says. "University of Missouri turned me down."

She looks up at him, her heart sinking. "Oh, no. How could they? Why?"

"Went to a Missouri resident. Maybe get partial."

"I'm so sorry. They're such stupid-heads."

"Way it goes," he says cheerfully. But he looks totally bummed.

The waiter brings their main courses.

She wants to give Moony something to remember her by. Her flask comes to mind, but he wouldn't like it. She would gladly turn her grandpa's money over to him, but it will never be hers to give. *Sacrebleu,* what he could do with it. He could go to any school he wanted. Pay for a whole flipping building at the University of Missouri. The St. Moony Physical Rehabilitation Center. It wouldn't warp him, it would fortify him. Goodness would spread out into the world via all the disabled people he would return to function and health.

She grips her thighs. "No matter what, I want you to know that you've been the best, most wonderful friend I've ever had. That you've helped me as much as anyone possibly could have, during . . . a hard time. That I only want what's best for you. That I love you." It's all she has to give.

He grins like a little kid. And gazes at her. "You're so beautiful," he says softly. "You don't always let people see it."

"What?"

"Sometimes, your expression, can be . . . defensive. Not to me," he says, "but to some."

She's not a complete chicken, contrary to what he thinks. She takes his good left hand. And clasps her fingers with his. He falters for a split second, but keeps talking. She's surprised him and she's glad. He smiles. Not a goofy smile, but an *I don't know what to do with you* smile that goes along with someone shaking their head in frustration. Only he doesn't.

Once again, her hand in his feels so right it scares her. She wants to let go, but she makes herself hang on. She closes her eyes and feels that electricity, that force in him, flowing into her through their touching skin. It's powerful. It feels like it could melt icebergs, or even frozen continents.

She squeezes his hand, then releases it so he can eat his tahini. She switches to his right hand, hard and curled like a beige and pink seashell. He doesn't pull it back, and she caresses the taut skin stretched over his misshapen bones. Then he takes her hand with both his strong one and the damaged one, as she closes her eyes memorizing this moment.

He gently lets go and continues to feed himself both his and her dinner.

Why can't she hang on for Moony's sake? Another day, another week. Love Moony and stay alive.

She does love him. All of him. So much it threatens to drive her bananas.

They pay and she walks him to the Métro.

At the top of the steps, Summer pulls Moony to her and hugs him hard, desperately, feeling his muscular and lumpy, bony body close against hers. His warmth and love make Kurt's poisonous iciness a distant memory. She doesn't want to let go.

He hugs her back. "What's this for?" he asks, smiling.

"I'm not leading you on," she warns. "It's . . . nothing special. For being there. I'm going to be sort of busy the next couple of days, so just in case I don't see you. Before I leave. Good night." She kisses him smack on the lips.

Adieu, dear Moony.

FORTY-NINE

That evening at Mom's apartment, the doorbell rings. Before she checks the peephole, Summer knows who it is.

Kurt stands there, with a huge armful of flowers—white lilies.

"*We got no reason, no reason to go onnnn!*" he belts out. She opens the door and he hands her the elaborate bouquet. Their sweet scent doesn't begin to cover up Kurt's malodor. She looks at him quizzically.

"Kentucky Morris," he says, as he walks passed her and tosses his coat on the Louis XV table.

"I know. No kiss?" She doesn't regret their encounter last night. Funny thing.

He kisses her gently on the mouth. She coughs.

"Cool flowers," she says. She takes them to the kitchen and puts them in a crystal vase full of water.

"Big, big night, little darlin'," he says. "Love of my life."

"Hmm-mmm," she agrees.

"Let's go for a walk. Plan our future together."

"How romantic." She gets her jacket. A stroll, hand-in-hand on this, her last evening, is perfect.

They end up on a quay by the Seine and light cigarettes. The river air wafts around them damp, dark, and cold, although streetlamps every so often cast pale yellow pools on the stone path and the embankment wall beside them. Kurt holds her hand. His touch is warm and reassuring. “My favorite,” he says, as they stare at the swirling black water, supposedly at a ten-year high.

“You think I should jump into the river?” It’s not appealing.

“You’re an excellent swimmer.”

“Thank you.”

“But it’s faster and more violent beneath the surface than it looks. You could always put stones in your pockets.”

“Like Virginia Woolf.”

“Exactly.” He blows three smoke rings.

She stares at the fast-moving current. Strange shapes seem to bubble up to just below the dark surface, before being sucked back down. She shudders. “Yeah, but it’s full of chemicals and rats and two-by-fours and stuff.”

“It’s not that bad.”

From Kurt’s gift flask, she takes a swig of aged Armagnac. She hands it to Kurt. The mellow fumes fill her nose and entire head. It *is* better than the Monoprix stuff. The bottle was hidden in the back of the big living room bookcase. Mom will have to find a new spot.

Actually, she won’t.

A brightly lit Bateau Mouche forces its way against the current. Hundreds of people are seated on the lower deck inside. A few tourists have braved the cold and sit on the open upper deck. One guy does a double take at them. Kurt waves at him. He waves back.

“You do know a lot of people.” She laughs.

“Yep. Never met a stranger.” He winks at her, then hands her back the flask. “But I know some people much better than others.” City bus brakes squeal on the quay road. Kurt says, “You could step in front of a bus. They’re heavy enough that one tap—”

She pictures herself sprawled in the middle of a cobblestone street. “No. Kids might be on it.”

“I’m telling you, the river is a winner,” he says, after taking a long draw. “Step into it right now and be done with it.”

Summer stares into his sultry eyes for several beats. "I have some questions for you."

"Oh?"

"Now that I'm . . . committed."

He purses his sexy lips, and crosses his arms. "All right, then. Go ahead."

"So, who are you, exactly?"

"I'm who I say I am."

She rolls her eyes. "Could you elaborate?"

"I'm your lover. Your partner. Your soul. Your friend."

"Were you that guy's friend? The one who jumped off the overpass at Les Halles?"

He smiles like he's impressed. "Yes. That was a messy affair. He jumped *and* was hit by a truck but lived for three more days. I did try to talk him into something higher and more effective. But it had to be there."

"The druggie we went to the Catacombs with?"

"He was a disappointment," Kurt says primly. "We were all set for an OD, but he *chickened out*."

She doesn't rise to the bait. "The—lady of the night who got into a Peugeot with you?"

Kurt nods. "Very good."

"And the woman in the Métro? The first one . . ." She already knows the answer.

"Of course."

She stops and puts one hand on her hip. "What's with this? All these people you know and destroy?"

"They actually do it to themselves."

"Just answer me. I have a right to know."

He runs his long fingers through her hair. "There are many people for whom this world is unbearable. And for whom it has been unbearable for a long time. They live in hell and finally, one day, cannot hold on any longer. They yearn for the freedom from pain and despair that *only* death can bring. They only have one choice."

"Hmmm."

"I help them see that. I'm their counselor, their guide. Like I was for your father."

Her throat thickens. "Why do you think Dad did it?"

" 'Why' is not my department. Besides, you know full well. Same reason you will. The world is too much for them. In the end everyone's reasons are essentially the same."

"And Mom? What about her?" Summer puts her hand over her eyes. "Poor Mom. To lose your . . . whole family . . . this way."

"Serves her right."

"No it doesn't. She'll be traumatized."

"She'll get over it."

"I hope so. I guess she did once before." Summer knows Mom will be more than traumatized. But in the end, she, too, will be much better off. Summer starts walking again. "So, what is it that you *do* exactly?"

Kurt falls in beside her. "I help you see the way. Come to a balanced decision. The one Camus says is the only real question. Ditto, Hamlet, er, Shakespeare."

Summer pictures Mom's dog and smiles. "Right. I mean at the moment I . . . do it."

"You'll see."

She takes his hand again, then drops it. "You have a bad habit of cutting out right at the end. When you're most needed."

"I'll be there, when you take the big step. Don't worry, little darlin'."

He's mimicking Winston. She rolls her eyes. "And then, that minor business of whether or not there's life after death?"

"Are you asking?"

"Yes."

"Would it make any difference?"

She snorts. "No. Hell or black nothing, anything's better than this."

"There you go." Kurt smiles. "Other questions?"

"What about—Is this, like, something rich people . . . is this like a first-world problem?"

"Freedom from want, indeed privilege itself, brings many people face-to-face with the emptiness and pointlessness of life. But deprivation and especially oppression send 'em into my arms in droves. *Ma chère,* despair is universal."

"So that's a 'no.'"

"Yes," he says.

She studies the speed of the current in the river. "If you're so convinced it's the way, why don't *you* do it?"

"That would be like asking Neptune to drown himself."

"Huh?"

"I suppose I should emphasize: I can only take my beloved so far." He says it so quietly she almost can't hear him. "Fine print: It's still your decision, your choice, in the end."

This gives her pause for thought. "It doesn't feel like it," she says.

He steps back and puts his hands up. "Hey. I'm right here with you, and like I said, to the bitter end. But I'm not forcing *anybody* to do *anything.*" He flicks his cigarette butt into the Seine.

"Okay, okay. Fine." Forcing people to do things. Isn't he sort of forcing her? But the thought floats away with the butt. She unstoppers the flask and takes another slug.

"My friend Moony recognized you."

Kurt blinks in his slow reptilian way.

"Why did he think you were Egyptian?"

"Your father thought I looked like Charlie Shoemaker."

"Who's that?"

"Major League baseball player from way back. Kansas City Athletics. That man on the boat saw a Marilyn Monroe impersonator wearing his mother's raincoat."

"Wait." Summer turns and stares at him. "Really?"

He holds his chin with his thumb and forefinger and gives her a mock *You don't say* look. "And not everyone sees me."

This thought needles her. Then Kurt's not exactly . . .

Solid?

"Seriously? Not everyone can see you?" She shakes her head. "No wonder people look at me like an insane person when I'm talking to you."

It doesn't matter. He's more real and powerful than anything she has ever known.

"What do *you* get out of it?" she asks, moving forward again.

"The pleasure of doing my work well. I'm very good at what I do." He bats his eyelashes. "Helping people. And don't forget population control." He grins.

"That's not funny."

"None of you has a sense of humor."

She scowls at him. "I used to. And if I still had it, I wouldn't be talking to you."

"Touché."

It's no use getting mad. She can only muster a ghost of her former indignation anyway. She takes his hand again. "Let's not argue."

"I want you to know that I'm grateful for this intimacy with you," says Kurt softly, interlacing his fingers with hers. "It doesn't usually work out this way. It's true I lusted after you first, but a strange thing has happened. I've come to respect and really admire you. I so want to see your suffering end. And for you to be content." He pauses. "I love you."

"Thank you," Summer says sincerely. "I still want to know *why* you do what you do, though."

"Everyone has the capacity within themselves. It comes with free will. It's in my job description to move things along."

"I don't understand. Job description? Is someone paying you to do this?"

He laughs. "I volunteer out of sincere concern for people's suffering. The razor-sharp, multiton, hot tar, icy, deep-ocean torment that you, my friend, know too well. It's torture of the most devious and inescapable kind. I'm proud to be relief."

"Relief is a feeling. So's contentment."

"Yeah?"

"You have to be alive to feel a feeling."

"I think we should get on with things," Kurt says, stopping. "All this discussion serves no purpose. Once you've decided, you must *act*."

He's right. But agitation buzzes inside her. "I told you I'm committed," she huffs.

A couple strolls by arm in arm and ignores them. Moony's lopsided smile fills Summer's head and her chest tightens.

And what does life expect from me?

She says, "Humans are capable of incredible things. Full recoveries are against the odds."

"Nonsense," he barks. "You know you can't go on like this."

"I know. But I don't have to do *this,*" she whispers. "Right?"

"Ah, the ambivalence. 'Should I or shouldn't I?' That and lack of energy are my two biggest obstacles. But you're my favorite type. Inebriated, depressed, suicidal, impulsive—*and afraid of backing down*. Plus your brain is too trashed to do anything as complicated as getting a new outlook on life."

"Go to hell."

"Are you ready?"

"Yes. But not the river." She takes a long pull from her flask and then offers it again to Kurt.

"To your health. So what's your idea?" he asks.

"I'd like to go up," Summer announces. "To the Eiffel Tower. Late tonight, right before it closes so there won't be any families there."

"Hmm," he says, holding his chin. "Poetic choice. Only they've made it very difficult to do up there. You'll need some good wire cutters and the stealth of a black cat."

"I know. It's under control."

"Good for you. Sure you don't want to step off the bank here? Or ingest the rich harvest from your mom's medicine cabinet?"

"Eiffel Tower or nothing."

"Okay, that's the spirit." He glances at his watch. "I've got a couple of things to take care of. I'll meet you there at ten thirty. Turn your phone off and keep it that way."

He walks away.

With hands on her hips and tapping her boot, Summer says, "Um, Kurt?"

He turns around, grins at her, then grabs her around the waist, twirls, and kisses her.

"Wow," she says, smiling, when they come up for air. "No more questions."

FIFTY

Summer heads for a taxi stand, and is about to turn her phone off but checks it first. Two messages and one missed call from Moony.

She clutches her mobile to her chest. Oh, Moony.

Before she can talk herself out of it, she calls him back.

It rings and rings. And rings. His voicemail switches on. Listening to his voice in a sort of trance, she doesn't disconnect quickly enough, realizes the beep was seconds ago, and says, "Oh, uh, hi. Saw you called. And well, I wanted to say good-bye. Since I'm leaving tonight. And all. Love you, Moony." She hangs up. She's an idiot. She told him she was leaving Saturday. But she's glad she left him a message.

She passes a Monoprix and ducks in. Heads straight for the candy section and grabs a large bag of gummy bears. In the office supply aisle she uncaps a permanent marker and writes across the package: "Do no open until after operation. Love, S."

Then she hails a taxi and gives the driver Moony's address.

Because it's after 5:00 P.M., the outside door of Moony's building is locked and Summer can't remember the code. So she waits. A few minutes later an old man opens the door and Summer smiles at him reassuringly then slips in. She climbs up to the Butterfield apartment and rings the bell.

No one answers. She buzzes again, longer and harder. Come on. Someone's got to be there.

No one's home. She slumps.

She's disappointed and relieved. All her feelings seem to have two sides—a hot and a cold. A heads and a tails. A truth and a dare.

Mostly cold, tails, and dare.

The timed light in the hallway blinks off. She stands in the dark for a long while, finally leaving the package on the welcome mat.

FIFTY-ONE

Back at Mom's apartment, Summer gets her wire cutters, changes into her black jeans and long wool coat, and writes a note that she leaves on Mom's bed:

Dear Mom,
Totally sorry for everything.
Love, Summer
PS Wayba knows nothing.

It's lame, but she can't think of anything else and has a feeling she misspelled Ouaiba. Her message was lame. The gummy bears are lame. It's all lame, but if she doesn't leave these small signs of herself behind, there will truly soon be no trace of her. She's been riding a wave of resolute energy, but it's fading. She needs all her strength for what's coming, so she spreads Nutella on a hunk of baguette and forces it down.

Camus follows her around the apartment. Their friendship has been a bright spot these last weeks. "I'm sorry, Camus," she says. "To leave you." She picks him up and rubs his head and behind his ears. "You're a good, good dog. You love your family. You don't complain. You spend most of the day alone. You try to do the right thing." She carries him under one arm where he seems content.

Her phone sings. It's Moony.

Should she answer it? Camus licks her hand. Okay.

"Where are you?" He sounds frantic.

"I'm at home. Where are you?"

"Concert Choir performance! Intermission."

"Oh, yeah. 'Feliz Navidad.'" She's supposed to be there. Didn't even remember to blow it off.

"You okay?"

"Definitely. I'm fine."

She pauses. What if she just said, *I'm getting ready to off myself?* She stifles a sigh. No way. She's not going to ruin it now. And a tiny part of her doesn't want Moony to think she's any more of a freak than he already does. Until after she's gone.

"Summer, that guy? Seen him lately?"

"He's not really a problem anymore." She notices the clock. "Oh, shoot. I gotta go."

"Why?"

"I'm supposed to be somewhere."

"Where?"

"Um, I, well, the Eiffel Tower."

"Why?"

"You know, since I'm leaving. Tourist stuff. I love you, Moony." It gets easier and easier to say. She hugs Camus good-bye, lets him lick her chin, and puts him down. "Gotta run."

Heads you win. Tails I lose.

FIFTY-TWO

Summer stands alone beneath the massive soaring steel girders of the Eiffel Tower, out of the freezing rain. Only a few tourists wander about. It's 10:32 and Kurt's nowhere to be seen. They're going to close soon.

She stubs out her last cigarette and shoves her hands in her wool coat pockets, feeling the wire cutters.

No problem. She'll do it alone. It's now or never. One simple goal that she actually can attain.

She marches toward the elevator.

Kurt falls into step beside her. "*Bonsoir,* mademoiselle." He looks straight above them. "Ah, Jules Verne." He means the expensive restaurant on the first platform. "Shame we couldn't have a romantic dinner first. Champagne, of course. Some escargot, maybe . . . *poulet cordon bleu.* But you have to make reservations months in advance."

"Another time," she says. "Oh. Wait. No more times. Where were you?"

"Watching you from over there. Lovely in your solitary determination."

The elevators and therefore the tower close at eleven. Only a young Japanese couple is ahead of them when they get in line. She already bought her ticket. Kurt, of course, has lifetime privileges.

He's dressed in his usual impeccable style, but his skin and teeth are mellow yellow in these lights, his eyes ringed with dark shadows. In fact, he looks old and ghastly. Summer would be repulsed if he weren't such an intimate friend. And even in the cold, he smells like . . . *les égouts.*

"Have you been, like, partying? Staying out late?" she asks him as they stroll into the room-sized, industrial elevator. Only the operator, the Japanese couple, and three loud, hammered Russian men who push their way on, occupy it.

"Why, yes."

"That would explain the dark circles under your eyes."

"The better to see you with my dear."

The uniformed male operator keeps turning to stare at them. The Japanese quietly back into the far corner.

"By the way," she says, hooking her thumb at the operator. "Can he see you?"

"Amy Winehouse," he mouths. As Kurt winks at Summer, she startles. The set of his eyes reminds her of the newspaper photo of Dad.

I wish I'd known, Dad, she thinks. I guess I was too young to really understand. I know now. I understand completely. How you felt. How you didn't feel.

And you knew Kurt. What a small world. She doesn't really believe there will be anything after she hits the ground on the Champs de Mars, but a little part of her wonders if she'll see her Dad again. Or Kentucky Morris.

Doesn't matter. Leaving this one is all that does.

Kurt laces his long fingers through hers. "Can I hold your hand?" he asks, after the fact.

No one else gets on. The elevator jerks into motion and they ascend. Looking out at the Quai Branly, the street along the Seine by the tower, Summer catches sight through the steel girders of a scooter as it bounces up illegally on the wide walkway. It speeds across the plaza under the tower, and screeches to a stop. Then her line of sight is obstructed by too much steel. At the first platform cveryone has to get out. There are still quite a few people milling around. Summer and Kurt make a beeline for the lifts to the summit.

A sign by the smaller elevators to the top says they close at 22:30. 10:30. "Too late!" Summer cries. She can't believe it.

"Here, use the wire cutters," Kurt says. Following his instructions, she uses the short blades as a sort of wedge-lever, and forces the doors partially open. Then they are easy to part. Inside, he points to the main power switch. She flips it. The lights blink on and hum.

"We're in luck. Now, push that," he says. She does; the doors close and they move up.

The lights of Paris, in fact all of the Île-de-France, spread out twinkling for miles and miles. They watch in silence as everything slips farther and farther beneath them. It's spectacular.

"'The carriage held but just ourselves,'" he quotes. "You are brave and true, to leave this vale of tears for . . . you'll see. Freedom. From pain and strife."

"I know. Speaking of strife, I'm sorry I won't get to see my relatives rip each other apart over that money."

The ride is long, compared to the first elevator. "This is taking forever," Summer says. "You know, it would be nice to see the sparkling lights. Before I jump." She wants to see them, from within them. "They come on at eleven."

"It should work out about right," he says, glancing at his flashy watch. The elevator grinds to a halt. "Next stop. Eternity." As if he were Prince Charming, Kurt offers his hand to her. "Come, Razorback."

She takes it.

They emerge in an all-dark, closed observation area. A couple of SORTIE lights glow pale green. A chain blocks the stairs that leads up to the very top deck. They slip under it, climb and emerge onto a metal walkway. The wind blows so hard and loud, frozen pellets of rain sting her face like BBs. A small, enclosed room is ringed by the open walkway. Way above, the giant searchlight sweeps the city. Right below it, on the roof of the enclosed apartment, are antennas and other high-tech paraphernalia. Bright red lights glow on each corner of this last platform, probably for airplanes. Heavy metal fencing curves up and over them like a cage. Meant to impede people like her.

They push past a dark window.

"Ack," Summer screeches. "There's someone sitting in there!"

"Look again," Kurt yells back. Light spillover from the huge searchlight momentarily illuminates a life-size wax dummy of Monsieur Eiffel in his late-nineteenth-century waistcoat and jacket, forever at his drawing table.

"Creepy."

Frigid air blasts from the northwest and the English Channel, whistling—screaming around every wire and solid surface. They struggle to the south side of the deck and stare out at the million lights of Paris way, way below. Above, it's starless. Even in the lee of the covered observation area, the noise is fierce and their coats slap their legs. Her face is numb. She fishes the wire cutters out of her coat pocket.

She squeezes the handles as hard as she can, working on one bit of the surprisingly thick wire above the wooden banister, atop a denser metal mesh railing. She works with concentration she hasn't had in years. The wind is too loud for conversation anyway. The Champs de Mars park stretches out far below.

"Need bolt cutters," Kurt yells into her ear.

Her hand aches. The tool is simply too small for the thick wire. "You could help, you know."

"Nope. Not my job. Besides, I'm saving my strength for the important part."

"Running away?" she mutters. She does wonder what he means. Will he push her or something? No. But she already knows he'll desert her, as usual.

It doesn't matter.

She pulls a flap of the wire backward and tears her leather glove. She works at it a little longer. It's ridiculous, it will take weeks.

"Kurt. Can you just give me a hand here, please?" she yells.

He shakes his head. With effort, she dislodges another piece of the cut metal and with the blades, pushes it back. Great. She has a five-inch hole now.

"If your cutters are too wimpy," he says into her ear, "there's always the river."

Summer nods. "Yep. I guess you were right. Maybe we should just head on down there—"

Over the roar, they feel rather than hear the clunk of the elevator below them on the lower level. Kurt holds his hand up, as in *Wait and listen*.

Some security person has come to bust them. It might even be the police.

She pulls Kurt by the arm. They move farther along the walkway behind the apartment and wait. There's too much noise to hear anything. Summer leans out from the wall to see the spot where the stairs come up. Her pulse is banging in her ears.

Nothing.

But two seconds later, a figure appears at the corner of the deck, illuminated in the glow of the red and white tower lights. It's Moony! She could recognize his tilted silhouette anywhere. He sees her and yells something that's lost in the wind.

"Get rid of him," growls Kurt, stepping back farther into the shadows.

She steps out. Moony has on only his thin navy fleece jacket, and no gloves or hat. Or cane. He limps over to her moving as quickly as she's ever seen him move. He's panting and wild eyed.

"What're you doing?" he demands between gasps.

She doesn't know what to say. It seems kind of obvious standing there with her wire cutters.

"Someone with you?" His hair is plastered to his forehead and his jacket and eyelashes are beaded with rain.

"No," she lies.

"Come on. Get hot chocolate." He reaches for her hand.

She steps back against the railing and wire cage. "Moony, please go."

"No way." He takes her by the arm. Over the wind, a siren wails far below.

"You're being a *helper*," she says, an attempt at a low blow.

But it doesn't work. He won't let go of her arm.

"Why are you even here?" she demands. The powerful beam of the searchlight shoots over their heads and their shadows spin beneath them.

Moony says matter-of-factly, "I love you."

His brown eyes lock on hers with defiance. She lets her breath out and looks away, then back at him. "I know. I love you, too."

There. They both said it. They love each other.

But it's not enough.

"I still have to do this."

"No. You *absolutely don't*!" he screams into the gale. "Let's go home."

"I guess it's silly to expect you to understand." She's contemplating her options. No matter how she kills herself, she has to get him to leave. If she talks to him calmly, reassures him—

He wraps his arms around her and holds on. She struggles to break free of him but he's stronger. She pushes him off, huffing. He grabs her again.

"Let me go! You've ruined everything!" she cries. She's got to get away.

"Going over with you then," he says.

"Oh, for chrissakes." He will not let go. Summer looks around for Kurt. He's going to have to help if he wants her to do it tonight.

He's nowhere to be seen.

She'll have to plan this way better next time. She did, after all, call Moony and tell him exactly where she was going.

They stand as the wind screeches around them. Then Moony

pulls her, arms still locked around her, down the metal stairs to the elevators.

The sparkling lights are on. They can't help looking down at the wider sweep of the tower below and seeing the hundreds of thousands of lights twinkling.

A night guard waits by one of the elevators. He stares at Summer with dark Gallic wariness.

"Smile," hisses Moony. "Said you came up on a dare."

She forces a smile. Moony rattles off something reassuring to the man in French. He probably paid him off, too, to get up here. If he'd told them his real suspicions, there would be a squad of police with handcuffs waiting for her below.

When they arrive at the second platform, Moony drags her to the metal stairs. "Lower elevators closed. Gotta walk down."

As if she has any choice. "Okay, freaking let go," she says. "I'm coming with you."

FIFTY-THREE

It takes forever getting down the Eiffel Tower stairs from the second platform to the bottom even though Summer helps Moony the whole way. She has to.

"Why *do* you even like me?" she asks him as they round yet another landing. "It's sick to like me." She knows it, he knows it.

He hesitates, then says slowly, "On some level, suspected this."

"You mean . . . jumping?" She's shocked.

"Admire your attitude. Also sucker for lost causes." He smiles weakly.

"Now, that makes more sense. Damn straight."

Then he says what she's thinking. "They thought *I* was a lost cause. Proved them wrong." He goes on. "You think *you* are. Give anything if you could see through my eyes. What a gift and privilege life is. How it can get better." They pause on a landing and he gazes at her.

She shakes her head. He can't understand.

His face hardens. "Think it's all brave to want to die."

She takes his hand and holds it with both of hers. "Don't you see? I love you. Moony, I do. But I'm a black hole! Can you understand that? More than anything I don't want to hurt you. That's the only thing that matters to me."

He says nothing.

She adds, "I *don't* think it's brave. There's no way I can make you understand."

"You're wrong. I do understand."

"I can't bear living."

"Brave enough to die, then you're brave enough to live." He grips her hand. "Have the freaking courage to get help, to get better."

He makes it sound so straightforward and easy. "You have no idea. I've tried so, so many times. It's not a matter of courage. It's a matter of energy. Now it takes way more energy than I have. It's like I'm already dead."

"Bullshit," he spits.

It stuns her, coming from him. She pulls her hand away.

His eyes flash. "Can't believe how lame—how *pigheaded*—you're being. You *are* backing down from only thing that matters. Living."

"It's unbearable! I can't do it any longer!" she cries.

"You're the only one who can make it bearable!" he screams. "You! You! Not others!"

"But I can't. It's not worth it. And I can't hang on any longer. I don't want to live. I want to die." She drops her head in her hands. "I want to kill myself."

Moony bellows, "You have everything . . . you need . . . to get help . . . to find meaning. We all do. Fucking look for it! It's everywhere. So much you could do if you stop feeling sorry for yourself, being the world's biggest brat."

Summer's jaw drops. "But—You—I—You're not supposed to say that to a suicidal person."

"You're saying . . . *everything* . . . I *fought* for . . . suffered for, since accident, is . . . worthless!" He shakes his head in disgust then glares at her. "Should be executed."

"Me? Oh, that makes a lot of sense! Go ahead. Please! Shoot me now. And while you're at it, fuck you."

"*You're* the one throwing away life." He takes a deep breath, then says quietly, "And love."

They walk the rest of the way in silence. Red fury at Moony bubbles. She hates him. She wants to kill him. No, she doesn't. Herself is enough. But her brain is a tilt-a-whirl bouncing around her skull. Which way is up?

Finally on solid ground again, he grips her by the arm, all the way across the plaza beneath the tower. The sparkling lights come on again, blinking all around them, like a fairy disco land. One whole hour has gone by.

It's midnight and December 17 is over.

"I am *not* riding that scooter all the way home. I'd rather be *executed*," she says, scowling and pulling her flask from her coat pocket. Strangely, a part of her doesn't want it. But she *does* need it right now. Plus it will annoy the hell out of Moony.

She takes one sip. Then holds it up for him.

Moony sighs. "Taxi, then." To her surprise, he takes her flask and throws his head back. Two, three glugs and hands it back empty.

"What?" he says.

"Nothing." But it bums her out, if it's possible to get any lower. She's why he did that.

As they pull his scooter over to a bike rack and he locks it, she contemplates bolting. Moony is only delaying things. But her energy is gone.

He takes her by the arm again and they walk to the street. It's thirteen minutes past midnight, an impossible time to find a taxi in Paris because it's the same time everyone goes home from dinner out. Plus it's still drizzling. Moony calls for one, and gets a recording. They try to flag down two taxis to no avail.

"Anyone at your house?" he demands.

"No."

"Staying with you. Métro," he says, fatigue flattening his voice. He gazes down the Seine. "Bir-Hakeim's closed. Trocadéro." The two nearest metro stations.

Now Summer just wants to go somewhere and sleep. They cross

the bridge. She doesn't look over the side at the dark river because Kurt might be loitering beneath like a troll.

They shuffle past the big fountain, heading for the wide plaza and museums of the Trocadéro and the Métro entrance there. The rain has stopped.

Moony calls his mom and says he's taking Summer home and will stay at her house.

They climb all the Trocadéro steps. Moony drags. They pause to rest finally on the plaza and look out at the Eiffel Tower on the other side of the river, and the shimmering lights of the city beyond.

She takes his hand. "Please don't be mad. I've never had a friend like you."

"Never had a friend like *you,*" he says. They laugh. His gaze says . . . what, she's not certain. Not *sorry,* that's for sure.

"I'm not saying it's worthless," she says softly.

"You are," he insists. "But I'm not you. Haven't lived your life."

"I just can't stand it anymore," she murmurs.

Moony closes his eyes, as if to end any more discussion. He grips her hand.

Underground, the next train isn't due for six minutes according to the electronic sign, and is the last one. Her trainophobia disappeared. Of course, she thinks. Trying to jump off the Eiffel Tower cures it.

No, she's not afraid because Moony is with her.

"Summer?" he mumbles. "You'll get help? This iss serious." He slurs his words.

She nods, and means it. A bit of her has thawed somewhere.

They sit in two plastic seats bolted to the mustard-colored tiled wall, leaning against each other. The lights above them gleam harshly. Moony looks ill. There's no one else on their side, and a bum sleeps against the wall directly opposite them. Moony slumps against her in exhaustion.

"Jeez, Moony. I've got to get *you* home. By the way, did you see your present before . . . you came to find me?" she asks.

"Present?"

"In front of your door."

"Never went up. Jus' got the scooter."

"Oh. Then you'll see it tomorrow. It's for after your operation." She clears her throat and holds his curled hand. The pathetic bag of gummy bears is the *only* thing she's ever done for him. He just saved her stupid, hopeless life.

And for what?

Her eyes look down the empty tunnel, then follow the curved ceiling above them, down to the platform on the other side of the tracks.

In a hot-orange seat with his legs crossed, sits Kurt. He moves his ankle in time to some inaudible beat. Behind him is a huge wall ad of a naked woman for Acide perfume. He winks at Summer.

She glares at him and wishes with all her being he'd just give it up for a while. He walks out the exit to the stairs to the main level.

The hairs on her arms rise. She's not only ready to back down, but to run like hell.

"Moony? Um, maybe we should take the scooter," she says, standing, but thinking of him having to walk all the way back. Her mind is racing. Could they find a taxi easier on this side of the river? Or call a car service? Could she carry him piggyback? "I, uh . . ."

"Train'll be here, three minutes," he murmurs.

Already Kurt appears out of the passageway on their side of the tracks. He strides toward them, staring at Summer. Here he is, she thinks. Prince Not-So-Charming. Wrong guy at the right place and time. A groan escapes from her throat. Moony turns to see.

"You," he says, standing unsteadily. "I knew it."

FIFTY-FOUR

Kurt saunters over, trailing his pungent smell. He and Moony scowl at one another.

"Introductions not needed, then?" says Summer. Her mouth is dry. Moony not only sees but knows Kurt.

"We're acquainted," Moony says. He puts his hand over his nose. "Whew."

"When did you know Kurt?" Summer steps between them.

"Azzy," Moony corrects. "Several times—post-rehab depression, when addicted to painkillers. And . . . a time or two lately." He sighs and sinks back into the seat.

"We're old pals." Kurt smiles and pats Moony on the back. Then pulls Summer to him.

Summer says, "Oh." Moony knows him all right. But how did he . . . avoid him?

He said *lately*.

Kurt grips Moony's weak shoulder. Moony holds his forehead in his good hand. "Swear, though. Wonder why I fight it. Him."

"What?" says Summer. Her scalp and neck prickle.

"Not going to make it to old age anyway."

"Don't say that," she says, grabbing his other shoulder and stepping away from Kurt.

"This operation. So sick of it all," he whispers. "Would be so. Much. Simpler."

"Moony! You'll do fine!" she insists.

He shakes his head.

Kurt says, "You *won't* make it, brother. Sadly, it's a hopeless situation this time. But you can still take control. Keep your honor and dignity." He pulls Summer to him again.

"How do *you* know?" demands Summer, shrugging Kurt off.

"Really? You doubt me?" he asks.

The train approaches.

Kurt takes Summer's hand. "Come, Razorback. It's time."

Do I doubt him? What *is* true? It doesn't matter, she thinks. Ambivalence is a funny thing. I'll destroy myself. I'll live. I won't. I will. It can all be over, *now*. She still wants that. The date doesn't matter.

But what about Moony?

Kurt extends his other hand. "Come, my brave Moony." He grins. "How romantic. A love triangle." He raps, "You love each other. You both love me. That makes us a threesome . . . for eternity."

"Spare us," says Summer.

"It's best," says Moony, standing unsteadily.

"What?" cries Summer. "You're Super Moony. You help everyone. Don't help him!"

Moony doesn't look at her.

"Kurt and I are one thing. But you're entirely another. You're the only true thing I know!" Summer wails. "You just told me that meaning is everywhere. Wait!"

From the tunnel at the head of the station, the rumble of the coming train amplifies.

"No waiting," Kurt says. He pulls them to the edge of the platform. The headlight is now visible in the tunnel.

The old guy against the opposite wall stares at them with a worried expression. He catches Summer's eye and shakes his head.

Dad chose to go with Kurt. Isn't she just like him? He's the one who told her to not back down.

They balance on the concrete edge. The familiar stale air pushed out of the tunnel by the oncoming train washes over them, along with the scent of old urine, and even a pungent whiff of the bum's unwashed body. In addition to Kurt's stink. In her line of vision, the toes of her boots emerge from the bottoms of her jeans out over the gravel, the silver gum wrapper, torn chips package, and the tracks.

The face of the driver in the illuminated cab rushes toward them from the darkness. A woman. She observes them without expression, then her eyes widen.

Summer's left hand is in Kurt's. The deafening thunder of the train reaches its highest pitch, and she looks over. Moony's eyes are closed. He holds Kurt's other hand.

Moony took Kurt's hand with his weak one! Saint Moony, what-does-life-expect-from-you Moony is holding Kurt's hand.

And not hers.

He fooled her! Moony was so strong for her, always there when she needed him, always ready to forgive and extend yet another kindness to her.

She thought she was just like Dad. Dad thought so, too. He was crying when he hugged her because he was *worried* about her. He loved her and wanted what was best for her.

Sweetheart, you are not like him.

And Moony loves her. But his incredible will to survive and his love of life—his fairy Hope—have given out. She thought she was sacrificing herself to protect him. A sacrifice that takes him, too, would be a *sacrilege.*

A blowtorch ignites in Summer. The lights in the station flicker. Brighten.

She's not afraid of dying. She's afraid of loving.

She *is* backing down. From loving Moony.

FIFTY-FIVE

The speeding, roaring train is meters from entering the station, and a few more meters from the threesome.

"NOOOooo, let go!" Summer cries, releasing Kurt, pulling toward Moony. But Kurt holds her fast.

For chrissakes! Dad wasn't talking about soccer coaches or gangbangers. He meant don't back down from *life*!

"Step forward," commands Kurt over the thunder.

Dad was *afraid* she might one day do what *he was going to do*. He wanted her to do better, to stay and fight and love and triumph.

Living is freaking hard.

Mom's voice through the door—*You have your own strength*.

She's not her father. Or her mother. Their choices are not hers.

What life expects from her . . . is to have Moony's back.

The flame of hope and attachment to this dark world blazes, and the anger she has felt for so long focuses into a laserlike beam as she struggles against the fake, sleazy liar who is using her to rob the world of someone who is . . . everything she isn't.

She spews a lifetime of fury at the most worthy target possible.

"You ASSHOLE!" she screams. She jumps back, yanking herself from Kurt's grasp. She grabs Moony from behind. Her tae kwon do kick into Kurt's back pushes him in front of the train, a nanosecond before it roars past.

At the same time, Summer pulls Moony with every ounce of her strength.

Moony is torn from Summer, his body knocked by the train.

Brakes screech forever.

Summer lands hard on her butt, slams her head, lies sprawled on the concrete.

Perfectly alive. She is Summer and she's free.

A groan down the platform.

"Moony!"

Summer pulls herself to her knees, stars flashing, head spinning, and crawls to him.

She gasps. His eyes are closed but moving beneath his lids. His marble-white face glows with perspiration. He groans again but is unconscious.

"Oh my god, oh my god, someone help us!" Summer screams.

FIFTY-SIX

The following hour is as if Summer is under water, in the dark, with earplugs. Suddenly people are all around and tired faces are getting in her face. Some are concerned looking, some brusque. As paramedics examine Moony, a man gently pulls her aside and shines a penlight into her eyes. She's aware that her head and her tailbone really hurt, and that she feels like she's going to barf. They make her lie on a board, put a plastic thing around her neck, and check her over.

A man in a dark uniform squats beside her and asks her what happened in French.

Summer doesn't answer.

He demands in English. "Mademoiselle, what happened?"

She cannot begin to explain what has come to pass, and so says nothing.

When they take Moony away on a stretcher, Summer tries to get up, but realizes she's strapped down. Two guys carry her out.

Above ground, outside the Métro entrance, too many red lights are flashing. Too many people loiter. The guys put her into the back of one of too many vehicles. She lies there mutely, praying that Moony will be okay.

A woman officer, or maybe she's a paramedic, uses Summer's cell phone and contact list to call her mother, who is asleep in a hotel in Geneva. The lady talks briefly then hands the phone to Summer.

"Summer? Darling? Are you okay?" Mom sounds a little hysterical.

As if swimming up to the surface to answer, Summer musters every bit of coherence she can. "I'm okay, Mom," she says, taking pains to pronounce each word clearly.

"But you're on the way to the hospital! It's one thirty in the morning!" Mom's flair for the obvious. But the pain and fear in Mom's voice is concern about her.

"We were too near the platform edge when the train came, and Moony"—she gulps, almost chokes—"got hurt."

"Why did they call me? What's wrong with you?"

"I fell on my butt. I'm a little dizzy, I guess."

"I'm calling Monsieur de Villefort. Don't answer any questions until he comes."

Summer shuts her eyes. Probably another lawyer. Mom's worried about her saying something wrong or incriminating. She's fully responsible and will tell anyone who asks her.

Mom continues, "I'll be there in a few hours."

They leave the Trocadéro with sirens blaring, *weee-ooo, weee-ooo, weee-ooo*. Before long, the truck stops and they pull Summer out in time for her to see two men rolling Moony from another truck through the doors of the emergency room. His eyes are closed and he's so still.

It's the last glimpse she has of him.

Summer's rolled into a room where a doctor examines her. Again, the woman is kind enough to speak English and Summer realizes it's just another way in which she is spoiled.

She has a mild concussion, a cracked tailbone, and a week-old fractured rib from the catacombs. The doctor gives her a prescription for something with instructions to rest.

Mom's French lawyer is tapping his foot in the waiting room when she comes out, unmistakable in a dark suit and tired expression. A serious-looking guy in a *police nationale* uniform stands with him. The doctor hands them a piece of paper and discusses something. Summer sits by dumbly, not even trying to understand.

Summer's never met him, but Monsieur de Villefort says with a thick French accent, "Mademoiselle, please explain what happened." The police officer frowns at him.

She says, "It's my fault. That . . . we were . . . too close to the edge. I—I tried to pull Moony back."

It is the truth. Somehow in all the confusion, pain, and uproar, she decides that she will try to tell the truth from now on. As best she can. Especially to herself.

Glancing at Monsieur, the police officer says, "Did you consume any alcohol?"

"Yes. Earlier this evening."

"When?"

"At around six thirty or seven." With Kurt as they strolled by the Seine.

"How much?"

"I guess one or two drinks? I drank brandy. Twice from a flask." And then just a sip to piss off Moony at the base of the Eiffel Tower. Which was nothing for her.

Moony finished it.

Monsieur-the-lawyer says, "Bah, that was some eight hours ago, and would have no effect at the time of the accident."

Summer is more sober now than she has ever been in her life. It's almost overwhelming, but it's here and now and she will not back away from it.

Ever again.

The officer asks a few general questions about her friendship with Moony, school, and where she lives. She tries to be helpful but her head and tailbone hurt and focusing is taking every bit of strength she has left.

Monsieur and the officer discuss her and the accident. Mom's friend seems to shut down further questioning.

"I will take you home," he says to Summer. He has a 2:00 A.M. shadow that's as good as a full beard.

"No. Thank you. I'm staying here. I have to find Moony."

"He is in surgery. You must go home and rest."

"No," she says firmly. "I'm staying here until he comes out."

In exasperation, Monsieur calls Mom, explains, then gives up and leaves.

Summer finds the surgery waiting room. A grim-faced Karen is on the phone to Moony's dad in Kuwait City. She waves at Summer when she sees her.

Karen slips her phone into her pocket and hugs Summer. "Are you okay?"

"Yeah, I'm fine. What are they doing to Moony?" A silent, old-model TV flickers above them. A fake evergreen wreath with a droopy red ribbon hangs on the wall.

"He's going to be okay," Karen says forcefully. "They're pinning his arm bone. He has a bad break, and a couple of other fractures." She takes Summer by the shoulders and looks her in the eyes. "What happened?"

Summer stares at Karen's double-knotted tennis shoes.

She must tell the truth.

At least her truth. Her secrets have held power over her for too long.

She sucks in a deep breath. "I—I was . . . going to . . . ," she swallows, ". . . kill myself."

Karen sucks air in through her nose, eyes wide. "And he stopped you." She steps back. "Of course he did."

"Yes."

"The police said that the driver said Munir hit the moving train. That you guys were horsing around too close to the platform edge."

"Probably what it looked like," Summer says softly. "Was there— Did they mention another, um, person?"

"What?" Karen snaps.

"Never mind."

"What do you mean another person? Was there someone else?"

"Um. A friend of . . . we saw—No. There was no one." No body on the tracks. Or tall, handsome stranger in a black coat. Or an Egyptian athlete with a *ghutrah* who escorts people to their self-inflicted demise off train platforms or towers.

She hopes he was shattered into a million pieces.

Karen says with quiet fury, "Do you have any idea what you've done to Munir?"

Summer drops her head, and nods, unable to keep from crying any longer.

"He may *not* be okay. His body can't take this. He may die in there. You realize that, right?"

Summer nods again. Tears stream down her face.

"Because of you."

Summer blubbers, "You can be as mad at me as you want. I completely understand. But I can't leave here. He saved my life. And . . . I . . . can't leave." She was going to say she loves him, but Karen's furious enough already.

"Here." Karen impatiently holds out a tissue. "Wipe your face. And Summer? Get some help." Then she says, ice cold, "But I insist that you leave. And never contact him again." She walks to the other side of the room and pulls out her phone.

Summer turns to go.

FIFTY-SEVEN

That evening after the accident Summer trudges around the Place Victor-Hugo to St. George's Anglican Church, not far from Mom's apartment. By saving Moony, she saved herself. But given what she knows about Kurt, he could easily show up again. And she could put herself in another dead-end situation.

If Moony needed help, then she can damn well admit she does.

She knows where she has to start.

She arrives early for the Alcoholics Anonymous meeting and sits gingerly in a hard chair on her very sore tailbone. At the right time, she says, "Hi, my name is Summer. I'm an alcoholic."

"Hi, Summer!" everyone answers enthusiastically. Over the next six months, she goes daily to meetings at several locations in Paris. She pretends Moony is sitting next to her at each one.

The week after the accident, she officially flunks out of PAIS just like all the other schools. The upshot is that she, Mom, Winston, and everyone finally understand that doing yet another term anywhere will be a ludicrous waste of time.

The following days both speed up and slow down. Living them soberly brings them into painful focus, like being awakened in the middle of the night only to be pushed into noonday sunlight and a pool of ice water. Naked. And then jabbed with salad forks. But she's in charge. She will not back down.

Summer goes back to Dr. Garnier and this time she tells her the truth about her drinking and substance abuse, and about Kurt—how and when she saw him. So she is put on suicide watch. They work out a routine and Summer agrees to stick to it. Rising time, bedtime, AA meetings, regular meal times, exercise time, reading and journaling time. And meds.

Mom sends Moony an oversized flower arrangement with balloons and gummy bears. Karen calls Summer's mom to thank her and updates her on Moony's tentative progress, but allows that at least for the present he has two useless arms. His other corrective surgery has been postponed.

At her one-month sobriety date, Summer writes a letter to Moony. No one she knows within thirty years of her age writes letters. But putting her thoughts down in careful longhand, on heavy cream-colored paper in blue ink, does something to clear and settle her mind. Plus it's less intrusive than a text, and more respectful than an e-mail.

And she's always liked stamps.

January 19

Dear Moony,

I hope you will read this and not tear it into little strips. I know how angry you must be with me and I just want you to know that it's totally cool. All I want is for you to know what you mean to me and how much of a difference you made in my life, and my almost lack-thereof.

First, I hope you're feeling okay and that your injuries are healing. That you're resting and taking care of yourself. You'll be happy to know that I'm praying for you. There is something larger than me or I wouldn't be here. Every day. I picture you playing soccer, although I don't care if you ever do that. It just seems a healthy thing to visualize. Incidentally, that's the New Age part. It's all pretty unorthodox but it's mixed in with some Christianity and I've been reading about Buddhism and Islam. Thanks for that, too. The permission to do it my own way.

Last night I got my one-month chip at the AA meeting I go to, a little piece of plastic symbolizing thirty-one days of sobriety. That's longer than I've been sober since middle school. I know I've got a long way to go, but I want to thank you so much for showing me how to get started.

I'm seeing a psychiatrist and working as hard as I ever have on anything. I call it UN-kidding myself. I'm happy to say it doesn't involve math of any kind. But it's difficult. Today is a good day.

I also want you to know how deeply sorry I am that I put you and me both in the situation I did. I will be eternally grateful to you for saving my life. Repeatedly. And eternally devastated that I almost was the cause of you losing yours.

Well, got to go now. I have my AA meeting and then dinner with Mom to look forward to. The days are just packed. I love you, Moony, and always will and pray that one day you will forgive me. I hope also that your mom will one day forgive me, but that's more an exercise in loving kindness because I know she'd like to kill me, since I failed to do it myself.

Love,
Summer

She mails it, but never gets any reply or acknowledgment.

FIFTY-EIGHT

Almost four months after the accident, in mid-April, Summer and Mom sit at the kitchen table by the French window on the courtyard, eating *salades Niçoises*. Camus lounges beside them. Mom has a glass of Pouilly-Fuissé and Summer drinks sparkling water. Sometimes they sit in silence, which is fine with Summer, but Dr. Garnier has encouraged her to engage with her mom. And she has something important to ask her.

"Mom," Summer says, "I'd like to hear about Africa. Your project in Cameroon."

"Oh, I already told you all about that, didn't I?" she says, flaking the tuna in her bowl with her fork.

"Uh, no. I don't know anything about it. I'd like to." Summer takes a sip of water and looks at Mom expectantly.

Mom glances warily back at her, probably to see if she's being sarcastic. Summer tries to look encouraging.

"In the village in northern Cameroon where we're involved, we've built a new schoolhouse with six rooms, and a kitchen with gardens." Her eyes brighten. "The best part is that we've just hired a great head teacher. She's from the city and also spent some time in France, but knows rural ways. She's gentle and diplomatic—a really good role model. She just charms the families into letting their girls go to or keep going to school. You know, some of them don't want their girls to go."

"How come?"

"They need their help at home." Mom takes a sip of wine. "They also fear it, I think. It's a change for them. Sophie shows them how it's a win-win situation."

"That's really cool, Mom," Summer says sincerely.

Mom pulls her shoulders back and looks at Summer again as if to measure whether she should keep going. "We're expanding into other countries. Other NGOs out there have the same idea, but we're one of the lowest cost and quickest. We get things set up, and then get out of their way." Mom looks animated and, frankly, happy. She would rather mother the continent of Africa than Summer, but what the heck. Maybe Africa is easier.

Summer pushes an anchovy aside and takes a big bite of hard-boiled egg. "How do you know where to start?"

"It's a fairly long process. We meet with authorities for the village, and village elders. We try to *listen*. It's important . . ."

Summer raises her eyebrows but says nothing. Mom listening carefully to anyone is pretty ironic.

There's a long pause. Mom says softly, "I wasn't really listening to you, was I?"

"I guess not," Summer allows. Interesting that right now they are both paying close attention to the other. And trying to be gentle. They have a lifetime to catch up on.

Mom presses her lips together and examines her lettuce. "I'm sorry, sweetheart. I really am. I just want you to know that." She squeezes Summer's hand. Her touch feels warm and nice. "That I'm sorry for my big part in all this. I'm not one of those 'helicopter moms.' I had to take care of Liz and myself when we were kids. I guess I thought all kids should do that. But I didn't realize that I was . . . dangerous." Her eyes glisten.

"It's okay, Mom." She's being a little dramatic and making it about her. But it's a start.

"I'm trying to be better."

"I know. You haven't left here for ages. For goodness sakes, take a trip," Summer kids.

Mom's face lights up, pleased Summer has noticed. "And I'm really proud of you. How well you've done these last months."

The compliment lands gently on Summer's shoulder like a yellow songbird. "Thank you." It's funny, though, that Mom will still never utter the word "suicide."

"I have to say, proud also that you've managed to keep that weight off." Mom spears greens.

Summer just nods. "Yeppers." She takes a sip of sparkling water. "Mom, I know it might seem like running away or escaping, but Paris is very hard for me."

"Harder now?" asks Mom.

"It's always been hard and still is," Summer says evenly. "I was thinking that I'd like to go back to the US as soon as it's okay. I think I can make better progress there—"

Mom's pale eyes open wide. "I don't think that's a good idea at all!"

"Okay," Summer says, despite heavy disappointment. "I've been thinking a lot about it, and I did discuss it with Dr. Garnier, but you'd have to be on board."

Mom's face droops into wrinkles. She puts her fork down. "Why? Why is it so hard here?"

Mom thinks it's about her. And it is a little bit. But it's way more than that. "Because every building, every tourist landmark, every bus and Métro, and every freaking cobblestone, remind me of what I did. To Moony. To myself. To you."

Silence settles over the table. Mom takes another bite of salad and frowns in thought. "Where would you go then?"

"I'm thinking San Francisco, where I could stay with Aunt Liz for a while."

Now Mom looks sad. "I know she'd like that. Have you talked to her?"

"No. I wanted to ask you about it first." It would be better for them both. Later she and Mom can carve out a way to coexist.

"What about school? And university? And the will?" Mom

demands. "Are we just going to give up? I wasn't going to bring it up yet, but you're kind of forcing the issue."

Summer chews the inside of her cheek and reminds herself that Mom has every right to be worried about her inheritance, even if she's not. "No. I'm not giving up. I don't know what I'll do about that. Anyway, I won't be twenty-two for years, and I've got bigger chickens to fry right now."

Mom's mouth twitches. "I know."

Summer says, "I appreciate your watching out for me about that, Mom. Really. But you want something for me that I don't."

"I want you to have the option. Not to throw it away, for heaven's sake."

"I understand. Can we just let it ride for a little longer?"

"Do we have a choice?" Her shapely eyebrows arch.

Summer smiles. "No."

Mom smiles, too. A small one. "Let me think about it for a couple of days." She sighs. "About logistics and all. I'll talk to your doctor, I guess."

"Thanks, Mom." Summer gives her a kiss on the cheek.

FIFTY-NINE

With the blessings of Dr. Garnier and Mom, near her five-month sobriety date on a Saturday afternoon, Summer calls Aunt Liz. It's nine hours earlier in San Francisco.

"Hi, sweetheart. How nice to hear your voice." Aunt Liz sounds a little sleepy.

"Wait," Summer says, looking at the clock. "I think I messed up the math. Don't tell me it's only six A.M."

Her aunt laughs. "Okay. I won't tell you that."

Good work, Summer. She covers her face with her hand.

"You can call me at any hour. You know that."

She and Liz get along great, but Summer doesn't know how far it goes. And she's about to ask her something big and hard, and it will really knock her stuffing out if Liz refuses.

Liz goes on, "I'm so sorry you've been having such a hard time. I've been keeping tabs, thanks to your mom. Did you get my messages?"

"Yes. Thank you for those. And for the cards and flowers. I just haven't really called anyone back."

"I understand. And you're welcome. How are you, pumpkin?"

For the first time in weeks, a baseball-sized lump rises in Summer's throat at the sound of Liz's soft, concerned voice. She's going on nineteen years old and she feels like a little child. She says as steadily as she can, "I guess better than I was."

"You're doing great from what I've heard."

"Um." Summer hesitates, then blurts out, "Can I come live with you for a while?"

Aunt Liz pauses. "Oh, I . . ."

Summer interrupts, "It's okay, if not. I understand it's a lot to ask." Aunt Liz won't say "suicide," either. And who in their right mind wants a suicidal kid in their house? Even though she isn't now.

"Summer," Liz says firmly. "I'd love it. Nothing would make me happier."

"Really?" Now Summer's eyes fill. Funny how it's kindness that slays her.

She'll run one more time, to San Francisco.

"Of course. Your room is waiting. Your mom and I have already discussed the possibility. She's graciously agreed."

"I'd have to get set up with a shrink there and everything. And not fall off the wagon and all."

"No problem. We'll take it one step at a time."

"Thank you, Aunt Liz."

SIXTY

Summer finally purchases a one-way ticket to San Francisco for June 20.

At her last session in Dr. Garnier's wood-paneled, musty office, Dr. G leans back in her leather chair and asks, "Now that you have a departure date, how do you feel about leaving?"

"Petrified," says Summer.

Dr. Garnier taps her pen on her notebook, a sure sign she's pleased. "Could you elaborate?"

"I *did* want to leave Paris like I always wanted to leave a place. To escape my life. But now it's different. In San Francisco, I have to find work, stay sober, go to school eventually, and all that stuff. I'm really worried about being able to pull if off." She adds, "But I still think it's a good move. And that I can do it."

"Why do you think this?"

"Because I have to. I want to." Summer focuses on the glass coffee table and the large book with all four of The Beatles' faces on the cover.

Dr. G nods at her to keep going.

"And I do feel sad to leave here. Usually when I bolt, I don't look back." She crosses her arms and swallows hard. "The thing that really makes me sad . . . is Moony."

"You've still had no communication with him?"

"No." She squeezes her knuckles. "I know he's okay because my mom talked to Karen."

"Does he know you're leaving?"

"Yeah, I told him in my last letter. And Mom told Karen. She'll talk to my mom, but not to me."

"How do you feel about that?"

"Terrible! She's a flipping witch." Summer toes a tuft of the white shag carpet. Dr. Garnier looks at her indulgently, as if at an overwrought third-grader. "But I kind of understand how she feels. Plus, while she might toss out my letters, I doubt that she's deleted my e-mail or text. Most likely, he just doesn't want to answer."

"Is he capable of answering?"

"I think so. He's had two surgeries and his left arm is mended. He's graduating this month with his class. I saw online that he's planning a road trip through the US this summer with some old friend, so that's good." She clasps her hands beneath her chin. "But maybe that's part of it. Even for Super Moony, things are hard right now. He needs to be more selfish. So, I'm glad." She pauses. "And maybe he hates me."

"Maybe he needs time. He likely has had to acknowledge the self-destructive part of himself." Dr. Garnier crosses her stockinged legs. "You mentioned you sent letters? Texts and e-mails?"

"Five letters now, about one a month. Only one text and e-mail each, back in January."

"How will you deal with his noncommunication?"

"I won't, like, stalk him, but I'll keep trying every month or so. I'll let him know what's going on with me anyway. If he tells me to stop, I will. It's a little like Kentucky Morris. He's gone, but his music isn't."

Dr. Garnier raises one eyebrow at her analogy. "You said earlier that this process is surprising you. How do you mean?"

"I expect to get better because I'm busting butt. It surprises me that it's so slow. Some days I panic that I'm falling back apart. But I haven't so far. And the next day is usually better."

She taps her pen again. "What is different than before?"

Summer props her head in her hand, noting a whiff of ammonia glass cleaner. "I don't know. That I was shocked out of my rut? Out of being suicidal?" She pauses. "What is it with suicide? Do all depressed people want to kill themselves?"

"No, thank goodness," Dr. Garnier says. She shifts in her seat at the thought. "Most suicidal people are depressed. But most depressed people are *not* suicidal. It's a small subset."

"Oh." Summer crosses her arms again. "What causes it? Being suicidal."

"A number of factors contribute. One's mental 'wiring.' And as I mentioned, almost always along with depression. She counts off on her fingers, starting with her thumb. "Isolation and/or lack of support. Any history of abuse or trauma, such as the loss of your father, especially coupled with a hostile social environment, so most recently your experience with the young man and his 'cyber-bullying' at St. Jude's—these would all qualify."

"Hmm."

She pauses and looks Summer in the eye. "And substance abuse."

Summer nods.

Dr. Garnier says quietly, "History of suicide within the family can also be a factor."

"Yeah." She folds her hands in her lap and stares at them. "I guess I did sort of know. Didn't know it, exactly, but felt it."

Dr. Garnier nods. "Children can be remarkably perceptive."

"So you're saying if I stay connected to family and friends, sober, and busy, I can be okay? Maybe a few meds?"

She smiles. "Along with an awareness of your predisposition, yes."

"Okie-dokie. No sweat. Can I go now?"

The doctor looks at her watch. "Not yet." She contemplates

Summer. "What else changed for you? Why have you embraced this process now, and not before?"

"I realized that I truly wanted to live," she says matter-of-factly, "but . . . that I need help."

"Yes. How?"

"At that, um, moment, I knew I had to save Moony. I was the one who brought him to that awful point. But that Moony knew Kurt shocked me."

"Go on."

"He was more fragile than I thought, and it made me realize that everybody's fragile, given the wrong circumstances, and that *I* was, and that I needed to get over myself, and freaking get help."

Dr. G taps her pen on her notebook.

"Now I care, I guess."

"Did you not, before?"

She looks at Dr. Garnier in exasperation. "No, I did. Care. Totally. Too much. I was so . . . overwhelmed, I guess."

"Suicide is an attempt—a desperate, even blind one—to escape pain that's become unbearable. We were not made to support the weight of the world alone, especially when damaged and depressed."

"Right on."

Dr. G smiles "Anything else?"

"I was drunk all the time, maybe a little stubborn? Now I'm focusing more outward, not inward? You tell me, doc. Wait." Summer glances at The Beatles book and puts up a finger, "*Don't* tell me. 'All You Need Is Love.' Right?"

"*Mais oui*. 'I get by with a little help from my friends.'"

"You've helped me a bunch, Dr. G," Summer says, grinning. Dr. Garnier's a well-paid pseudo-friend, but she's grateful all the same. Summer gives her an awkward hug before she leaves. "*Merci beaucoup*."

SIXTY-ONE

Six months after the accident, Summer clears security at l'Aéroport de Paris-Charles-de-Gaulle and arrives early at the gate for her flight to San Francisco. She plops into a seat, takes a couple of "cleansing" breaths to relax the tension in her shoulders and neck, and puts in her earbuds.

She skips an old favorite Kentucky Morris song on her playlist and shuffles to a catchy, Bollywood-inspired dance hit from Scratchy Sponge Hearts. The slight tang of body odor lingers from whoever was sitting there before.

Out the massive window, a giant airbus taxis out to the runway while ground crews crisscross the tarmac between passenger buses, long strings of baggage carts, fuel and catering trucks. The sky's a crystalline June blue above the curved modern lines of the airport.

Summer feels her phone buzz.

Two texts: one from Lila, her AA sponsor. And one from Mom.

Disappointment stings Summer. A tiny part of her is still hoping to hear from Moony. In her last letter she told him exactly when she was leaving. She'd give a front tooth for a *Farewell,* a whole digit for *Safe travels.*

She'll keep sending letters until snail mail is phased out, or he tells her to stop.

Or he answers.

A girl can dream.

Lila's text reads:

Bon voyage! One day . . .

"At a time," Summer finishes. She smiles. Lila is another one who has helped her so much.

Mom's says:

Proud of you. Text when you arrive no matter the hour. Kiss Aunt Liz. Big kisses for you xoxox Open card now.

Mom hovered the last months. She has no clue how to hover and tended heavily toward annoying. But Summer appreciated the attention.

They even started to talk about Dad; his death and his life.

She opens the card Mom gave her when they said good-bye. It's an old black-and-white photo of some man. Underneath, it says, "Albert Camus: 1913–1960. French Algerian philosopher and author. Father of the absurd."

She chuckles. An absurd guy named after their dog.

Inside the card is scrawled in Mom's handwriting:

In the depths of winter, I finally learned that there is within me an invincible summer. —Albert Camus

Mom! Knock me over with a silver spoon.

Acknowledging and enjoying good moments like this has been an important part of her strategy lately. She'd love to share these words with someone, but there's no one nearby except a fatigued-looking Indian businessman.

Gratitude is important, too. She texts back to Mom:

Thank you for everything, Mom. I love you. Invincible me.

She's traveling alone—which she's been doing since she was twelve years old—but this time feels different. A strange tightness has been squeezing her ribs and throat since she woke up this morning, and it's getting worse.

What is it?

Leaving Paris? The parks in the city are full of geometrically arranged beds of vibrantly colored flowers. The days are infinitely long now and it doesn't get truly dark until close to midnight. Summer solstice, and the all-night party that is la Fête de la Musique is tomorrow evening. She's sorry to miss some soft version of it, and she and Paris are on better terms, but leaving is still the right thing to do.

Maybe it's leaving Mom—after finally finding a semblance of a mother-daughter relationship. There's a part of her that always felt homesick anyway when she left Mom's or Aunt Liz's, either one.

But no. It's bigger than that.

Is it fear that she'll fall apart again, tumble into that abyss of despair?

Always. But that's not it either.

She used to have three speeds: stuck in despair, rage, or retreat. But if there is one thing she's learned, it's that she has to recognize and *feel* scary sad or angry emotions. Jump right into the middle of them and swim around. Not freeze them away so that they pile up, hard and sharp, ready to crush her.

Gripping the armrests, she closes her eyes and concentrates.

This ache is not fear of despair. With all her might Summer suffers it and names it.

Moony.

Through bleary eyes, she stares out the airport glass wall, but pictures the sprawling city that's just forty-five minutes south. Moony is there somewhere, probably in pain, but positively persevering.

She's doing the same.

What's absurd is that they're doing it alone.

She was deluded to think he'd tell her to stop sending letters. He's not going to say anything to her ever again. It's okay. But she knows his schedule and routines and pictured him in his room as he recovered. As she *hoped* he recovered. Even though she got precious little information, through all her dreary days, and all her worry of how injured and messed up he was, she took great comfort that at least he was nearby.

Soon he'll be half a world away.

It's over. It was over already. She's been holding on to that thin shred of hope for six months.

Summer's hand flutters to her throat at the memory of their kiss. She can't go there. Instead, she pictures him on the soccer field with the team, clipboard in hand, yelling encouragement as gold leaves swirl around him. Possibly, occasionally, thinking of her. Probably in exasperation.

Maybe, maybe, someday he can forgive her.

Closing her eyes again, she leans into that one hug at Moony's apartment door: his wheaty scent laced with traces of Ariel laundry soap; his warmth and easy energy, as they stood at the nucleus of the twinkling city of Paris spreading out amebalike—moving, living, pulsing—around them and how the entire universe at that moment felt so perfect and infallible.

So right.

She buries her head in her hands.

Grief, gratitude, fear, and loneliness shoot off like fireworks as Summer's heart cleaves in two.

SIXTY-TWO

She fishes around in her backpack for a tissue, but has nothing. She can't stop the tears and the Indian businessman is looking at her with alarm. A mom with a squirming toddler sitting opposite regards her with concern. Summer tries to smile reassuringly at them. Not to worry, just a little breakdown here.

She stuffs her music paraphernalia into a backpack pocket and charges for the ladies' room. A toilet paper face mopping, nose ring wiping, and a splash of cold water later, she ducks into a café. There's still time before they board and she could use some caffeine. Or something.

Summer sits at a white marble table by the window.

Now, she can't stop the sound in her head of the train screeching in, or the sight of the lady driver going wide eyed; Kurt gripping them both, and Moony's pale, unconscious face, his body sprawled on the concrete. It's playing on an endless loop in her brain. Over and over. She shreds her paper napkin. Rubs her eyes trying to shake the loop loose.

The waiter brings her an espresso.

All the time, distance, and effort in the world can never undo what she did, she thinks. Second chances are glowing stars, but some memories are black holes. Somehow, she's gotten sucked too near to the edge of this one. That point where light no longer escapes.

She's panting. Yes, she must deal head-on with negative emotions, but this is obsessive. Unhealthy. She's dangerously close to a panic attack. Get a grip.

A sip of too hot coffee burns. She swallows. Counts backward and slows her breathing.

She sniffs the scent of the toasty butteryness from baking croissants. Then pictures breaking a warm one apart and slathering it with raspberry jam. Too bad she's not hungry.

She takes another sip of coffee. Then another. This flood of emotions, roller-coaster highs and lows, has taken her by surprise here at Charles de Gaulle. Maybe caffeine's *not* such a good idea. She's too damn *awake.* Like her skin is on inside out. She wishes Dr. Garnier were here. Or even Mom.

She pulls out her phone, and stares at its blank face. Calling will worry them. She's better now. Just give it a moment.

Deep breath.

An American family with two sulky preteens steers past her table headed for a booth. Someone else follows close behind them, but stops beside her table.

Summer looks up.

Kurt smiles down at her.

SIXTY-THREE

"How—?" Summer gasps, knocking over what's left of her espresso. The liquid darkness seeps across the marble and drips into her lap.

"*Salut,* Razorback." Kurt's wearing a black windbreaker and jeans. "Mind if I sit down?"

"Yes," she croaks, as her pulse pounds in her ears.

He pulls out a chair. "It's been so long."

"Definitely not long enough."

The concourse entry is way on the other side of the room. There's an emergency exit next to the kitchen. She's got to get out of here.

She slumps back in her seat. It won't make any difference.

Kurt clears his throat. Sounds like he has a cold.

His shirt is stained and frayed at the collar and all that big hair could use some shampoo. "You don't look so good," she says.

"I feel great," he says, then coughs.

"So what brings you to the airport?" His hands are dry and flaky.

"I wanted to see you. Wish you bon voyage. And maybe make a date in San Francisco. I plan to be out there soon."

"I bet you do." She mops up the mess with napkins the waiter brings.

It's funny that Kurt's waited all this time. Lots of bleak days populated the last months, especially in the beginning. A few were worse than others. When getting out of bed and putting one foot in front of the other took all the will, energy, and James Brown lyrics she had. He could have showed up on one of those.

He didn't.

Maybe because she was working so hard? Staying focused. Staying sober.

She just picked up her six-month plastic chip at her AA meeting the night before last. Not being hammered all the time has its small rewards.

She stopped smoking.

Thanks to GED international testing options, she has now "graduated" from high school.

She's taken up tae kwon do again and can make it through a whole hour now without having to collapse on the floor in a pool of sweat every ten minutes to rest.

Last week, she mailed a completed registration form for the first prerequisites for an education degree to a San Francisco community college. Classes start in late August.

Aunt Liz's friend runs a French bakery in their neighborhood and he's hiring dishwashers and food servers. Summer will apply as soon as she arrives. She's also exploring volunteer positions working with kids.

She's inching ever closer to her own center and knows now she is an important, if small, part of the whole, this life, this world.

Even though she'll never be more than *half*, without Moony.

Kurt taps his fingers on the table.

The wrong jerk at the wrong time. She sighs. Maybe suicide will hang there as an option for her, forever, dangling like some foul air-freshener card looped over the rearview mirror.

Especially when the world is shifting beneath her feet. Kurt was just waiting to kick her when she's down. That he might keep popping into her life like this sucks more than she can stand.

He says, "I was thinking about grabbing a quick drink at that bar down the concourse."

"Go for it," she says.

"Care to join me?"

"Nope. Not today."

"But I never drink alone. Just one, for the road. For the big trip. For luck."

"Kurt. I don't know what freaking language you need it in, but I said no. Why are you here again?"

He doesn't answer. Examines his ragged nails.

Summer knows why. Her throat closes and her eyes fill again.

She must *really* let go of Moony. Believe it.

No more letters. No more false hope.

Accept that she must mourn the loss of him and feel sad, probably forever. Ha! That's an understatement. Some primal part of her believes that letting him go will destroy her. It's irrational.

She'll be okay.

She nearly killed him. There's no choice but to make his sacrifice worthwhile by getting healthy and moving forward with her life.

The morning sunlight slants through the window. It leaves a brilliant pool of platinum on the white marble table and spotlights slowly waltzing dust motes.

So beautiful, it aches.

"Summer?" Kurt lasers his sexy smile across the table.

His shoulders are broader, his features more symmetrical even than she remembers. But he's slouching, his skin is coarse, and his face is lined.

"Yes," he muses, studying her. "The last months agreed with you incredibly." He makes goo-goo eyes at her as the scent of something acrid and sharp hits her, like mothballs mixed with cat urine. He'll slide over and nuzzle her neck in a few seconds if she doesn't do something.

Summer stands, pushing her chair back with a screech. "Get the fuck out of here."

Heads swivel. The four American family members turn in unison to stare across the room.

Kurt adopts a shocked, hurt look. "That's no way to talk to an old friend. And, hey, maybe I want to order something."

"But you can't pay for it, now, can you!" She's still standing even though her knees are wobbly.

His left eye twitches. "No need to be so hostile, is there? I've been thinking about seeing your beautiful face and hearing your voice for months. Years. Eternity." His dark eyes intensify and melt at her. He murmurs, "I don't think you understand how much I've missed you."

The sound that comes from her vocal cords is bitter, not really a laugh, but it gives her strength. "You've got some nerve showing up now. Or ever." She points to the door. "Go. Away."

He scowls, coughs. Waits one, two, three beats, then rises slowly and leaves.

Summer sinks into the chair even though right now she could soar out of it. It's like tapping ruby slippers together three times.

It was there all along. And she's floored with the power of it.

Grateful.

So *many* things to be grateful for.

One day at a time. It *is* a good strategy. She's got today, thanks to Moony, and what life expects from her is that she make something of it.

SIXTY-FOUR

The final boarding call for Summer's flight crackles over the PA system. She pays and leaves the café. Air France agents are herding stragglers in the now almost deserted boarding area.

Near the gate, in the middle of a bank of seats, sits a lone young guy, reading. One leg is sprawled at an angle. A cane leans against the seat next to him. He reminds her of . . .

Moony!

Unbelievable.

"Ohmigod!" Summer exclaims, breaking into a run. She stops.

She closes her eyes and breathes out, then walks over.

"*Excusez-moi?*" she says.

Moony looks up slowly as if so engrossed in his book that he can't tear himself away. "Yes?"

His clear brown eyes sweep her mind clean of all thoughts, except that he looks older. She stutters, "I . . . er . . . you are . . . uh?"

"On this flight."

"What are the odds?" she murmurs.

"Low."

"It was a rhetorical question."

He grins. "Traveling around the States this summer. Part of my graduation present."

"Oh, right. I heard. Are you staying in San Francisco?" She tries to tamp down the sheer joy in her voice, but doesn't do a very good job. Feeling and acknowledging emotions is one thing. Frightening people with them is another.

"Yep. With family friends. Then meeting an old PAIS buddy in Los Angeles next week. Traveling across the Southwest with him, end up in Missouri."

"Missouri! Are you studying there then?"

"Hmm-hmm. Full ride. Premed."

"That's so awesome!" she cries, reaching out to clap him on the shoulder. But she stops short. Touches her throat. "You're feeling . . . good then? I mean, you look great." He looks thin. She can't help glancing at his arms bones jutting under his long-sleeved T-shirt. His color is good, though. And his eyes are twinkling.

"I am."

"I'm . . . I'm so happy to see you." She's full of understatement today. Keep cool, Summer, don't blow it, she reminds herself.

"Happy to see you," he says with his sly smile. "You look really good, too."

"Um. So can I give you a hug hello?"

"Why not?"

He stands, pushing up awkwardly from the armrest.

Summer embraces him. Lightly, carefully. She breathes in his warmth and grassy, limey soap smell and they don't let go as the loudspeaker announces in French, then English, that this is truly the final boarding call and the door to their flight is closing.

Or as the woman's voice blares, "Passengers Munir Al Shukr and Summer Barnes, on Air France Flight eighty-four to San Francisco, please proceed to gate fifty-four immediately. The captain has ordered the aircraft doors closed."

"I guess it's time," says Summer finally, unentwining herself from Moony. "You're on this flight," she repeats. She still can't believe it.

"Not yet."

"Heh."

She studies him closely as he fishes out a boarding pass, then slings his backpack over his shoulder and grabs his cane. He moves stiffly, but his left arm seems to work okay.

The annoyed flight attendant takes their boarding passes.

"I hope you plan to fill me in on everything that you've been up to," Summer says. "You know what *I've* been doing."

"Yep. Pages worth."

"One thing's for sure," she says. "Someday, we'll look back on all this"—she reaches for his curled hand—"and probably change the subject."

Moony laughs, deep and true.

As they walk down the ramp, Summer gets it. In a new, wide, forever way. While one day at a time is an outstanding concept—really, she only has *this moment.*

Ever.

Presently, it happens to be the totally astonishing gift of Moony's hand in hers.

No matter what happens, in all the moments from here on out, it's enough.

SUICIDE PREVENTION RESOURCES

National Suicide Prevention Lifeline: 1-800-273-8255 (TALK)

If you are feeling suicidal or believe that someone you care about is, call the number above.

The Trevor Helpline is a 24-hour suicide prevention line aimed at gay, lesbian, bisexual, transgender, and questioning teens.

1-866-4-U-TREVOR

http://www.helpguide.org/index.htm

http://www.sptsusa.org/ **Society to Prevent Teen Suicide**

http://www.apa.org/research/action/suicide.aspx **American Psychological Association**

http://www.nimh.nih.gov/health/publications/suicide-a-major-preventable-mental-health-problem-fact-sheet/suicide-a-major-preventable-mental-health-problem.shtml **National Institute of Mental Health**

FACTS ABOUT SUICIDE AND SUICIDE PREVENTION AMONG TEENS AND YOUNG ADULTS

From the National Institute of Mental Health (NIMH)

Some common questions and answers about suicide:

Q: How common is suicide in children and teens?

A: In 2009, suicide was the third leading cause of death for young people ages 15–24. In this age group, suicide accounted for 14.4 percent of all deaths.

While these numbers may make suicide seem common, it is important to realize that suicide and suicidal are not healthy or typical responses to stress.

Q: What are some of the risk factors for suicide?

A: Risk factors vary with age, gender, or ethnic group. They may occur in combination or change over time. Some important risk factors are:

Depression and other mental disorders
Substance abuse disorder (often in combination with other mental disorders)
Prior suicide attempt
Family history of suicide
Family violence including physical or sexual abuse
Firearms in the home
Incarceration
Exposure to suicidal behavior of others, such as family members or peers

However, it is important to note that many people who have these risk factors are not suicidal.

Q: What are signs to look for?

A: The following are some of the signs you might notice in yourself or a friend that may be reason for concern.

Talking about wanting to die or to kill oneself
Looking for a way to kill oneself, such as searching online or buying a gun
Talking about feeling hopeless or having no reason to live
Talking about feeling trapped or in unbearable pain
Talking about being a burden to others
Increasing the use of alcohol or drugs
Acting anxious or agitated; behaving recklessly
Sleeping too little or too much
Withdrawing or feeling isolated
Showing rage or talking about seeking revenge
Displaying extreme mood swings

Seeking help is a sign of strength; if you are concerned, go with your instincts and get help!

Q: What can I do for myself or someone else?

A: If you are concerned, immediate action is very important. Suicide can be prevented and most people who feel suicidal demonstrate warning signs. Recognizing some of these warning signs is the first step in helping yourself or someone you care about.

If you are in crisis and need help: call this toll-free number, available 24-hours a day, every day **1-800-273-TALK (8255).** You will reach the National Suicide Prevention Lifeline, a service available to anyone. You may call for yourself or for someone you care about and all calls are confidential. You can also visit the Lifeline's Web site at **http://www. suicidepreventionlifeline.org**.

For more information on suicide visit the National Library of Medicine's MedlinePlus **http://medlineplus.gov** En Español **http://medlineplus.gov/spanish**

For information on clinical trials, go to the National Library of Medicine's clinical trials database at **http://www.clinicaltrials.gov**.

Information from NIMH is available in multiple formats. You can browse online, download documents in PDF, and order materials through the mail. Check the NIMH Web site at **http://www.nimh.nih.gov** for the latest information on this topic and to order publications. If you do not have Internet access, please contact the NIMH Information Resource Center at the numbers listed below.

National Institute of Mental Health

Office of Science Policy, Planning and Communications Science Writing, Press and Dissemination Branch 6001 Executive Boulevard Room 6200, MSC 9663 Bethesda, MD 20892-9663 Phone: 301-443-4513 or 1-866-615-NIMH (6464) toll-free TTY: 301-443-8431 or 1-866-415-8051 toll-free FAX: 301-443-4279 E-mail: **nimhinfo@nih.gov** Web site: **http://www.nimh.nih.gov**

Discussion Questions

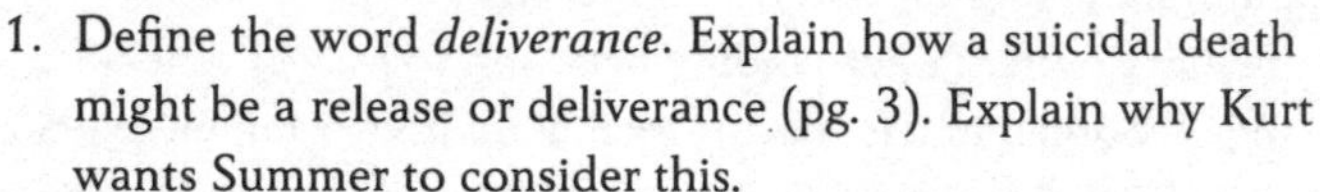

1. Define the word *deliverance*. Explain how a suicidal death might be a release or deliverance (pg. 3). Explain why Kurt wants Summer to consider this.

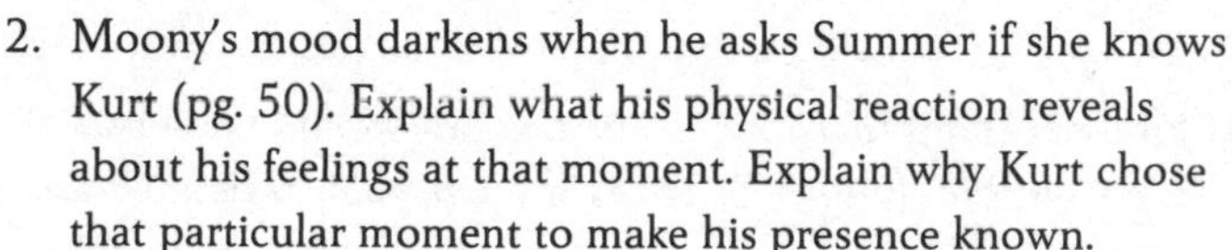

2. Moony's mood darkens when he asks Summer if she knows Kurt (pg. 50). Explain what his physical reaction reveals about his feelings at that moment. Explain why Kurt chose that particular moment to make his presence known.

3. Compare Moony and Kurt by discussing ways that the two are similar. Contrast these characters by listing their differences. Discuss how they each affect Summer in different and similar ways.

4. Discuss what being "Trapped in a giant cobweb of blah" (pg. 66) means. Explore what this description reveals about Summer's state of being at this point in the story.

5. Explain Summer's overreaction when Moony stumbled while going through the metal detector at the U.S. ambassador's residence (pg. 71–2). Examine the underlying reasons behind her mood swing.

6. Discuss why Kurt encouraged Summer to go to the Paris sewers with him. Tell why he told her that she would "love" it (pg. 82–85). Explain the motivation behind this action.

7. Summer wonders how Moony is able to manage pain and still apparently enjoy life with "gusto and, like, grace" (pg. 95). The word *grace* is defined as kindness, goodwill, and compassion. Describe ways that Moony extends grace to Summer and others. Explain his motivation for doing so.

8. Analyze the feelings of "hollowness," the "rush of deep sadness," and the energy "vacuum" Summer experiences following her first kiss with Kurt (pg. 119). Explain what is happening to Summer at this moment in the story.

St. Martin's Griffin

9. Summer's entering Karen's classroom generates a fond memory of her father holding her hand (pg. 146). Consider the emotional impact of this moment with her father. Explain what his holding her hand means to her. Explore Summer's feelings for her father.

10. Summer states that "to become the girl [Moony] deserves is impossible" (pg. 171). The word *impossible* is defined as being intolerable, unreasonable, and hopeless. Explain why Summer feels deserving Moony's affection is a hopeless act.

11. Discuss why Kurt does not carry money. Tell what this detail reveals about his character.

12. Summer tells her mother, ". . . graduating will be moot if I'm not around to inherit" (pg. 190). By saying these words, is Summer indirectly making a call for help? How so? Consider her mother's response to Summer. Is her mother missing the true intent behind Summer's comment? If so, why?

13. How does the news of the death of singer-songwriter Kentucky Morris impact Summer? Explain why.

14. Consider Summer's statement (pg. 218), "Humans are capable of incredible things. Full recovery against the odds." Is Summer capable of full recovery? Do you agree with this statement? Explain your answers.

15. Moony takes Kurt's hand with his weak one (pg. 238). Explore the symbolism behind this act. Discuss why the act of holding hands is meaningful to Summer, thus causing Moony's reaching out to Kurt to be more poignant.

16. Consider the meaning behind the phrase "She's not afraid of dying. She's afraid of loving" (pg. 238). Explain how loving is a risky act, more daring and terrifying than the act of suicide.

17. Explain Kurt's physical transformation from having a young "handsome profile and shiny disheveled hair" and "perfectly shaped fingers and nails" (pg. 20) to developing coarse skin, a lined face, and ragged nails (pg. 267). Consider Kurt's seemingly gradual aging and increasingly foul body odor. Tell what these physical changes reveal with regard to his character and Summer's feelings for him.

18. Return to the early pages of the novel. Explore the phrase, "She knows the guy can't read her mind and doesn't mean anything by those words, but there it is: the real, and growing reason why she's got to find someone to love" (pg. 3). Discuss how these words of exposition inform the novel's resolution.

19. Discuss the role that alcohol plays in this story.

20. Moony asks Summer, "But what does life expect from you?" (pg. 93). Interpret the meaning behind his words. Predict how Summer's response to Moony's question might have changed from the midpoint of the story to the end. Explain the causes for the change in Summer's outlook on life. What about you? Describe what life expects from you.